He Has Her Heart

Cynthia Marcano

Feeding Thousands Publishing

Copyright © 2017 by Cynthia Marcano.

All rights reserved. No part of this publication may be reproduced, distributed or transmitted in any form or by any means, including photocopying, recording, or other electronic or mechanical methods, without the prior written permission of the publisher, except in the case of brief quotations embodied in critical reviews and certain other noncommercial uses permitted by copyright law. For permission requests, write to the publisher, addressed "Attention: Permissions Coordinator," at the address below.

Cynthia Marcano/Feeding Thousands Publishing

Publisher's Note: This is a work of fiction. Names, characters, places, and incidents are a product of the author's imagination. Locales and public names are sometimes used for atmospheric purposes. Any resemblance to actual people, living or dead, or to businesses, companies, events, institutions, or locales is completely coincidental.

Book Layout ©2017 CynMar Designs
Copyright © 2017
First Edition 2017 – He Has Her Heart: Spring Love Series
Author: Cynthia Marcano
Library of Congress Control Number: 2017900352
ISBN-13: 978-1535403443
ISBN-10: 1535403446

THE HOLY BIBLE, NEW INTERNATIONAL VERSION®, NIV® Copyright © 1973, 1978, 1984, 2011 by Biblica, Inc.™ Used by permission. All rights reserved worldwide.

For my grandmothers.

In Dedication to Monse Marcano.
"Sank" you for always being you.
Te amo.

Chapter 1

How sobering acknowledging that her parents had been right about her all along. In fact, her friends hadn't been far off either. Her big mouth always landed her in trouble. There! She could admit that now. Too bad it only took twenty-six years to reconcile herself to that accurate assessment and their belief that not every thought had to be voiced. That sometimes, it was better to keep one's mouth shut. Like a puff of smoke, a scripture to the same affect clouded her head before dissipating almost as quickly as it manifested.

Oh how she wished she could have come to the stark realization before she began cheering at the top of her lungs like a banshee, for the team with the cute outfielder. On second thought, why should she aim to please a stadium full of complete strangers? The last time she checked, she lived in America and had the right to cheer for whomever she pleased. Freedom of speech and all of that other patriotic good stuff. It wasn't her fault that Mr. Strong-Arms, just so happened to be on the opposing team.

At least if she continued repeating that sentiment to herself, the glares from her best friends being escorted out of Citizens Bank Park by security officers, wouldn't make her want to go bury herself under the pitcher's mound. How could a little harmless cheering erupt into such an unnecessary riot? Perhaps if baseball wasn't as exciting as watching water freeze, Dream could have found something else to occupy her attention. Or perhaps someone. Someone other than number twenty-three who she could swear just winked at her as the crowd cheered her exit.

Clutching her purse to her midsection, Dream turned from the field and kept her gaze firmly to the stadium steps that led to the concourse, as her platform sandals carried her further away from the game. She ignored the white tee that stretched keenly across Max's back and the jeans that hung nicely from his waste. Redirecting her gaze to the concrete, she remembered what was important. Technically, all of this was Max's fault.

If he, who had her teetering on the brink of love and loathing from one minute to the next, would quit playing hard to get, they wouldn't be in this predicament. Unfortunately, today, attraction to the dunce who couldn't recognize a good thing if it clobbered him over the head with a bat, swung her love-hate pendulum towards attraction.

It had to be the stupid red Phillies baseball cap. He'd always looked good in a baseball cap. A mixture of boyishly handsome and rugged good looks drew her attention like a magnet to her grandmother's refrigerator. When he had the audacity to turn his cap and face its bill backwards, affording her an unobstructed view of his hazel eyes, her heart skipped two beats. One for his beauty and the other because this man was off limits. Sourly, Dream snapped back to the crisis at hand.

The last person she needed to feel all mushy inside for was Max Davidson. The current look in his eyes communicated anything but tenderness of heart. If she knew him at all, and she did, he was biting back a growl. A weekly occurrence since junior high school. Alas, there was no time to think about that now. Eventually he'd get over it. At the very least, he'd add this situation to his growing list of reasons to keep his distance.

As of now, security was kind enough to walk the rabble-rouser and her cohorts out of the stadium, in order to protect them from being maimed by the vicious crowd. Philadelphia fans really did earn their reputation of serious fanatics.

"Thank you Officer-" Dream searched for a name on the gold plated badge but found only a red P logo that represented the ball club. Adjusting her purse strap over her shoulder, she offered her most grateful smile. After all, he'd held back the fans spewing hate at her and in return kept her back from the one loudly disapproving of her shoe choice. As if a man wearing a dingy baseball cap and sandals with socks could ever give her fashion advice.

"Ma'am I suggest you and your friends make haste getting out of here." The middle-aged man cuffed his thumbs into the belt holding up his tan trousers, a nervous glint in his eye. That certainly didn't bode well for her physical well-being, but she refused to be bullied. Three self-defense lessons had her primed and ready to take anyone down. Hopefully, she could remember everything she learned back in college years ago.

"Aren't you escorting us out of the parking lot?" Dream's sculpted eyebrow rose a degree.

"No." He dipped his chin, his one word answer unyielding. "Go Phillies," he let out as he walked away.

"Unbelievable." Dream turned to her friends. Each set of eyes peering at her, loaded, aimed, and ready to shoot. Suddenly she felt like she'd been lined up before a firing squad, blindfolded and hands tied behind her back. "What?"

"You could have gotten us killed." Tami tossed her hands up and walked to the passenger side of her husband, Jonah's, car. Her best friend had always been a bit of a jellyfish. In high-pressure situations, the woman would literally pass out whether behind a steering wheel or the middle of a restaurant. It'd been a while since her last spell, but lately she seemed to be on edge. The last thing Dream needed was Tami sprawled out on the hot concrete.

"That's a little overdramatic don't you think?" Dream fisted a hand and situated it on her hip.

"Overdramatic, was you screaming as if a chainsaw were coming at you rather than a home run ball. Then tossing it back onto the field because it was 'dirty'." After his air quotes, Drew folded his arms into themselves and chuckled. God bless his heart. Someone wasn't so crabby about the simple misunderstanding.

"Did no one else see where he scratched before he pitched the ball?" Aghast, Dream tossed her hands up and searched each of her friend's faces waiting for someone else, anyone else, to be appalled by such a public display of crude behavior.

"He was adjusting his...cup." The petite woman to her right blushed and Dream could barely contain her amusement. Nicole wasn't shy about most things, but there were a few topics of conversation that could color her cheeks like a cold winter's day. Add athletic supporters to the list, right under anything regarding, Drew, her fiancée.

"Cup? Oh that's too funny." Dream contained her amusement. Laughing aloud bordered on poor taste given she wasn't exactly everyone's favorite person at the moment. Belittling their concern only served to irritate them even further.

"Did you have to pour your soda on the guy sitting next to you?" Nicole bit her lip, eyebrows burrowed.

"The degenerate *accidentally* rested his hand on my thigh. He's lucky that's all I did." Could no one see how this really wasn't any of her fault?

"He did what?" Tami closed her car door and rushed over to Dream. "Why didn't you say anything?"

"Yeah, Dream. You should have told one of us." Jonah turned away from his wife, concern etched in his features.

"I handled it." Dream waved it off. A few strands from her long dark ponytail found their way to her shoulder courtesy of the warm breezy air.

"Dream, you could have really gotten yourself hurt. I'm not justifying the behavior of some of those fans, but there are lots of people out there that don't care if they hurt a woman. Many of those men are riled up, far from sober, and at any moment ready to lose all self-control." Jonah opened the driver-side car door. "I think we should get out of here before we all end up in a brawl."

"I'm really sorry guys. I'll make this up to you. I promise." Dream beamed a bright smile hoping to smooth away any remaining ruffled feathers.

Tami quickly embraced her best friend. Dream chuckled as they rocked back and forth. "Yes. You will."

Several hugs later, Dream waited before heading for the Philadelphia subway. Not remembering which way to go, and not bothering to ask directions from the few fans lingering that she may have enraged, she walked out of the nearest exit. Following the signs directing traffic toward Broad Street, the unmistakable sign for the Septa transit system beckoned her.

With the stadium falling further away with each step, the sounds of American baseball and its fans began to dwindle. Having left the game during the fourth inning, the foot and car traffic were blessedly minimal. She was sure to find a seat on the train unlike her initial trip but no use in complaining about it now. Other than being jostled on a moving train while standing, and being ogled by a pubescent teenager, it hadn't been too bad. Repeating the experience wasn't at the top of her list of things to do, but it was her only means of getting home, so she'd have to endure it.

Shielding her eyes from the sun that sat up high and bright in the clear blue sky, Dream waited for the lone car to pass before she could leisurely cross the wide street that led to and from the stadiums. Reaching into her bag pushing her sunscreen and cell aside, she opted for her larger sunglasses that added more coverage, swapping the pair she had on. Hopefully, grandpa would pick up the pace and drive pass, by the time she finished her exchange so she could cross.

"You lost?"

That voice was all too familiar. The richness it exuded since he was a teenager had only deepened over the years. Masculine. Strong. Was there anything about this man she didn't like? Yes! The fact that he didn't feel the same way about her. Now if she could get her heart to accept what her mind had already resigned itself to, life could move on.

"Nope. I know exactly where I am and exactly where I'm going." *Mostly.* Dream situated her purse on her shoulder and smiled.

"Where's your car?"

The appreciation for a deserted sports arena street had suddenly lost its appeal. What she needed now was a rowdy crowd of fans to get lost in, or a long line of impatient drivers obnoxiously beeping at cars that currently stopped in the middle of the street to talk to a woman walking alone. With no plausible reason to dodge his question, Dream aimed for being vague. "In a parking lot." Short and simple.

"How'd you get here?"

"Train"

"You took the train? Alone?" The edge in Max's voice could offer hope to a woman in love, but years of pining for a man who'd mastered keeping his distance stripped away any such notion.

"My mommy said it was ok." Dream chuckled and waved. "I'm gonna miss my train if I don't get going." Technically, it was true. The train had to leave the station eventually, even if she had no clue when that was.

"Get in." Max rolled up his window cutting off the protest she formed with her lips but wasn't given the opportunity to articulate.

Trying to reason with a pane of glass was pointless, not to mention ridiculous. Walking around to the passenger side, Dream chastised her stupid heart for its irrational thumping. It was just a ride home, not into the sunset. She couldn't remember the last time she had been alone with Max.

The click of her seatbelt echoed in the quiet. Never one for awkward silences, she tried thinking of a topic that wouldn't end disastrously. Little chance of that, since small talk was meaningless and life was too short to waste on dead end conversations, which she wouldn't attempt. Nope, she'd rather get to the core of people. Dig up truth and what they are really thinking while they are spewing generic answers to equally generic questions. Alone with Max for fifteen minutes was an excellent opportunity to probe into his world. She had to make the best of the situation with the time that God had gifted her. Forget safe. That wasn't part of her nature. She preferred real.

"So? Dating anyone?"

"Next topic."

"Huh." Dream considered his reply. "Normally, that means a person is a lonely as a stray dog with fleas. Yet, with you it could mean you actually prefer to keep your personal life private."

Max remained quiet.

"Not even a hint? Fine. Me, you ask? No, I'm not dating anyone right now." Hint. Hint. "Focusing on work, oh and Cecelia, remember her? She was at Tami's wedding."

Max shook his head, his eyes never leading the road.

"She was the red-head that wore that hideous orange dress. Her shoes were cute though. Anyway, she is organizing a huge community wide fundraiser, and asked if I could help with the budgeting. What are you up to these days?"

"Right now. Taking you home and then going home to catch the rest of the game."

Ok, so today wasn't going to be the day she broke down walls, but if the years of unrequited love were any indication, Dream could be plenty patient with Max. Right now, it was best to try to keep quiet, but no promises were being made.

The vexing woman was full of secrets and a heap load of trouble. What in her right mind would make her antagonize a stadium full of fans? Therein was the problem. Dream was hardly ever in her right mind. She'd nearly gotten his brain bashed in by the brute two rows back that made it clear he valued baseball over human life and apparently really wanted the homerun ball that put the Phillies up by a run. The one she tossed back because of the pitcher's decision to…adjust beforehand. Not to mention pouring her ice-cold soda on the man's lap that sat beside her. Actually, he couldn't fault her for that. The scumbag had it coming.

Playing the knight in shining armor was never his style, but he'd lose an arm before he let a man put his hands on a woman he cared for. That was the kind of man his dad had been and the kind he strived to be. It was a good thing he hadn't found out about Mr. Loose Hands touching Dream until after being escorted out. That probably would have ended badly.

As if that weren't enough, she came into the city alone on a train. Granted it was daytime, but that hadn't stopped the feeling of dread that sank to the pit of his stomach, much like Tami's cooking. The desire to protect Dream from surly fans hurling insults or possible assailants in a subway, wreaked havoc in his carefully compartmentalized brain. Feelings for Dream were tucked away in the recesses of his mind, under lock and key, in a vault, behind a fortified wall. The key tossed away long ago, deep in his mental ocean of common sense, never to be found.

After Jonah and Tami pulled out of the parking lot with Drew and Nicole, Max would just wait for Dream to drive out right after. Once she was out of the parking lot with no potential threats of crazed fans following her home with ill intent, he'd wait for her to get a good lead, inconspicuously follow her into Jersey before venturing off to his Dream-free thus, sane life. When would he ever learn that nothing was ever simple when it came to Dream?

Since no man walks earth without suffering, rather than seeing Dream's oversized SUV, he spotted her walking out of the parking lot on foot, heading to the only logical place he could surmise, the subway. Not wasting another second to ponder why, he'd set out to intercept her and had succeeded. Succeeded into driving himself to the edge.

A perfectly good summer afternoon of baseball wasted. And all for what? The centerfielder that wasn't worth his weight in tinfoil. Honestly, who rooted for a player because he was cute? Women.

"Are you going to tell me why you took the subway into the city?" Maintaining a level of civility could only aid in getting answers. At least, he hoped. Turning onto Broad Street, he slowed as the first traffic light they approached changed from yellow to red.

"Are you going to tell me about your love life?" A hand flew to her mouth, covering it, her eyes pinched shut. Under her breath, she mumbled to herself. Had it been anyone else he would have found the behavior strange, but odd was normal in Dream's case. For some reason, he couldn't help but think that on some level she enjoyed being illogical. Her eyes began to flutter open and he turned his attention to the line of row homes on

Philadelphia's South Side rather than be ensnared in her gaze.

If he didn't know better, he would think she was fighting to keep her mouth from shooting off. Unless she stapled her hands in place, she would lose that battle. He could feel her glare burning into him as he lurched forward into the exit lane. She wasn't seriously awaiting an actual answer, was she? As if he'd ever want to talk about his love life with *her*. It was a blessing that he'd always kept that part of his life personal and he aimed to keep it that way. That meant, denying her request to grant access into his affairs.

"No." His denial was short and to the point.

"Then, no," she replied.

It was probably for the best that he didn't try to understand why Dream did the things she did. The inner workings of her mind was a maze he'd rather not get lost in. Danger and deranged crossed her paths wherever she went, leaving trouble in her wake. The less he knew, the safer he'd be from men twice his size ready to pound him, almost being carted off to jail, forced to bid on lunch and fun dates with the seniors from her church, listening to her argue her views on why massages are beneficial to a person's health, and likewise nonsense. But most importantly, safe from her.

The ride over the Walt Whitman Bridge into Jersey was quiet, with no traffic. As he merged onto the highway, he longed to get her out of his car. The scent of sunshine mixed with her perfume made his stomach queasy. It was the only scent he ever remembered her wearing, and it became entangled with his repulsion for falling for her. Over the years, it began to revolt him. It was one of the main reasons he avoided close proximity to her. Focusing on the destination helped distract him and he lowered the windows despite the heat. "Where's your car parked?"

"At the police impound." The crazed woman folded her hands onto her lap demurely as if she had simply commented on the weather.

"Home it is." No sense walking onto that landmine.

"That would be perfect. Thank you." Focusing her attention out the passenger side window, they rode in silence. A blessed understanding between them. He wouldn't ask and she wouldn't tell.

If by some miracle, Dream managed to find a man willing, although more likely coerced, to marry her before Max took his last breath on this earth, he'd be sure to say a prayer for that poor guy. As for him, he had plans for his future and none of them involved Dream Collins. He'd learned the hard way that feelings couldn't be trusted. Emotions could change like the direction of the wind, blowing strong one way, one minute, gentle in the opposite direction the next. Feelings were sometimes more of a complication, than a help in life. Especially when it came to relationships. Yet, he couldn't deny wanting a stable relationship, with the right person of course.

Dumbstruck it hadn't occurred to him sooner, he wondered if his best friend Emily Serrano would be his bride. A proposal would probably send her reeling, being that they weren't dating and never had, but they had been best friends since high school. Weren't married couples supposed to be best friends? They were half way to wedded bliss already. All that remained was training his heart to see her as a woman.

No doubt, Emily was a woman. A few admirers had taken notice, from what he remembered, although he didn't see her in that way. Not that it mattered. Beauty was in the eye of the beholder and Emily was the sweetest and most creative person he'd ever known. That was the beauty he sought. Not a tall slender body that rivaled the ones of the models he used to photograph gracing the cover of magazines. Not a long dark mane that called out to his hands to run his fingers through it. Not a smile so bright that could light up a room, no matter how dark.

Nope. Beautiful was the woman that he could share a normal life with and never have to worry about being arrested with, for any number of insane reasons. A woman, excited to mother his many children and maybe teach them how to draw and write, and become aspiring authors like Emily was what he wanted. Definitely not a woman that stirred irrational emotions within him with just a glance. Instead, he needed someone level headed, down to earth and….meek. Yep. That was the word God used. Meek was exactly the wife Max needed.

How he arrived at Dream's he couldn't remember. She gathered her bag and hesitated before turning to him. *Please don't linger.*

"I'm sorry about today. Thanks for the ride."

Max nodded, accepting her gratitude. She looked like she wrestled to say more but refrained. Relief flooded him. He waited for her to exit his car and enter her front door before pulling away.

Come next week, he'd be engaged and the insane desires within would have a very solid reason to be denied, a fiancée that deserved, and would undoubtedly receive his loyalty.

Chapter 2

The glare of red and blue lights illuminating her rear window was the icing on the cake of this crummy morning. If she didn't make it to work within the next ten minutes, her boss would surely make her the company to his misery. Being pulled over five minutes after leaving the impound lot had to be a record. Reaching into her glove compartment, Dream snatched the white envelope with all the appropriate paperwork. At the knock on the window, she lowered the volume of the radio followed by the window.

"Do you know why I pulled you over?"

The familiar voice made her flesh crawl. She was going to be fired and David Escobar would be the reason why.

"No *Officer*, I do not." Attempting to be cordial was a waste of time and frankly she hated being phony, or what Tami insisted was tactful. "And please don't give me one of your cheesy lines. I already told you that I don't want to go out with you."

"Cheesy?" His voice pitched. "Words from the heart are never cheesy."

"Oh please! Your come-ons could top a pizza."

"From what I remember, you love pizza." The flirty smile made her teeth clench.

"This has to be an abuse of power. I'm going to be late for work, so if you don't mind." The faint buzz of her window going up as she dismissed him halted when he exercised his authoritarian voice.

"License and registration, please." His voice softened again. "You have a tail light out."

The very real thought of speeding off rather than handing her personal information over to this particular police officer morphed from a seedling of an idea into the planning stages. If she waited for the light ahead to turn green, she could floor it. It would take him a few seconds to get back to his squad car. Then again, the size of her SUV would slow her down. Perhaps she could turn into an alley like they did on...

"Ms. Collins, there is nothing more that I'd like than chasing you, but a car chase wasn't exactly what I had in mind. Besides, it would only further delay you getting to work. Now, license and registration please." Stretched lips gave way to his too perfect pearly whites.

No human on earth should have a mouth full of impeccably flawless teeth. In fact, he was just too ideal for her taste. His chiseled features, perfect skin and fine manners paired with a selfless, heroic career in which he wore a uniform that fit rather nicely made her want to gag. His whole being was simply too...good. He was like a human Ken doll. Barbie, she was not. She smiled at the accuracy of her comparison. Officer Escobar cleared his throat disrupting her thoughts.

"Make it quick." Handing over her paperwork, she reached for her phone and dialed the office as she watched Ken - David, walk to his car to verify her information. Even his commanding gait made her want to roll her eyes. Why did she always attract men she never found the least bit interesting?

No answer. Why wasn't Lily at her desk? *Why aren't you at work?* A quick glance at her car's clock and she growled. The morning meeting was starting. Before she could think twice, her hand slammed against the horn.

David better hurry with whatever game he was playing. After a few more minutes he returned to the car, his jaw clenched.

Handing back her paperwork, he held tight as she reached for it. "Two warnings Ms. Collins." The teasing grin had vanished. "I won't cite you this time. Go straight to the car parts store and get the lightbulb replaced."

No ticket. Thank God. "And second?"

"Don't ever blare your horn at an officer ready, willing, and able to properly cite you. Believe me. That won't go over very well."

Heat rose up her neck. Perhaps, she had crossed the line a teeny tiny bit. Wasn't the first time, and as much as she wished it would be the last, it was naïve to believe so. Nevertheless, he was right. "Sorry about that."

"Good. I know you're running late, but no speeding." A long finger pointed at her in warning and she offered a polite smile in return. No use in scowling at his mothering tone when he had just cut her a break.

Leaning out the window, she called out to him. He returned, his eyes filled with uncertainty. "Out of curiosity, what's your middle name?"

"Kenneth. Why?"

"Of course it is!" Dream cackled. "Bye Ken!" She rolled up her window and left a stunned Officer Escobar standing on the road watching her as she pulled away.

There was no use in rushing now. No matter if she arrived with the next two minutes or twenty, she was late and Mr. Littleton would apprise the entire department of his disapproval. Keeping true to her word, she kept within speed limits but decided to replace her tail light after work. Stopping at the coffee bar downstairs for a much needed caffeine boost, she added a muffin to her order before trudging her way to the elevator.

Straightening her spine, she girded herself for the verbal assault her quick-tongued boss was ready to dish out. A solid faith in God kept her from fearing most things, including her boss. That and remembering the sage advice, *sticks and stones may break my bones, but words will never hurt me.* It wasn't scripture but growing up it was her answer to every tormentor. A smile played across her lips remembering the first time Max nicknamed her 'Nightmare' and she chose those precious words as her defense. An eight-year-old saying such was expected but a bra-wearing, purse-toting fifteen-year-old daring to spout it left Max wonderfully stupefied.

"You're so immature," was all he could manage. Repeating her favorite words again, further infuriated the usually cool Max. Kicking the pebble beside him, he sent it sailing into the street and nearly into the neighbor's new window. He stomped away grumbling under his breath. She laughed at how often she bested him since then with such simple words.

The ping of the elevator brought her back to the present. Schooling her features, she exited through the double doors and toward her cubicle. Lily, the department's secretary, sped toward the ringing phone and quickly turned back, pulling Dream's arm. "Dream! You're here. Littleton was on a morning call and it must have been bad because he's in a foul mood."

"Bad fish foul or sewage foul?"

"Definitely sewage. Rumor is we've been bought out and some of the changes have come through and it's not looking good." The ringing of her telephone had her stubby and unshaved legs, speeding off before she could elaborate. Rather than try to decrypt the latest rumor mill gossip, Dream made a mental note to email Lily reminding her that shaving and skirts went hand in hand. It was the least she could do as many times as Lily had covered for her.

Settling in quickly, she fired up her computer. If Littleton had been on an important call, he may not have noticed her absence. As if summoned by her thoughts, Littleton's booming voice vibrated off the walls as he exited his office. He peered at her as he passed, shooting daggers with his calculating eyes. Crud! He noticed.

If she were going to enjoy her coffee and muffin, now was the time. Once he returned, her brew wouldn't taste as rich or the muffin as sweet. Littleton had a way of making everything less enjoyable. Pulling the cup to her anxious lips, she blew then sipped the hot coffee; its strong flavor warmed her tongue.

"Collins! My office! Now!" He didn't even look in her direction as he headed back to his lair.

Startled, the hot cup slipped from her grasp and landed on her lap. Quickly standing to her feet, the cup landed on the carpet with a splat. The hot coffee burned her hands as she desperately tried to keep it from scalding her legs. That miserable man!

Once she left the ladies room, she headed toward what was sure to be fifteen agonizing minutes regarding office etiquette and protocol. Before she could knock, he waved her in. Not offering her a greeting or a seat, he pounced.

"You were late." Brown client folders blanketed his large oak desk. The view of the parking lot was depressing. He moved the mountain of files in search of something. He huffed, unsuccessful in retrieving whatever was lost in the mound.

"There was a misunderstanding with a police officer." Offered or not, she took the seat closest to the door.

At her words, Mr. Littleton, stopped shuffling the files and eyed her. "A misunderstanding?" He sat back quietly, his way of inviting her to explain further.

So much for keeping personal matters private in the work place. "I was pulled over. I explained that I was running late to work, but he didn't seem to care."

"And?" Placing his elbows on his desk, he sat forward and steepled his fingers.

"And then I left and came straight to work. He warned me not to break the speed limit, so I didn't."

Rubbing his temples, he sat back. "Let me see the citation." Each word dragged from his mouth slowly and painfully.

"I didn't get one." She sent a quiet thank you up to God.

"Ms. Collins, you're fired."

Dream shot up from the chair. "Fired? Why?"

"Excessive tardiness. Now, I value myself a fair man. I have given you many opportunities and have given you enough written warnings in hopes that you would improve in this deficient area of your employment but you have mistaken my kindness for weakness."

"I've only been late twice."

"This week," he interjected. "A person either has to have the worst luck on all of earth to land in as many predicaments on the way to work as you have or a person is a pathological liar. Now, had you produced a ticket as proof then perhaps, I could have overlooked this latest violation of policy buying you a few more weeks. However, you have no proof, therefore I can only conclude that you are being untruthful and I see no need to drag out the inevitable."

"Let me get this straight, I'm fired because I *didn't* get a ticket? And what exactly is the inevitable?"

"No. You're fired for being excessively tardy. We've already covered that part. The inevitable, Ms. Collins, it that we've been bought out and are being forced to downsize. We need to make cuts and naturally, you are at the top of my list." Mr. Littleton began to pile his folders into a semi-neat stack before he stopped and returned his attention to her.

"Naturally?" Today God presented the perfect opportunity to exercise patience and she aimed to do right by Him, otherwise she might end up on the nightly news.

"You're not a bad accountant," he continued, "you just so happen to think that order, rules, and the proper way of things are merely suggestions. You can't expect to ever stay employed with that attitude. You're a superior's nightmare." Pushing the intercom button to speak to his secretary, he inquired after a client file, effectively dismissing Dream.

"Nightmare." There was that word again. Dream calmly approached his desk. The tight grin across her face held no humor. "Mr. Littleton, sticks and stones may break my bones, but words will never hurt me."

With her head held and her coffee-stained skirt, Dream walked away from Smothers and Regal Accounting Firm, never looking back, not even when her heel broke off in the parking lot and she proudly wobbled to her car.

Not many things could coax as wide a smile from Max like watching David walk into their weekly basketball game wearing pink yoga pants and a black compression tank with a hint of his navel peeking out. Slowly the sounds of basketballs pounding the wooden gym floor were replaced by whistles and hooting. Approaching with a scowl, David pulled the tank down in an attempt to hide his midsection that rode up with each step.

More than seeing the self-proclaimed gift to women, David, looking completely ridiculous, it did his heart good to know that Dream turned David down. Again. "Why do you keep doing this to yourself?" Max gripped his shoulder and tried to contain his amusement. "Let it go. She won't bend." *Thank God.* If Dream was anything, she was as stubborn as he was. Most days that resulted in a tension, but today it was a blessing. Not because he had a vested interest in her love life, of course, but simply for her own protection. David wasn't quality boyfriend material. "This is a stupid bet you made with yourself. No one cares if you quit."

"All a man has is his word. Even if it's only to himself. Dream Collins will agree to go out with me. Until then, women's extra-large it is." Looking down, David pulled his tank down again. "Does this make me look fat?"

"Are you asking me to check you out?" Afraid he'd reply, Max left him standing alone.

"Of course not! Max, hold on. That's not what I meant!"

Straightening his shoulders, Max kept his chuckle to himself. Teasing David was too good to pass up. "Shirts and skins! Oh wait, David is both." The riotous laughter echoed. Ever the good sport, David joined in.

"Alright. Alright. Can we just play ball?" David turned and held his hands out to catch a pass. Iron on letters sprawled across his backside set off another round of jeers and whistles.

"Juicy? No chick is worth this humiliation." Romeo, the newest member of their informal league, and rookie police officer crossed his arms, smirking.

"That's because you haven't seen her, Casanova." Admiration twinkled in his David's eyes. "I will convince her. Just you wait and see." Dribbling the ball a few times, David took the shot. All net. He winked and sprinted to catch his rebound, pulling his tank down again.

"It's Romeo and don't forget it!" Romeo charged after the ball taking advantage of David's distraction.

Any other time, Max would have found the scene entertaining, but something in David's determination to win a date with Dream churned his gut. He quickly checked the feeling and ran out onto the court catching a pass of his own, heading straight for the basket. She was off limits, and if his friend wanted to pursue her, there wasn't much he could do about it.

After an hour of shoving, yelling and shooting, Max's team lost to David's by a hard-earned point. The constant streaming of jesting ceased when David slammed in the game winning dunk. Women's athletic wear or not, he played hard. Everything he did emanated an all-in attitude. Apparently, even getting a date.

The men congregated catching a breath and downing water as if they just had just crossed a Mojave, the light chatter revolving around the Phillies loss to the Mets the night prior. Sunlight flooded the gym door as Drew entered, his youth group trickling in behind, their boisterous voices taking over the subdued atmosphere. The rowdy bunch had a love for Basketball Summer Camp.

Picking up their bags and plastic bottles, the men heeded the presence of the youngsters as their queue to exit the building and exchanged goodbyes by way of man hugs and handshakes. Drew approached, greeting each man and sharing a laugh when he eyed David's getup.

"You might want to hurry on out of here before my boys see you and tell the neighborhood they saw a police officer wearing women's clothing." David masked his anxiety and bid farewell once more before exiting the building discreetly. Max couldn't blame him, street cred was important in his line of work.

Picking up his duffle, Max held the strap on his shoulder and faced Drew handing him an envelope. "Thanks for letting us use the gym. The guys thought it was only right we make a donation to the church for allowing us to play on Saturdays."

"I'm just the coach. All other matters go through Pastor Collins. I saw his car out front. He must be in his office." It would only take a minute to drop the envelope off personally and check in on his old friend. Max nodded and set out to find him.

"What's up with David's getup?" Drew asked stopping Max in his tracks.

He wrestled with the idea of telling Drew. Dream had become Drew's unofficial baby sister and he was sure to disapprove of whatever David was trying so hard to accomplish. Yet, keeping it from him would make things worse, were Drew to find out later. Pulling a hand down over his face, he blew out a breath. "David is trying to get a date with Dream and every time she turns him down, he's promised to come to our games looking like that." He pointed toward the door David had exited.

Eyes wide open, Drew leaned in. "Our Dream?"

"She's not my Dream," Max scowled. "But yes, the only Dream I know."

Grooves formed in Drew's brow, his mouth in a hardened line. "But why? What does dressing ridiculously accomplish?"

"Nothing, if you ask me but he won't back out of his own promise. No one is holding him to it but he refuses to let it go." Max crossed his arms. "Pride I guess."

"How many weeks has this been going on?"

Heat crawled up his neck and suddenly it felt too hot. "This is the fifth week."

"Max," Drew hissed. "You know she isn't going to like this once she finds out."

"I don't know about that." Looking beyond Drew's shoulder to the boys beginning to roughhouse, Max couldn't bring himself to look into Drew's anxious expression. "She likes attention. She'd probably get a kick out of it."

"You can't believe that. She's lives in her own world, but that's very different from appreciating being made a sport in David's dating games. The man has more women than arrests." Planting his hands on his waist, Drew's agitation became more apparent.

"Well, she has turned him down every week, so I'm sure he'll give up soon enough. There's only so much rejection a man can take before he gets bored." What did

Drew want him to do? He wasn't Dream's keeper. Whom she dated was none of his concern. Besides, it's not as if she was actually dating David and he was fooling around behind her back. That would require intervening. The man couldn't even get her to say yes, let alone string her along. No use in worrying over a problem that didn't exist.

"Or her rejections could fuel him to be more persistent. Do you know the man to be a quitter? I haven't known him long but from what I've seen he's got determination oozing out of his pores." Drew turned back at the escalating shouts of the boys. "I've got to get practice started before Lucas organizes a mutiny. After all of these years, the kid still doesn't like me." Placing the whistle to his lips, Drew sounded off grabbing the attention of all the boys in the gym.

Drew's barking orders faded as Max stepped into the passageway that led from the gym to the church and headed to Pastor Collins office. While he wasn't a member of Christ Community Church, he was the former Basketball Summer Camp Coach before handing over the reins to Drew a few years back. The hallways of CCC, as it was known, were familiar and strangely comforting. He was at ease here.

The steady clicking of typing confirmed Drew's conjecture and Max knocked on the opened office door before entering. The high back chair spun to face him and when a pair of dark eyes stared back at him, he kept his features schooled. Dream's long hair flowed over one shoulder, the shine as good as blinding him. Her beauty was not a characteristic he found wanting. In fact, she had more than her fair share of allure. Unfortunately, the woman was as nutty as crunchy peanut butter.

"Sorry to bother you, I was actually looking for your grandfather. Drew saw his car outside and thought he'd be in here."

Unlike him, she didn't mask her surprise and the bright smile that stretched across her face made his heart speed up a fraction. "Sorry to disappoint you, but it's just me. He's out changing the bulb in my tail light while I catch up on the accounting. Maybe I can help you with something?"

"Now that you mention it, I guess this would end up in your hands anyhow." Stepping further into the office, he approached the desk and placed the envelope on the desk sliding it towards her. Without hesitation, she picked up the envelope and peeked inside, her eyes widening. "The fellas and I wanted to make a donation since we use the gym almost every Saturday."

"That's quite a donation." Her eyes met his, astonishment dancing in the depths.

"We've been collecting it for a while. It's the least we could do." There was no need to mention that he was the main benefactor of the sum she held.

Lifting the envelope, Dream narrowed her eyes. "I'm guessing there's a couple of thousand dollars in here."

"Give or take a few dollars," he held her gaze refusing to squirm under her accusing scrutiny. "Like I said, we've been collecting for a few months." That was only part of the truth, but technically not a lie.

Standing, she left the desk and approached him. Sirens went off in his head as if a three-alarm fire was in progress. Before he knew what she was about, she wrapped her arms around his middle and squeezed. Like an ice cube thawing, her touch warmed him, cracking the carefully constructed walls he'd built. The scent of her hair was alluring before her perfume took over and he nearly gagged. Oh how he hated that perfume. Thanking God for saving him via designer toilet water, or what could have been actual toilet water, he yanked free from her warmth, taking a step back. "I gotta go."

Her shoulders shook as she chuckled. "See you Sunday, Mr. Davidson."

Her words slowed his hurry to escape. Mr. Davidson was his father. Yet, he found that he liked hearing it. Was God confirming the yearning in his heart to leave bachelorhood behind? There was no time like the present to resurrect Mr. Davidson and all that entailed. Family, children, a dog, and even the mini-van. The idea made him smile.

Stepping out into the sunshine, the urging to begin his own legacy deepened. A longing to be more than just a wealthy man giving away money. It was noble but he had more to give than money. Valuable lessons to teach his children. Love to shower his wife with and spoil mercilessly. However, that would require actually having a wife. Blessedly, he had the perfect one lined up and it most definitely was not Dream Collins.

Chapter 3

Firecrackers exploded nearby, startling Dream out of her skin. Retreating footsteps mingled with the snickers of Drew's young neighbors hauling rear opposite of where she stood. She could almost swear the rapscallions waited behind the hedge, day and night for an opportunity to torment her. Already in August and they hadn't ceased with the fireworks. Ringing the doorbell, Dream swatted away thoughts of revenge, along with the odor of burnt paper and smoke filling her nostrils.

Nicole yanked open the door creating a breeze that sent her ponytailed tresses swinging from the sheer force of her agitated welcome. "Hey, Dream." Slumping shoulders followed by a relieved huff, Nicole moved aside to allow Dream to enter the bachelor dwelling that had as much warmth as a Northeast winter. Would it kill Drew to add a little color to his drab place? Even the mammoth leather bound Bible displayed on his coffee table was a boring brown that enticed her to yawn.

"I can't decide if you looked relieved or agitated?" Dream set down the two small trays of cookies.

Nicole's tense expression softened. "I thought you were the fire department."

That couldn't be good. "And why would I be the fire department?" Her shoulders dropped knowing all too well why. "Please tell me those rowdy little snots were in here setting off fireworks and that Drew didn't just cajunize my dinner. Start talking medicine woman."

"Medicine woman? Not another nickname."

Clapping accompanied Dream's chuckle. "I've been waiting for two weeks to introduce it into the rotation."

"I guess it's better than Florence Nicolengale." Dream hugged the future anesthesiologist tightly rocking backing back and forth in amusement, not releasing her until she heard Nicole giggle. Moods officially lightened, she sought answers for her growling stomach. "Dinner?"

"I haven't seen the boys all day, but I guess you have." Nicole wrapped her arm around Dream's shoulders hiding her amusement and guided Dream toward the kitchen. "Sorry. Jonah's manning the grill."

There went their perfectly laid out plan up in flames. Literally. The whole purpose of rotating Sunday dinner was to keep Jonah from grilling every Sunday in his backyard. If he hadn't figured out how to barbecue in two years since being gifted the mother of all grills, what was the likelihood he ever would? Yet, that didn't stop him from taking over and serving well beyond done fare with more char than any actual meat.

A wooden stool beckoned her and she willingly answered it, lowering into it, resting her forearms on the Formica countertop. "How many more summers can we go on eating ashes on a bun? I'm developing gallstones from the excessive amount of ketchup I need to make a hot dog pass as edible. The ones I can chew anyway. I volunteer to tell him he is banned from the grill." Dream sat back giddy at the idea. There was a longstanding joy, she found in irritating the goody-two-shoes of the group. Inexplicably it made her world just a little brighter, even if Tami insisted it was mean.

"Tell who, what?" Drew slid the glass patio door closed, his long strides making quick work of being in their immediate vicinity. Opening the fridge, he removed a tin foil covered container. Turning to the pair, he awaited an answer.

"I'm just going to go make my rounds." Abandoning her seat like it was on fire, Dream barely escaped Nicole's protest of abandonment. Drew was Nicole's fiancée. It was reasonable that she should explain to him that his cousin's cooking was atrocious and the only thing that ought to be fired was Jonah. For a moment, she recalled how terrible it felt being canned and felt a touch of remorse in wishing it on a friend, up until her stomach growled chasing the infrequent emotion away.

Warm air assaulted her as she slid the patio door open, its normally sticky traction gliding along more smoothly than she's ever experienced. Max held the handle on the other side, the explanation for the ease in getting it open, before he nearly charged into her. Dream stepped aside unscathed, allowing him to enter.

"Sorry about that." Max patted her arm as he whizzed past.

Warmth penetrated her arm despite his frosty demeanor. One day soon, Max was going to fall for her again and she'd rekindle what had once looked promising. Obviously not today, but really soon. His barely there, little sister contact, only served as a reminder of the one-way attraction.

Sitting alone at the round patio table, the monotone blue stripped umbrella providing desperately needed shade, Tami concentrated on the screen of her cell phone. The summer sun still sat high for early evening, casting sharp shadows. "What's got you so sucked in?"

"Binge watching a program on Netflix." Tami rose to her feet and encased Dream in a hug. "And waiting for everyone else, so we can get dinner started. I'm starved."

She returned the hug then sat. "Which show?"

"Nothing you'd appreciate and I'm not in the mood to defend my brain washing television choices."

"Unabashed honesty. I love it! There's hope for you yet Tamryn Davidson."

"Wells." Tami shot her a pointed look.

"Sorry to rain on your parade Tamryn *Wells*, but I'm pretty sure Nicole and Drew are making out in the kitchen, Max practically ran me over trying to get somewhere else, and dinner doesn't appear to be...ready?" If that were what one would call burning everything to a crisp.

"He's getting better," Tami, pleaded through a stifled chuckle.

"I guess marriage deludes people." Dream moved the patio chair further into the shade. "Among other things." Boy oh boy she hadn't seen Tami's acne flare up so bad since junior high, before she began to manage the breakouts. "Did you run out of facial cleanser?"

"Do you always have to be so...Oh! Never mind. What did you bring for dessert?"

"Later for dessert. I'm hungry. Is there anything your other half didn't ask the devil to breathe on?"

"The salad," Tami joked smugly.

"Leaves and grass are not real food, and shouldn't be allowed at any decent barbeque. What kind of joint is Drew running here, anyway?" Dream stood canvassing the small patio for anything passable as a food table. Jonah walked over with a tray, and a smile. Great. Now, she'd have to sample whatever he was peddling.

"Hey, Dream. Hungry?" Jonah set the tray down. The hot dogs had stabs wounds, as if they had been tortured before being burned at the stake. Sweet sausages, he was offering her Joan of Arc hot dogs. The hamburgers, more char than not, had shrunk down to hockey puck size, and were probably just as hard.

"Actually,"

"She's starving," Tami finished.

"Oh yeah?" Jonah asked. "I cooked the hamburgers a little longer. I know you don't like pink in the middle."

I don't like burnt in the middle either.

"You are too sweet, honey. I'm sure Dream appreciates your extra effort. Don't you Dream?"

Jonah turned and faced her, hope in his puppy dog eyes in search of a "good boy" and a scratch behind the ears. Unfortunately, for him, vulnerability didn't sway her in the least. The swift kick under the table to her exposed shin, however, was much more convincing.

"No one puts in more effort than you Jonah." The last few years of summer grilling was evident of that. "I'll just grab the plates from inside to set the table." Dream pointed toward the apartment, bee lining to safety. Watching Drew and Nicole maul each other wasn't going to be much better for her stomach than consuming not-dogs, soot-sausages, or puck patties, but she could just hide in the bathroom for a bit.

Entering into a room of raised voices wasn't what she expected, but God liked to throw her a bone every now and then. Nicole and Drew's heated discussion was getting hotter by the second. Occupying her once abandoned stool, Dream took in the show already in progress, hoping she hadn't missed anything good.

"When are we going to pick a date? We've been engaged for over two years." Nicole flustered was definitely new.

"You said you wanted to wait. Why do you want to rush into marriage now?" Drew lowered his exasperated voice, raising his arms in question.

"I do, did want to wait, but I think we've waited long enough and it's time to set a date. Why are you making such a big deal about this?"

Drew dragged his hand down his face. "Marriage is a big deal, Nicky."

Pastor Pretty Boy was losing his cool. Oh, this was too delicious. It was also probably a private conversation, but since neither had asked her to leave, so it must be ok to stay. Moral support and all that stuff, or referee the way this was headed.

"I didn't say it wasn't. I know marriage is a big deal, which is why I wanted to wait when you were ready to elope. I just don't understand why, now, you are..." Nicole paused, her posture straightening.

If Dream had a remote, she would have checked to see if she'd accidentally pressed pause, but this was real life and the look in Nicole's eyes did not bode well for Drew.

"*No lo creo*. I can't believe I didn't see this sooner. You're having second thoughts, aren't you? You don't want to marry me." Unshed tears glistened the brim of Nicole's eyes.

Dropping his arms, Drew stepped toward Nicole and lifted her chin. "Of course, I want to marry you. Don't ever doubt that." Sliding his hands over her shoulders, he rested them on her naked forearms.

"*No me toques, Tonto.*" Nicole removed herself from his hold gently. "Actions speak louder than words." She said barely above a whisper and walked away, her spirit crushed. Poor thing.

Storming off would have been much more appropriate, but Dream could coach her for future couples spats. A wedding gift of sorts, *if* they ever got married.

As if on cue, Pastor Pretty Boy pulled out his pocket Bible, thumbing through it. Since being dunked two years ago, Drew had gone from loud and proud bachelor to monk. Any given day he bordered inspiring and irritating.

"Hoping to find a wedding date in there?" It was too difficult to keep her grin from spreading across her face, hearing her own joke.

"How much did you hear?" Drew looked up, defeat in his eyes. Compassion wasn't one of Dream's God-given gifts, but they were alone so unfortunately, the burden to lend an ear fell on her shoulders. It was too late to run out of the room now. Served her right for being nosey, she supposed.

"All of the juicy stuff." Dream reached over to the variety tray of chips and palmed a few pretzels.

Closing the Bible, Drew tapped it against his leg. "Do you know what she said in Spanish?"

"We haven't gotten to 'How to Argue' in Spanish class just yet, but she did call you an idiot." Dream tossed a pretzel into her grinning mouth.

"I take it your class already covered insults."

Dream dusted her hands free from the salt. "I aced my exam."

"Do you think she's really upset?"

Slouching in her stool, she narrowed her gaze. "Why do you ask me questions you already know the answer to? I can tell you, that I was a few seconds away from jumping on your back myself."

Offering her a look that conveyed it wasn't the time to tease, she continued.

"Drew, you know you are like the brother I never wanted, but Nicole and Tami are the closest to sisters I'll ever have, and I will always have their back. So stop being a *tonto* and set a date already."

Drew considered her words.

Gesturing toward the front door Dream shouted. "Go!" Pocketing his Bible, Drew followed Nicole's earlier path through the living room, making it only a few steps before Dream's stomach protested, reminding her, they hadn't eaten yet. "Hurry! Some of us would like to eat sometime today," she called over her shoulder

---

Nicole cleared the table as Drew carried out Dream's cookie trays. The plastic lids crackled as he removed them. He sat after snatching up a chocolate chip. Nicole returned, sitting as far away as she could.

"I guess I'll go first." Drew volunteered.

Dream kept the eye roll in check, hoping he wouldn't turn their weekly tradition into a Bible study again this week.

"Low point of the week," Drew fiddled with the cookie, "is arguing with Nicky. No matter what she thinks, I love her more than ever, and I do want to marry her."

"That's so sweet." Tami teared up.

Nicole didn't seem convinced. She turned toward Dream lifting her chin in defiance.

"My highlight of the week is the Summer Basketball League has found enough sponsors to host a community championship tournament."

Although not the sentimental type, the news made Dream's heart leap for joy. It was a great program, her grandfather founded for the local children, hoping to keep them out of trouble. Over the years, its success continued to surpass the year before. Christ Community Church was making a difference. Dream joined in cheering and clapping. Shoving Nicole's foot when she remained quiet, though she looked ready to burst.

Support inevitably escaped her tightened lips. "Congratulations. The boys deserve it."

Locking eyes with Nicole, Drew continued. "And lastly. News I need to share. By this time next year, I will be a happily married man."

Despite her best effort, Nicole was unable to hold back the grin. "I guess that's my cue. My highlight of the week is this very moment."

The group chuckled, though Dream's gag reflex wasn't to be ignored. Nicole and Drew were painfully sweet, which in real life only resulted in stomachaches and cavities.

"My low of the week was losing a patient at the hospital. Oliver finally succumbed. It was so heartbreaking."

"I thought he was 'the meanest *viejo* to ever roam earth?'"

"Dream. The man died. Do you have to speak ill of the dead?"

"Me?" She laughed. "I was only repeating what you said."

"Please don't remind me. I feel terrible. He was just lonely. He caught me praying over him last week. Since then he'd been a little nicer to me. I think I was the only person to care about him one way or another."

"That is so sad." Tears streamed down Tami's face. "Nicole can't participate anymore. I can't take all this talk about mourning business." Tami teased as she wiped away her tears.

Good grief, Dream couldn't agree more. "Her or her man, if you ask me. Must you two make us an emotional mess every Sunday?" That was a rollercoaster ride of emotions all within the span of a few minutes.

"Well, no one asked you," Drew chimed in as he winked.

"No one is getting banned. Nevertheless, I'm sorry for your loss Nicole. Here. Eat a cookie." Lifting the tray, Tami slid it in front of Nicole before glaring at Dream between sniffles.

"Thanks." Choosing her favorite, Nicole nibbled absent-mindedly before moving along. "Anyway. Any news I need to share? Not anymore."

Max sat back in his chair, brow furrowed. "How come?"

"Because I'm not single, after all."

Drew snapped his attention to Nicole. "Nicky," he growled.

Max chuckled and Dream could drown in that full smile. He caught her watching, his amusement faltering. In no rush, she casually diverted her attention elsewhere.

"Dream?" Tami urged her to go next.

"Me? Ok. My low for the week. That's easy. Being fired. My highlight was getting my car back. News I need to share-"

A chorus of voices competing with one another stopped her from announcing her exciting news.

"Backtrack there for just a second. Did you just say that you got fired?" Drew's eyes widened like the basketballs he was so fond of.

Exhaling an agitated breath, she prepared to explain, what she was hoping would have bypass quickly. Wishful thinking. "Enough with the interrogation. I'll talk."

Tami chuckled. "One question is hardly an interrogation. Now let's hear it. And don't leave anything out," she warned.

"Settle down there Little Bit. I'm getting to it." Her friend had obviously had one sugar cookie too many.

Jonah pulled Tami to his lap. "Let her talk, babe."

Goody-Two-Shoes to the rescue. Not that she was surprised, or that she needed rescuing. "On Friday, I picked my car up from the impound-"

Max tsked as he shook his head.

So much for not judging during Sunday share time. Nicole patted his arm, discreetly scolding him with a look.

"I picked my car up from the police impound," Dream repeated. "And made it a block before David pulled me over. I had a tail light out. He went through the entire 'license and registration' process, and consequently I was late for work.

"Apparently tardy one time too many. Not that it would have mattered. I was specifically hand-chosen to be laid off come September. Mmm-hmm," she nodded. "'Not corporate material.'" She mimicked Mr. Littleton's condescending tone. "Company merged. Cutbacks were made. You know. All the good stuff."

"So sorry Dream." Nicole patted her hand. "What are you going to do?"

"I was getting to that. Is there anything, I need to share? Yes!" Butterflies fluttered as she prepared to share her exciting news. "I have decided to freelance my mathematical talents." It felt great to announce it aloud. Somehow, it made it official, despite not having a single client yet.

"And you've prayed about this?"

Had she been deaf and blind, she would have had no issues figuring out who posed the question.

"Yes Drew. In fact, I've been praying since my senior year at St. Johns and I truly believe this is the right time." Taking a leap to fulfill a goal was equally thrilling and terrifying. This is what tightrope walkers must feel like.

Her reply must have pacified Drew. Too bad for him, if it hadn't. Her mind was made up and she was not being talked out of the decision.

"Sounds like you've thought this through." The worry etched on Tami's face stirred a ripple of doubt within before Dream purged it from her mind. God was with her. No need to fear.

"More than you know. I'll start with some small businesses that can't afford on staff accountants. Maybe even a few churches." The silence wouldn't deter her. "Guys, I can do this."

"Of course you can!" Pounding on Jonah's knee, Tami jumped on the inspiration bandwagon. "And if you need anything from me, you just let me know." The others chimed-in offering the same encouragement and assistance.

"Actually, Max, I was wondering if you'd help me with some marketing materials. Business cards. Website. That sort of stuff."

Hoping, his picking at the table with his thumb in contemplation, and the tightening of his jaw wasn't indicative of turning her down, she shot up a quick prayer.

If push came to shove, she'd hire someone else if need be, but she'd rather give the business to someone she knew. A chance to support freelancers, and small business owners, now that she was one herself.

Not to mention that since leaving his photography career, much to her relief once she learned *who* he was photographing, Max had gone back to his roots in graphic and web design. If his tiny apartment was any indication, he could probably use the extra funds. Perhaps she should have led with that.

"I'd pay you of course." Fingers crossed, she hoped that would help turn the tide in her favor. Or not. It'd been almost a half-minute since she'd asked, and the silence was humiliating.

"Yeah, sure." A shrug of the shoulders was all she'd gotten, but she'd take it.

Rubbing the knee Tami had pounded on a minute prior, Jonah grimaced as he spoke. "I guess that means your next Max."

※

The tradition of Sunday dinner and Share Time had taken on a life of its own. Sometimes it was actually rewarding, but for a man with secrets, it could be torturous. Foregoing dinner altogether had been an idea quickly cast aside. His absence would just prompt his friends to ask questions. As long as he showed up and participated enough to throw off any suspicion, he was fine. Well up until Dream knocked his world off its axis with her revelations and requests. It hadn't happened often, but when it did, the effect was abounding.

Last year, a Sunday dinner resulted in Dream requesting the help of her friends for a church fundraiser.

A harmless request until he found himself in Mrs. Lugo's backyard, the eighty-year old woman sitting poolside in a bikini insisting he work his photography magic. The portraits would be a gift for her younger husband, to keep his eye from wondering. Wilfredo was seventy with eyesight as poor as baby Jesus.

For three nights straight, a raisin wearing a bikini haunted his dreams. He still couldn't eat the shriveled dried fruit without thinking of Mrs. Lugo in that swimwear.

Six months ago, Dream had gone on and on for fifteen minutes about a Spanish class she wanted to enroll in to help her communicate with others on an extended mission's trip to Mexico, she was planning. The woman obviously avoided the news, and how well received missionaries were in Mexico.

Three months ago, Dream announced she'd be cutting off most of her glorious mane to donate to charity. Hearing the news himself, made his heart dive before he checked the absurdity. She could do what she wanted with her hair. Besides, it was just hair, he reminded himself. It'd grow back. Currently, she sat across from him with her tresses to her lower back. Not that he was eyeballing her.

And now, as if she'd just announced what was for dinner, she'd admitted to being fired. No dejection. No dispiritedness. Her livelihood was gone and she seemed not to care one iota. Not to mention her joy at getting her car back from the police impound. The mere idea of why it was confiscated in the first place sent his nerves on edge. The woman attracted trouble like flowers did bees.

As if that weren't enough, she had once again solicited his help. Compassion led him to accept her offer.

Marketing materials could get costly. Unbeknownst to her, he'd do all the design work pro-bono.

Clearing his throat, Max straightened from his slouching position. "My low..." Accepting the job Dream offered, except he couldn't very well say that aloud could he? "Guess I don't have one. My highlight..." David waltzing into basketball looking ridiculous because Dream turned him down again sprang to mind. Stocks rising again, earning him a few extra pennies. Coming to a life-changing decision. "I guess it's been a slow week. I don't have one."

The grumbles subsided when Drew, in his big brother tone asked if perhaps Max had something to share that everyone needed to know. Dipping his chin, he gave the floor back to Max.

Meeting his gaze, Max shook his head. "Nope. Like I said. Slow week."

Drew was brewing beneath his carefully constructed façade of control. If Drew thought for one second Max would drop another bomb on Dream regarding David's ridiculous bet, he was sadly mistaken. She had one crazy week, already. His news wouldn't be the reason the woman finally cracked completely.

"You sure?" Drew insisted.

"Actually, I do. I did some graphic work for a friend and in exchange, he bartered a week at his beach house in Ocean City. I know its last minute, but this was the only week he had available for the remainder of the summer. Think you guys can make it down for the weekend?"

Tami sighed. "We could use a few days at the beach, right honey?"

Jonah shrugged. "Beach sounds good to me."

"Me too," Nicole chimed in. "Drew?"

Between gritted teeth and narrowed eyes, Drew replied his stare never leaving Max's, "I'll see if someone can cover me. The boys have practice on the Saturday. Which reminds me. Max, will you be at using the gym on Saturday morning? I know how much *David* and the guys appreciate the space."

Max's jaw tightened. "I won't be there. I'll be at the beach house."

The staring match lasted only a few moments longer before Tami interjected. "I don't know what all that is about, but if you two are done, Jonah and I would like to share our highs and lows together this week." Giddy as a teen at a boy band concert, Tami scooted her chair closer to her husband's, and waved to his phone as he began recording. "Our highlight of the week is that we had some pictures taken that turned out fabulous." Nonchalantly, she gestured to Jonah to continue.

Lacing his fingers through Tami's, he aimed the camera at his wife before turning it back to himself. "And our low of the week is that it looks like for the unforeseeable future, our finances are going to be a little strapped."

The silence wasn't surprising. The concern on everyone's face mimicked his own.

"And you two are grinning like idiots because?" Dream's bark was sometimes as vicious as her bite. Not that he could blame her reaction.

The odd desire to record themselves giving bad news paled in comparison to what Jonah had just admitted.

"Do you guys need money? Are you falling behind on your mortgage and bills?" They needed only to the say the word and Max would find a way to provide however much they needed to hold them over. Secretly, of course.

"Blessedly no, but that brings us to the something we have to share." The couple eyed each other before facing the eager expressions waiting in silence, turning the camera to their friends. "We are expecting."

Expecting what? To lose their home? Have their cars repossessed? Move into a boxcar in order to have a place to sleep? What exactly?

Jumping up from her chair, Nicole squawked like a deranged macaw, running over to Tami, embracing her before spreading her arms out wide, taking her in from head to toe. "I can't believe it!"

That was an understatement. What in the world was going on?

Dream stood and embraced his sister who had begun to tear up again. "Congratulations honey."

"Thanks." Wiping away the tears, Tami and Dream waved at the camera briefly before Jonah was interrupted.

Man hugging his cousin, Drew closed in on the camera, praising Jonah for getting the job done, as they shared a laugh. "I knew you had it in you Cuz."

Clearly, he'd missed something major. Meeting Tami's expectant eyes, he stood unsure what to say or do.

"Aren't you going to say anything? I expected you to be the most excited about being an uncle. I guess the photographer needs a visual to understand." Tami slid a sonogram photo across the table. "Here is one of the photos I was talking about."

A blob of black and white imaging stared back at him. An uncle? The understanding crashed down on him like a ton of bricks. How dense could he be? His sister was expecting a baby and he was going to be an uncle. Two minutes after agreeing to work with Dream, and his brain was already turning into mush.

Enclosing his sister in a bear hug, he lifted her from her feet and chuckled aloud. "I couldn't be happier for you, Hami."

"Whoa! Be careful there. Baby Wells is cooking in that oven."

Setting his sister back down to the ground, he remembered why Sunday dinners weren't so bad after all.

Chapter 4

A flurry of excitement coursed through her being. A million ideas filled her head and a million more in her notes. Logo ideas, colors for her very own website, and promotion ideas poured out onto paper into the wee hours of the morning. Tucking a small binder under her arm, Dream knocked on the paneled door. She was probably early, but the thrill of starting her own business robbed her of sleep and the sooner she got started the more she could say she accomplished.

Three knocks later, and a bit deflated, she turned away from the unanswered door back down the walkway, directly into a sweaty Max. His hands found his waist as he panted for breath. Even after a morning run, he made her insides turn into pudding. "Good morning. Did I confuse the time of our meeting?" They both knew he hadn't.

"I was just eager to get started," she confessed.

"I'd say. It's seven A.M." He cocked his head to the side, a teasing smile.

"Yikes. I hadn't even realized." She handed him a cup of coffee, wishing she could have drowned in it. There was eager, and then there was overzealous. "Black with sugar. Repentance for overlooking visiting protocol."

He hesitated before accepting it.

"Don't worry. I didn't poison it."

Tilting his head toward his door, he invited her to follow him as he sniffed the brew.

The morning sun entered the window above the television, illuminating the few dust particles floating midair. His apartment was small but neat. Even now, with unexpected company it was orderly. Everything was situated in its place, other than the scarf draped over the dining table that might as well have been surrounded by glowing neon arrows pointing to it. As if left there intentionally, it mocked her. And here she'd thought only dogs marked their territory.

Max set his coffee on the kitchen counter. "I need to shower. Give me a few minutes."

Snatched from her thoughts of the feminine accessory, Dream nodded as he excused himself. Pulling the chair away from the table, she eyed the scarf and then the door Max had disappeared into. Leaning in slightly toward it, she could hear the spray of a shower in use.

After a few minutes alone and being assured she had no audience, she picked up the scarf surveying every stitch from end to the other. Whoever owned the silk had expensive taste. It was a quality piece, with beading finely sewn on each end. One that her mom would probably love, therefore not her taste, even if she did like it. The faint smell of women's perfume lingered to the silk only noticeable if you held it as close as she was currently. A scent she didn't recognize, but one that didn't agree with her nose.

Before she could stop herself, the scarf clung to her hand as she covered her face during a fit of the sneezes. Quickly pulling the scarf away, she cringed seeing moisture spots absorbing into it. Waving it about, she hoped it would dry before Max returned. Other than flailing her arms like a mad woman waving a flag of surrender, the exercise was futile.

Pulling a paper towel from the holder, she wiped the scarf gently, but to no avail. Tossing the useless paper towel in the garbage can, she searched for a more successful solution. Rushing over to the window, she held it up to the window before pulling it back realizing it was overcast out. No sun meant no heat and no drying. Blowing on it, hadn't helped much either.

"I'll be right out!" Max yelled from the other side of his bedroom door.

In a panic and spotting the microwave, Dream marched over, tossed the scarf in, and nuked it before thinking twice. It took only a few seconds before a spark lit up the inside of microwave, followed by a myriad of fireworks along with a host of popping sounds. Yanking the microwave door open, she gasped at the burning odor that assaulted her.

Removing it from the dastardly electronic, she winced. The beading on the edges were blackened and melted. Tiny singes ran throughout the entirety of the scarf, ruining it completely.

Hearing the rattle of the doorknob, Dream shoved the scarf in her top, slammed the microwave door closed, and plopped into the wooden chair closest to her. Max emerged from his bedroom, but she hadn't the courage to face him.

The scent of his masculine soap reached her before he had, causing chaos with her sensibilities. She ought to be remorseful. Shameful. Fearful even. Yet, the urge to saddle up to Max and take a closer whiff, clobbered her upside the head.

His back to her, she risked a peek. Running a towel ruggedly over his head, she was fascinated with the movement. The tee clung to his back, every defined muscle evident, and she could only assume he hadn't taken the extra few seconds to dry it thoroughly.

It was ridiculous and wanton to envy that tee. Blessedly his voice brought her back to lucidness and she hurriedly evicted the corrupt thoughts.

"I hope I didn't take too long." Pulling out the chair across from her, he tossed the towel on its back, set his laptop on the table, beside a portfolio, and took a seat. "I have some samples to show you."

"Great." Gliding the presentation folder closer to her, she was grateful for having a reason to avoid eye contact a little longer.

"Let me warm up my coffee and then we can get started."

Terror seized her. If he opened the microwave and smelled the evidence of her mishap, she was as good as found out. The ringing of his cell phone interrupted the task. Never had she been saved by the bell and she thanked God for the rescue.

"Morning." Max leaned against the counter facing her.

Ear hustling, she turned each page after a reasonable amount of time passed, not having glanced at one business card, although, she'd leaned in a few times for what she hoped translated into getting a better look. If he asked, she wouldn't be able to recall a single detail of any.

What had her utmost attention was the fact that anyone calling this early in the morning had either, no shame or free reign, when it came to said man.

Choking on her saliva, she realized that sitting in Max's kitchen table at that early hour, qualified her to fit into only one of those two categories, and it flamed her face.

Now that she thought about it, whoever phoned had just done her a solid. Not only had they given her a chance to escape further humiliation, at least momentarily, they also helped her cast a bright light on her own imprudent behavior. Getting to her feet, she gestured to the door before making the universal sign for 'call me later' or did it mean aloha. Either way, it all boiled down to her leaving immediately.

Max dipped his eyebrow and raised a finger requesting she wait. And wasn't life full of irony. How many times had she wished he would've invited her to wait for a few minutes after Sunday dinner, for a private goodbye? Now that she needed to escape, he wanted her to stay. Men.

"As a matter of fact, you did leave your scarf here. I'll bring it with me when I come over for dinner." Max's eyes roved to where the scarf had been draped. Confused he tilted his head back, searching the floor under the chair, then around the table. His eyes locked on hers and he frowned. "Now that I have you on the phone. Where did you get the scarf? I was thinking Tami might like one. Maybe I can find one in yellow."

Max nodded as he listened intently to the caller. "Perfect. Thanks."

Like a kid awaiting to be punished, Dream's palms began to perspire. If his scowl was any indication, Max had already found her guilty and was about to sentence her, with no appeal.

He was right to accuse her of course, but it was extremely impolite to assume she'd actually done anything without the facts to prove so. Besides, the homewrecker that tried to mark her territory had it coming. Max was already spoken for, even if he didn't know it yet.

"Talk to you later, Mom." Placing the phone on the table, he trapped it between both palms, now flat to the table, as he continued his visual assault. His eyes hadn't stopped scorching her since he'd noticed the wrap missing.

He had just said mom, hadn't he? Dream pinched an eye shut as she gathered top lip behind her teeth. Taking in the severity of the situation, she realized that is was probably best to just confess without preamble.

Nonsense. She could get out of this. "How's Cecily?"

"Missing her scarf."

"A family heirloom?"

"No."

Thank God. "I'm sure it'll turn up sooner or later."

Max closed the space between them at a turtle's pace, yet menacing and calculating. "That's how you're going to play this?"

"Play what? I have no idea what you're talking about, and please stop looking at me as if I committed a crime so heinous that general population isn't even an option."

"What did you do with it? And before you deny it, I know you know where it is. You're doing that thing you do with your fingers when you're guilty."

Dream looked down to fingers twisting and interlocking on their accord. Forcing herself to cease, she slid both hands behind her back. "That is ridiculous."

"Dream, I am not above searching for it if I have to. If you think that I'm going to sit back and let you steal from me, you are sadly mistaken."

"Steal from you!" Slamming her fists to her waist, Dream took a threatening step forward. "Are you kidding me? I have never stolen a thing in my life and I'm certainly not going to start with a pink silk scarf that my mom, and apparently yours, have in their fashion arsenal. No offense."

Crossing his arms, his approach remained steady, forcing her retreat. "So you *have* seen it."

Two steps backward, and backed firmly against the counter, she refused to cave. "That is neither here nor there. What's more important is you owing me an apology."

Narrowing his eyes, he took the final steps trapping her. His forced whisper rode the thin line between poise and combustion. "Do I need to search for it Dream?"

Now only a hair's breadth away, the smell of fresh shower and soap enveloped her. If Max thought for one second, this scenario was intimidating, he was sorely deluded. The last time they'd been in such close, proximity was during a slow dance during her Junior Prom. She wasn't complaining then, nor was she now, but she'd play along if it meant he'd stay close for a few minutes longer. "You wouldn't?"

Ten minutes. That's how long he'd left her alone. It was the quickest shower he'd taken since living under his mother's roof, and being left without hot water after Tami hogged it all every night. And for what? Dream still managed to land him in a predicament without his participation. Again. He should have made her wait outside, no matter how rude it seemed.

Not that he'd ever carry out the threat to search her person for his mother's favorite scarf, but if she knew what was good for her, she'd realize he was not in a joking mood. The delicate swag reminded Cecily of a similar one his father had gifted her during their courtship. She'd even shown Max a photo where she'd worn the original that had looked vaguely similar to the now missing understudy. A tear escaped as his mom reminisced, battering his already bruised heart.

Now this woman, trouble in carnet, shows up, and risks disappointing his mom. Over a scarf, no less. No doubt, Cecily would brush it off, but he knew it would hurt.

Stepping in closer, the fact that Dream's scent made him gag, or that her long tresses, silkier than the scarf, made his heart race, had no bearing on his mission, to simply retrieve what was once safeguarded in his apartment.

"I haven't got all day."

The minute she began biting the inside of her cheek keeping her amusement in check, he knew what she about. The sneaky woman wasn't intimidated at all. Instead, Dream was enjoying the encounter too much. He'd change that soon enough.

"As soon as you apologize," she said.

"To you? For stealing from me? I don't think so."

Mouth hung up, she closed it, sparks flying from her coffee brown eyes. Dark and a little sweet, just like the cup, she'd brought him, and exactly how he liked it.

"I didn't steal it."

"Yeah, well you can explain it to David Escobar when he gets here, because I'm this close to calling the cops." The small distance between his thumb and index finger indicated the very little amount of patience he had left.

Although quickly masking the terror that flashed in her eyes, he'd seen enough to know his strong-arm tactic affected her. Granted, Dream wasn't afraid of the police. She'd been hauled downtown enough times for the threat to lose its sting. Calling David, however, was a newfound resource he wasn't afraid to exploit.

"Fine, but promise you won't get mad."

As if she were in control of the situation, she had the gall to request promises. One that he clearly couldn't honor being that he was currently on the brink, and ready to tip over.

"I promise no such thing."

Sidestepping him, she aimed to get around him moving toward the wall. "You're nothing but a stubborn bully."

Matching her move, he slammed his hands against the wall imprisoning her between his arms. "Sticks and stones may break my bones, but words will never hurt me."

Her eyes locked on his. She opened her mouth to speak then closed it again. Trying again, she failed at articulating a single word.

He'd effectively left Dream blessedly speechless. Pride swelled within, knowing he'd achieved something most had dreamed of, no pun intended, but never had the opportunity to accomplish themselves. Moreover, her own words had sweetened the victory. The feat was resume worthy. Perhaps it could be engraved on his tombstone.

The celebration for one came to an abrupt halt when the warmth of Dream's hands slid around his torso and locked around his waist as she tenderly brought her mouth to his.

The sirens sounding off in his head warning him to pull away, warred with the desire to wrap her in his arms, and kiss her until she begged him for air. Even then, he couldn't promise he'd comply.

Grateful for the shameful memories of his past he kept at the forefront, the desire to kiss her died a quick death. Nothing good would come from giving into the flesh again. He'd learned that lesson one time too many.

Yanking her arms from his middle, Max pushed her a safe distance away from him. "What are you doing?"

Dream's arms fell to her sides exasperated. "Apparently, failing miserably at distracting you."

Her confession had no business bruising his ego but the feeling was unmistakable. It made little sense, but his pride felt cheated. There once was a time she'd shown a genuine interest in him. Had she moved on?

Like a football punter, Max kicked aside the disturbing line of thinking, and circled the table adding more space between them. "Dream, us, working together, is not such a good idea." The panic that filled her eyes churned his gut. Refocusing his attention on anything other than her, he cleared his throat and continued. "I have a few contacts that can help you. In fact, most of them are better skilled than I am. My absence in this field is obvious. I'm just getting my feet wet again."

"Ok. I crossed the line. I know that." She neared. "And I'm truly sorry. Nevertheless, Max, this is the most important decision I've made in my life, probably ever. I plan to do any and everything to make a success of it. I know there are plenty of other designers that can help, but none of them knows me the way you do. That is essential for me."

He said nothing the silence prompting her to up the ante. "Starting this second, I'll be nothing but professional. I promise."

Running a hand over his cropped hair, he contemplated her ability to remain professional during their time working together, or even if he could remain so. He'd just barely dodged a mishap before regrets stepped in and done their job, keeping him in check.

Disgusted with his sudden lack of self-confidence, he adjusted his thinking. Of course, he could be a professional. He'd learned his lesson the hard way and matured since his early days as a photographer. If only to prove so to himself, he came to his decision. "Ok. You have a deal."

Dream nodded. "Thank you." Gathering her belongings, she headed for the door. "I think I'll just go, and pretend this morning never happened. Can we start later today?"

"Sounds good. Not here though." He was confident he could successfully take her on as a client but there was no use in stacking the deck against himself. Being alone with Dream could get stickier than syrup on a diner table.

Pink filled her cheeks. "How about at CCC? I'm doing some accounting there for a few hours and then I'm free for the rest of the day. How about one o'clock?"

A church where her grandfather was the Pastor and God was keeping watch. It couldn't get any safer than that. "Perfect."

"See you then."

"Dream?"

"Yeah?" Turning from the door, she faced him.

"The scarf."

"Right." Setting down her binder, she reached in her top and retrieved the scarf, as a magician would a string of tied up handkerchiefs from his sleeve. Walking it over, she captured her bottom lip between her teeth. "Obviously I have some explaining to do so how about, the whole professional-from-now-on thing start after that?"

Max dropped his chin and wondered if he really wanted to know why his mother's scarf looked like it had been in a war zone. This woman was going to drive him insane and he's just consented to let her.

Chapter 5

Arriving at the church, an hour early had its advantages. The quietude of an empty sanctuary was oddly comforting. Churches were meant to be filled with lost and found souls, nevertheless Dream basked in the peace of having the church, her great grandfather founded, and she grew up in, all to herself. Sometimes she just wanted her house to herself for a while.

The soft sound of the sanctuary door opening, followed by the soft whoosh of air signifying its closing, startled her. Her surrogate grandfather and Pastor of CCC waved from the door and proceeded down the center aisle toward the altar. "Good morning Twinkle. What brings you in so early?" Placing a kiss on her cheek, he settled in the cushioned chair beside hers.

She refused to let her cheeks flame being reminded of the circumstances that led her to being there at the unusual hour. "Nothing worth mentioning. How about you?"

"I'm actually a few minutes late," he laughed. "I always get here before Rosita. I like to pray alone in the sanctuary. I see you had the same idea. It's peaceful isn't it?"

"More than I anticipated." Getting to her feet, she reached down and pecked him on the cheek. "I'll let you get to it FauxPa."

"I didn't mean to imply you had to leave." Bracing himself, he pushed up to stand.

"Don't you worry a single gray hair on your head, old man. I've been here a while. The place is all yours."

"You know you're never too old for some hearty correction, don't cha?"

"FauxPa, you've threatened me with 'correction via rod' so often, the scripture is engraved in my brain. Right next to the fact that you've never laid a correcting finger on me in all of my days."

"Patience is a virtue, Dream and for your sake a blessing."

Laughter echoed off the empty sanctuary walls. "In that case, I owe patience and you, a debt of gratitude." She hugged him before smacking an unexpected and noisy kiss to his wrinkled cheek again. Remembering she'd done that twice before most of the Eastern Seaboard had enjoyed breakfast, she straightened and banished herself to her desk where figures, boring and constant, would monopolize her thoughts.

An hour into balancing Accounts Payable for the previous month, Rosita, the church receptionist, casually strolled in. An original member of the church, she rebuffed any mention of retiring her position despite her lack of ability, mobility, and sensibility. She could be as sweet as pie when inclined to, but other than being able to count money more efficiently than a bank teller, Rosita had become inept with most of her responsibilities.

FauxPa's soft spot blinded him to her inefficiencies. Correcting some of Rosita's errors, without anyone's knowledge, had only hurt her cause the two times she dared broach the topic of Rosita's retirement with Pastor Collins. With no real proof, he didn't as so much entertain the conversation. Being that she would never purposefully allow errors to go uncorrected, Rosita's job was secure until the day Rosita decided otherwise.

"*Dios te bendiga*. Drain." Her heavy accent changed Dream to Drain, but Dream had learned long ago, it was considered rude to correct an elder who couldn't help her native accent.

"*Dios te bendiga*, Rosita."

Rosita, tsked as she shook her head. "*Americana*," she huffed. Dream had also learned that it was perfectly acceptable for Rosita to publicly and openly disapprove of *her* lack of Spanish accent.

"I love being an Americana," Dream laughed.

"*America* is a wonderful country, but you are *Mexicana* too. *Aprende Español, Niña*."

Dream understood the importance of learning the language of her fore fathers and had already begun taking classes only three months prior. However, since grasping the concept of conversation as a toddler, she had never felt the inclination to explain herself then, and even less so now as an adult. Rather than expressing, what she figured would be rude, she changed the subject entirely.

"How was your vacation? Were you able to see your great grandchildren?" Dream tapped a yellow pencil against her chin as she leaned back in her swivel chair.

"Yes, but I no think they see me. All week they face stuck in the fancy phones." She lowered slowly into her chair. "My last vacation there. I too old to fly to Chicago for nonsense."

Rosita was the epitome of a shoot-it-straight woman. No mincing words. No beating around bushes. She gave it to you straight or not at all. A true role model if there ever was one.

"Why you here and no at you job?"

Although she could get out of hand sometimes.

"I wanted to get an early start. I have a meeting later."

"Ha. I very old woman. I raise fi daugh-ters." Rosita held up a wrinkled hand indicating the number five. "I have twelve *nietas*. Lots of girls in my family. And you forget that I know you since *pequenita*." She lowered her hand closer to the floor. Dream doubted she was ever that small, but she understood what Rosita meant. The woman had indeed known her since birth. "I know girl trouble, *senorita*."

Despite Rosita's glasses being thicker than Coke bottles, she could see what others couldn't. She could read people like a book with large print. However, that didn't mean Dream was ready to confirm or deny any of her keenly accurate suspicions. The woman was as much a gossip as she was wise.

Speaking of girl trouble... "I ran into Marciana last week. She wanted me to tell you that she was planning on stopping by for a visit, but I told her you were away. She's going to try again this week."

"*Ay! Por favor*. My granddaugh-ter is no coming and I no care. You tell Marciana I say, no sank you." Placing her purse in the bottom drawer of her oversized desk, she slammed it closed.

Dream bit the inside of her cheek to keep from chuckling. It was probably mean to goad a seventy-year old woman, especially knowing how she felt about the youngest of her granddaughters who shamed her *abuelita* more times than Dream could count, but it certainly was funny. The woman's tongue was spicy. Besides, it would keep Rosita focused on counting the donations, rather than on Dream's personal affairs.

With two weeks of donations counted then re-counted, Dream waited patiently for Rosita to finish verifying the deposit before signing the in-house record. If she rushed, she could input all of the data, and get a bite to eat before having to meet with Max.

"Sorry to interrupt." The timbre of Max's voice reached out and pulled her naturally toward him.

"Hi. Did I confuse our meeting time?" She teased, his earlier words coaxing a smile that made her heart sprout feet and race in place.

"Actually, something came up and I need to be somewhere earlier than expected. Could we meet now rather than later?"

Dream checked her watch. Eleven. She supposed the data entry could wait. "Sure. I just need to finish up with Rosita."

"No problem. Good morning Mrs. Perez." Max waved and smiled politely.

"*Dios te bendiga, mijo.* You two go. I finish," Rosita insisted.

"It will only take a few more minutes. I can wait for you to finish up." Dream insisted.

"I already finish. See?" Rosita signed the in-house record.

Ignoring the doubt in her gut, Dream didn't question Rosita's word aloud. The manic desire to oversee every single thing Rosita did, was driving her to obsession. It was only the thought that she'd double check things after her meeting that pacified her. For the present, she'd forego making Rosita feel incompetent in front of a guest.

"In that case, I'll be back in a bit."

Rosita waved her off. "*Vete.* Go, go, go."

Dream led Max down the corridor toward a classroom. "You can close the door." She pulled out a chair and sat. Contemplating the decision, he pushed it open wider than before. "It's probably best we leave it open."

All morning, she had kept her mind from wandering to the moment her lips had touched his stiff ones, the sting of rejection just below the surface. The humiliation flooded her once more.

In truth, she wasn't aiming to distract him, as she had said. Lost in the overwhelming connection she felt at that moment, and the proof that she had indeed made a viable deposit into his memory bank, sent her over the edge. It must have been her imagination that a longing in his eyes matched her own.

Dismissing the unfortunate memory from her concentration, she replied, "Of course. Whatever makes you more comfortable."

Max slid a black portfolio case on the table and set up his laptop. "I know you had a few ideas of things you like. Can I see what you have?"

"Sure. Rats! I left my notes on my desk. I'll be right back." Dream hurried to a vacant office. Rosita was gone, but her sweater remained on the chair, which meant she hadn't gone far. Dream was relieved Rosita had finished the deposit in short order. With that responsibility soundly put to rest, Dream searched for her binder finding it buried beneath a few files.

Heading back toward her meeting, Dream passed the foyer. A woman waiting expectantly snatched her attention. "Hello. Can I help you?"

"Hi Dream. How are you?" Marciana, dark circles under her puffy eyes, slurred her words. Rosita was not going to be happy about this.

"Hi Marciana. I didn't recognize you. Your hair looks...different." Ten shades off from the hair pulled closed to her scalp, Marciana's voluminous wavy ponytail stretched down the length of her back like a Barbie Doll.

She chuckled aloud before wincing, her hand pressing toward her temple. "It's fake."

As if anyone with eyes would believe otherwise. Unable to muster a single reaction Marciana was sure was appropriate, Dream cut to the chase. "I believe Rosita is in a meeting with the Pastor. Can you come back later?" *When you aren't hungover.*

"I'll just wait for her." Marciana slowly lowered into a chair, resting her head in her palms, evident signs of a terrible headache.

Leaving her to stew, Dream headed back to her meeting. "Sorry, it took so long..."

Max paced as he spoke on the phone, unaware of her return. "Could you hold the scarf for me? I can get there in two hours or so." He listened carefully as the other person spoke. "I understand that, but you can't take my payment over the phone and the scarves are sold out online. I live an hour away. It's going to take me at least that long to get there. Could you hold it for an hour, at least?"

Shoulders dropping, he smiled. "I owe you...what was your name again?" Max pumped his fist in excitement. "Jessica. I'll see you in an hour. Thanks again." Max stuffed the phone into his trousers pocket and began gathering his belongings.

"Everything alright?" Holding the binder to her chest, Dream stepped further into the brightly lit room.

"I have to reschedule. I only have an hour to make it to Delaware." He slid his laptop into its bag and clipped it shut.

"Is this about your mother's scarf? The one I damaged?"

Max frowned. "Yes, it is. The blasted things are discontinued, and the Nordstrom's at the Cristiana Mall in Delaware has one left. The cashier will only hold it for an hour."

"I'm coming along. I'm the one that ruined the scarf and I should be the one to replace it."

"It's not necessary, but thanks." Max pulled the strap of his laptop bag over his shoulder and zipped the portfolio closed. "I'll call you with a few dates we can reschedule."

"If I come with you, we can work in the car. You drive. I'll explain my vision. Two birds. One stone." If she allowed him to think about this too long, he'd be out of there so fast, he'd leave skid marks on the tile floor. "I insist. Besides, it's not fair making you pay for my mistake, especially now that you are strapped for cash."

Max stopped at the door befuddled. "What makes you think I'm strapped for cash?"

"I just assumed since you are out of work..." At the offended look on his eyes, Dream let the thought die.

"Didn't you just announce yesterday that you were fired?" Max trudged through the door, not giving her the opportunity to reply.

Dream ran to catch up. "Yes, but its only right that I replace what I damaged. And you should know me well enough by now. I'm coming whether you want me to or not. I have my own car and can follow you if I have to. Maybe we can race and see who gets there first," she joked.

Max exhaled. "So much for keeping it professional."

"Our business relationship will be strictly professional. But this is personal in which case I'm entitled to cross a line or two."

"No. You aren't." Max quickened his step.

"Give me two minutes to grab my purse." Ignoring his remark, she followed him into the foyer where Marciana had rushed away from the door they exited. She took a clumsy seat and avoided eye contact.

If Marciana thought for one second, Dream hadn't known she was listening in on their conversation, her ponytail was attached too tight. Dream could teach a class on eavesdropping for goodness sakes. The least Marciana could have done was exploit her state of inebriation. Fall to the ground in a drunken stupor or pretend to have forgotten where the bathroom was located. Anything other than rushing to her seat as if her feet had rocket launchers attached to them, her guilt as good as confessed.

No time to question her, Dream quickly entered the office penned Rosita a note and tossed it on her desk, only then noticing the deposit slip. Tsking, she snatched it from the desk and looked it over quickly. Everything appeared in order. Kneeling down, she opened the safe, relieved to find the deposit bag safely tucked inside. Quickly, she slid the deposit slip in the bag and closed the safe.

As swiftly as her feet allowed, she rushed passed a snoring Marciana in the foyer, and into the parking lot. Max had begun to reverse. Stepping off the curb, she waited for him to pull up to the curb. She waved and he stopped abruptly.

Dream pulled the handle but the door was locked. She bent down and looked into the window. Max was scowling as usual. She tapped. After several seconds, he unlocked the door.

Jumping into the hot car, she could feel the air-conditioner beginning to cool. "I thought you were going to leave me." She snapped in her seatbelt and offered up her most gracious smile. This ought to be interesting.

Chapter 6

For three miles, traffic on I-295 had been limited to one lane, eating up precious time. Without traffic, they were estimated to arrive in forty-five minutes. Now, he was lucky if he'd arrive before Jessica took her lunch break.

The lights of a police siren on the side of the road ahead, confirmed something had happened to cause such massive delays on the usually free flowing interstate. To the right of the road, a car was being loaded onto a flatbed, its rear crashed in completely. A second car sat on the shoulder, its front end in a similar predicament.

Just beyond, the traffic opened up to two lanes with minimal congestion. Accelerating, Max merged into the newly opened up lane.

From the moment, they'd left the parking lot, Dream had been absorbed into the samples he'd brought along and researching her competitors marketing tactics. She'd seldom spoken a word, other than to ask a question about design.

The suddenness of her voice filling the cabin caught him unawares. Head bowed, she prayed aloud for the drivers and families of the passengers of the vehicles involved in the accident.

A sense of shame washed over him as he chimed in with an Amen when she concluded. So caught up in getting to his destination, he'd not even thought about those involved in such a horrific accident. Dream went back to researching and he took the time to pray silently. Again for the passengers, to ask for forgiveness for his selfish attitude, and for the first time to his recollection, for Dream.

Finding the Women's Department in Nordstrom's hadn't been too difficult. Finding Jessica proved otherwise. Max approached the third register, Dream lingering nearby, perusing the purses. A slender redhead chatted up an older woman as she rang up her purchases. Max focused in on the nametag of the cashier. Jessica. Finally. He looked up to find her surprised eyes locked on his. Based on the placement of her nametag, it didn't take a genius to figure out what she was assuming.

Breaking eye contact, he waited patiently in line behind the woman who'd had more questions than a prosecuting attorney had in a career changing case.

Dream shoulder bumped him waking him from the hypnosis the monotonous floor pattern had invoked. "You ok? You look like the naughty cat that swallowed the pet bird."

"I just want to pay for this scarf and head back. I have somewhere to be." Nodding, he returned his gaze to the floor.

"I thought we established that I was paying for the scarf."

A mirthless laugh escaped. She wouldn't be quick to offer had she known the price. Jessica's sultry voice interrupted his thoughts. "Thank you Mrs. Perkins. Have a lovely day." The woman accepted her package and waved as she stepped away from the register. Clearing her throat, Jessica stiffened. "May I help you sir?"

"Hello. Yes. I called earlier. You were holding a pink silk scarf for me."

She said nothing but looked between him and Dream.

"Are you the Jessica I spoke with earlier?"

She instinctively covered her feminine assets. Yep, she'd assumed the worst. "You're late." Turning toward the register, she turned a small key, locking the register. Sliding the key in her pocket, she bent down and retrieved her purse, clutching it to her midsection as if he were a threat to dissolving her of it. Slipping from behind the counter, she squeezed past him, careful not to touch him.

"I'm only five minutes late."

Exasperated, she faced him. "Five minutes too late, sir. The sweet woman, Mrs. Perkins just purchased it."

"You saw me waiting in line. You could have held it for me."

"What I saw while you were waiting in line is despicable and you ought to be ashamed. Now, if you'll excuse me, I only get a half hour lunch break." At breakneck speed, she hurried out of sight.

"Jessica!" Max called after her.

Dream peered at herself in a nearby mirror modeling sunglasses. "What was she accusing you of exactly?" Sucking in her cheeks, she turned from side to side.

Max spoke to her reflection in the oval mirror.

"I was checking her nametag and she assumed I was checking her umm...."

Dream whipped off the sunglasses and faced him. "Her umm?"

Max scratched his neck. "Her... You know what? It doesn't matter. She sold the scarf."

Dream raised an eyebrow. "Were you looking at her umms?"

"Or course not, and could you focus on what's important?"

"Right." She placed the sunglasses on the counter. "Meet me at the car," she said as she rushed away from him.

"Where are you going?" Max tossed his arms up and let them fall at his sides.

"I have to pay a debt," she yelled back.

Max waited at the car for fifteen minutes. Any minute now, he expected to see Dream being escorted out by uniformed police officers. A tap to the passenger window startled him. Frantic, Dream jumped in the car. "Start the car quickly but don't make it obvious. The faster we get out of here the better."

"What did you do?" Max eased out of the parking spot.

"You just worry about driving." Dream haphazardly twisted her hair, and tied it up in a bun. Snatching the baseball cap Max kept in the backseat, she fitted it over her head. "Take this left," she said pointing toward the sign that directed drivers to the interstate. She looked back quickly.

"Are you going to tell me what's going on?" Ahead the streetlight changed from green to yellow.

"Floor it," she insisted.

"Have you lost your mind?" Max stopped at the now, red light. "What did you do, and I should I worry that I am an accessory to a crime?"

The blasting of a horn from a car in the lane beside them grabbed his attention. The customer from

Nordstrom, Mrs. Perkins, yelled at Dream from her window, yelling and waving liver spotted hands.

Raising her hand to block the view of Mrs. Perkins, Dream faced Max. "Why do you always assume the worst of me? And to be fair, I warned you to floor it. Maybe next time you'll listen."

The light changed back to green and with no other option, Max drove through the intersection, and onto the interstate, while Mrs. Perkins continued in her lane, honking as she drove along in a different direction.

"You want me to listen? To you? Did you not see the hundred year old woman ready to murder us?"

"Don't be so overdramatic? She's more like seventy." Dream sat forward and pulled a pink silk scarf from her back pocket. Pressing it to her leg, she attempted to smooth out the wrinkles. "I believe your gratitude is in order." She grinned and held up the scarf.

Snatching it from her hand, he tucked it under his thigh as he checked rearview mirror for the tenth time. "I specifically remember you telling me this morning that you have never stolen a thing in your life and now you are robbing elderly women." Rubbing his forehead, he felt a migraine coming on. "We are going to be on the evening news."

"I hate to break it to you, but purchasing a scarf is hardly exciting enough to be on the evening news." Dream reclined her seat back and closed her eyes.

"Purchase? What do you mean purchased?"

"My debt is paid handsome. Can we call it even?" She covered her mouth as she yawned.

"How did you manage that?" He divided his attention between the road ahead and the woman beside him.

"I gave the fifth Golden Girl a little extra," she yawned again, "for the scarf, than she originally paid. I may have also told her that you are the next Bachelor chosen for the television show, and wanted the scarf as a gift to present to a deserving young woman."

"What?"

"She totally believed me and mentioned something about a granddaughter needing a husband. Anyway, I got out of there as soon as she began following me. I had to walk into the mall and exit from a different door to dodge her. Pointless, she obviously she found us."

Unbelieveable. Dream was completely mad. The Bachelor? Maybe all women were completely off their rockers. Mrs. Jenkins appeared ready to maul him in pursuit of matchmaking. Again, Dream's fault.

"Come to think of it, you might be on the evening news after all. The Bachelor spotted in Delaware shopping for a woman, is gossip news-worthy." Her wide smile diminished as she fell fast asleep.

For a long time, Max said nothing. Dream's soft snores, the only sound disrupting the quiet, allowed him to think. Her method was abominable, but she'd come through for him. Then again, had she not ruined the scarf in the first place, none of this craziness would have happened. Nevertheless, she managed what he hadn't.

With no delays during the return trip, he'd made it back at a decent hour with enough time to deliver his donation to the senior center, before dinner with his mother. Of course, he'd have to drop off Ms. Mischief-Maker first.

Parking in the shade beneath the row of oak trees, Max turned to Dream to wake her but stopped short. Stray hair stuck out from beneath his Phillies baseball cap, yet, even in disarray, the woman was as beautiful, as she was odd. The rhythm of her inhaling and exhaling, hypnotized him. Taking his fill, he watched her sleep. Would the opportunity to admire her, unabashedly and without the complication of her talking, ever present itself again?

He chuckled. Probably not. Dream loved the sound of her own voice. How could he blame her, when hearing it made his own heart beat a little faster? She'd wiggled herself into his heart more years ago then he cared to admit. Calculating how long he'd denied himself was depressing.

Dream stirred, bringing him back to his reality. "Why are you staring at me?" Her eyes remained closed as she grinned.

Gripping the steering wheel, he straightened, "I, umm..."

"Do I have spinach in my teeth?" She interrupted. "Tami, don't laugh."

Furrowing his brow, Max risked another look in her direction. Eyes shut, she cuddled closer to the seat, her soft snores evident again. Relieved, he sat back in his seat. It was only fitting she couldn't keep silent in her sleep either, being she lacked the discipline while awake. It was alarmingly endearing.

Enough was enough. Clearing his throat, he tapped her shoulder, as he would, one of the fellas. "Wake up Sleeping Beauty." If only to convince himself, he infused disdain into the sentiment, immediately regretting the ploy to cover his true feelings. Knowing Dream so well, she'd deliberately ignore the barb and welcome it as flirting. The last thing he wanted was to encourage her.

Not that it mattered. She hadn't heard a word. Still sound asleep, Max tried shaking her again, but to no avail. Perhaps letting her sleep for a few more minutes couldn't hurt.

The confinement of the car must have robbed him of oxygen. Rather than give into the crazed, oxygen-deprived idea to let her slumber, Max honked his car horn like a lunatic, as he yelled out his window to an empty sidewalk.

Startled awake, Dream jumped into the upright position. "The rose is mine, Mrs. Perkins!"

Words rushed from his mouth. "Sorry about the horn. Sometimes people don't look before crossing the line...I mean street." Having been parked for five minutes and in no actual danger of striking a pedestrian, the fact would go unnoticed in her sleep-induced state. "The foot traffic gets crazy around here."

Dream rubbed away the heaviness from her eyes and looked around. The street was practically a ghost town. She raised a questioning eyebrow, the sleep confusion having worn off.

Refusing to speak again, lest nonsense fall from his mouth and onto her lap, Max waited for her to do or say something.

"How long have we been here?" she asked, the words stretched with her yawn and arms.

"Just arrived."

Brows dipping, she slumped in her chair. "I make a lousy road trip partner." Pulling the baseball cap from her head, dark tresses tumbled down her back and shoulders.

Max swallowed the lump in his throat as she finger brushed her hair. For his own sake, as much as hers, he denied himself the sight, instead, diverting his attention to nothing in particular. The zipping effect of an unlatched seatbelt scurrying back into place would be music to his ears. "Thanks for coming, and for the scarf." *Please take the hint.*

"Thanks for letting me tag along. It was fun."

Fun? The woman continued validating her lack of any sense. Being accused of being a pervert one minute, then followed by a groupie granny the next, was not what he considered, a good time.

As Dream exited the car, Max could feel the tension melting away from him and departing with her. Only heaven knows how he'd survive an afternoon alone with Dream. Barely.

Chapter 7

"Good morning Twinkle. Sorry to bother you, but Rosita wanted me to call. I'm running to the bank today, but Rosita can't find the deposit bag you two counted yesterday."

More reason to question Rosita's daily responsibilities. "It's no trouble at all Gramps, but the deposit is in the safe, as it always is. Is Rosita starting to forget things Gramps? I'm truly concerned about her."

"Actually, she checked the safe. It isn't there, which is why she asked me to call you."

"That can't be right. I saw it in the safe myself. Could you take a look? Rosita's eyes aren't what they used to be, God bless her heart." Dream learned a long time ago, if one added the sentiment after the insult, it would curb Gramps ire. He was fiercely protective of his flock not that she was complaining. It was commendable, she supposed.

"In fact, I removed everything and it's not there. I know how busy you are at work, but could you stop by on your lunch break?" FauxPa laughed.

"That was low. Even for you, Gramps."

"I couldn't resist."

"Obviously."

"Perhaps your concern is misguided since you seem to be the one forgetting where you're leaving money." The words still teased, but his tone spoke concern.

"Of course I can stop by, and I'm not forgetting anything. I'm sure it will turn up."

"I trust you. I don't have to tell you that the members of this church trust us with their faithful seed giving.

Financial seed unprotected somewhere doesn't sit right with me."

A spark of uncertainty heated the center of stomach. Dream thought back to the day before. She remembered inserting the deposit slip into the black bag, but whether she secured the safe afterward, escaped her. What she did recall vividly, was rushing to catch up with Max. The mere thought that thousands of dollars could be sitting somewhere it oughtn't, made her middle clench.

Admittedly, she had been distracted by a man, but surely not enough to forget the most important part of her job at the church. Not thinking twice, Dream grabbed her keys. "I'm on my way," she promised.

Racking her brain trying to remember every detail, she knew without a doubt that she had verified the deposit slip for accuracy. Due to the larger than usual amount, it was a detail she couldn't forget. Fear burrowed deeper into her pit churning her insides. The deposit contained two weeks of donations, including the large donation from Max's basketball league.

Arriving faster than anticipated, Dream eased into her usual parking spot, only a few other cars littering the parking lot. Entering in the glass doors, she waved hello to Mrs. Aviles, who came in a few times a week to pray for her sick husband, who'd been diagnosed with Alzheimer's.

Moving down the hall, Dream stepped into Gramps office. Sitting at his desk, he read a letter in silence. Not wanting to worry him without cause, she carried on as she normally would. "How you doing old man?" Grinning, she stepped around his desk, planting a kiss on his cheek.

"Good morning. Just reading a letter that came from the church we helped build in Columbia several years ago.

"Hope it's good news."

"I'll let you know once I'm done," he adjusted his spectacles as he returned his attention to the letter.

"I'll be in Rosita's office." Smiling, he nodded and continued reading.

It was her good fortune that Rosita's office was empty. She could search the safe again and not make Rosita feel like Dream thought her inept.

Not just her. Not that she didn't believe Gramps word, but Dream thoroughly searched the safe, just to be sure. He'd gotten up in there in age as well, and his eyesight not as keen as it once was. God bless his heart.

No money in the safe. Drat! She was truly hoping it had been a simple oversight. Now she'd have to search it out. Rummaging through every drawer to her desk, Dream came up empty. Baffled, she plopped back in her chair blowing out an exaggerated breath. Eyeing Rosita's desk, she contemplated searching it.

Rosita wouldn't like it, but it's not as if she were snooping through her things for fun. She was only looking for one specific thing, and nothing else would be of interest. Easily convincing herself that finding the money was worth facing Rosita's ire, she hopped up and pulled the drawer closest to her, only to find it locked. Trying the middle draw, it slid open easily. A small silver key sat in the corner beside some paper clips and pushpins. "Voile."

Five minutes and three drawers later, she'd found no deposit. Moving to the other end of the desk, she knelt, yanking open the sticky bottom drawer. A picture frame flopped forward, the wood banging against the drawer. Clenching her lip between her teeth, Dream removed the frame hoping she hadn't inadvertently cracked the glass.

A photo of Rosita at one of her milestone birthdays with a brood of young women, Dream could only assume were her granddaughters, Rosita looking happier than Dream had ever seen her. Slipping the photo back in its place, Dream closed the drawer, remembering Rosita's joy before moving onto to the next. Only thirty seconds into its perusal, Rosita entered the room. "Did you lose somesing?"

Hopping up, fixing a smile on her face, Dream situated herself behind the chair. "Hi Rosita. My grandfather called and said the deposit was missing. I was just looking for it."

Terror filling her expression, Rosita wobbled to her desk faster than Dream had ever seen her move. "In my desk? *Drain,* I never steal no money. *Ay Padre Santo.*"

Giving an auction master a run for his money, Rosita began reciting a prayer in Spanish faster than Dream's ears could ever keep up with, let alone decipher into a reasonable translation. Only, hands gathered before, a reverent head bowing, and closed eyes suggested she was praying.

Horrified, Dream moved beside the older woman. "Of course not. I simply meant to say that since I can't seem to find it, I wanted to see if it was accidentally misplaced amongst your files." For a long uncomfortable moment, Rosita contemplated the validity of Dream's words.

Sitting slowly, Rosita pulled the bottom drawer open, slipping her purse into it before gliding it closed. "You find it?" she asked.

Leaning against her desk, Dream huffed. "I didn't," she confessed. Every nook and cranny of the office had turned up empty, elevating her concern. Money didn't just disappear into thin air. "Rosita, yesterday before I left, the deposit bag was in the safe."

"*Si*. I know. I put it in there."

Which left only two questions.

The first she had contemplated since the phone call from Gramps. "Was the safe locked this morning when you came in."

After a few seconds to recollect, the woman finally shook her head, her short salt, and pepper hair barely moving. "Yes."

The one small word made every nerve ending calm so rapidly, she'd thought she lull herself to sleep. She hadn't even realized how tense she had been.

Remembering they were no closer to finding the deposit than they had been a moment prior, Dream's nerve returned to full alert status, although her guilt was assuaged.

"Rosita? Why didn't you and Pastor take the deposit to the bank yesterday?"

"My *nieta*, Marciana was here." Sparks flew from the woman's eyes. "She was drunk!" Rosita exhaled attempting to gain some self-control. "Pastor talked to her but I don't know what happen. She cry for long time." Lost in her own thoughts, Rosita wiped away a tear. It stirred Dream, seeing Rosita so vulnerable. "Drain, *mi nieta necesita Jesús*," she pleaded.

"Don't we all." Biting the bullet, she neared Rosita uncertain of how to comfort her. Reaching out, she rubbed her back and hoped she didn't seem too forward. Rosita sniffled a half minute longer before pretending she hadn't just broken down. Pulling her hand back, Dream didn't know what to say or do next. Following suit, she returned to her desk and prepared her head for what she had to do next.

With no place left to look, it was best to deliver the bad news sooner than later. Dragging her feet, she found her way to Gramps office. Being this was official church business, she put on her treasurer hat, and Gramps was now Pastor Collins. Rapping a knuckle on the door, she waited for his invitation to enter. Removing his reading glasses, he gestured to the seat opposite him. "That looks says a lot."

Lowering herself into the upholstered chair, she only used the edge of the seat. She was too wound up to sit back and enjoy the comfort of the chair. "I don't understand it. It was in the safe. I saw it myself."

Clutching the edge of his spectacles with his teeth, he contemplated before speaking. "Perhaps, you misplaced it. Did you look around?"

"Yes," she pleaded. "In and around my desk. I checked inside the safe twice. Still nothing. I even risked my life and searched Rosita's desk."

Sitting forward, his expression unreadable, he set his glasses down. "Are you alright? You seem distracted this week. Losing your job can have that effect on a person."

She'd not lie to her Gramps, yet she couldn't help but find it harsh that God would choose to test her obedience to be a better Dream, at this particular moment. "I guess so. Being fired was a little surprising. Alright, a lot surprising, but that isn't what has me distracted. I'm starting my own business and before you tell me all the reasons it's a bad idea, please know I'm truly excited about this. I guess to the point of distraction."

Astonishment registered in his features briefly before he masked it. "Your own business? When did you decide this?"

"I've been thinking about it for years. I began taking steps to achieve it, a few days ago." Shame colored her cheeks for keeping such big news from her family. She planned to tell them, once she had herself situated for success and it was too late for them to try to talk her out of her decision.

"I see." He looked up behind her, his countenance changing immediately. "Yes, Rosita?"

She handed him some mail and informed him that his ten o'clock appointment had arrived. Thanking her, he requested a few minutes of privacy and asked she close the door on her way out.

"I can see how that decision could keep you preoccupied. As your grandfather, I wish you had come to me sooner. I am always here to listen and support you. I hope you know that." The creases around his eyes multiplied.

"However, as the Pastor of this church, you have placed me in a tough predicament. You are responsible for the deposit that is now missing. I've never had this happen in all my years as Pastor. I'll have to be careful how I handle this."

"I get that. I know this can't be easy for you."

"I'm sure you don't Twinkle." Pastor Collins sat back in his chair a frown fixed on his face. "I won't show you favoritism, Dream. In fact, I admit that I hold you to a higher standard than I do others. I expect more from you. That's probably not fair, but it's true." Letting out a breath, she could see the struggle he faced. "I need to think about this and pray."

Nodding, she knew it was right. "I understand."

"In the meantime, it's best you leave your keys with me."

Oh how that stung. Her integrity had taken a serious blow.

"It's not a punishment. It's for your own safety Dream. I know who you are. Don't ever doubt that."

Fishing her keys from her pocket, she removed the church and office keys from the ring, placing them in his wrinkled palm.

Swallowing hard, she kept her voice steady. She had one more bit of news that formed the perfect storm. "I have to tell you one more thing."

"Yes."

"The deposit was for the past two weeks." Her stomach soured saying it aloud.

No longer attempting to hide his astonishment, he rubbed his neck.

Not wanting to wait another second to cleanse herself of the information that plagued her, she let out the rest. "The donation from the Saturday Basketball League was also in that deposit."

Never before had she seen her grandfather's eyes bug out of their sockets. The disappointment in his features flooded her with guilt. "Two Sunday's worth of donations and a large private donation?"

She nodded. The lack of oxygen, had little to do with the actual air in the room but with her ability to breath it in. "With Rose on vacation, I wanted to wait for her return to verify the deposit."

"Why didn't you ask me to verify it?"

"I didn't want to bother you. I know you dislike counting the donations."

"There are many things I don't like Dream, but that doesn't give me just cause to shirk my responsibilities. And in the future, allow me to decide for myself."

"Yes sir."

Running a hand over his face, Pastor Collins stared at everything but her. Effectively dismissing her politely, she abandoned the room, with the promise to receive a call soon. On some small level, she could relate to a prisoner awaiting sentencing.

Walking pass Rosita's office, more than anything, she wanted to tear it apart in search of the money. Alas, she was no longer welcome there. Whether for her benefit or not, the thought still burned a whole where her heart resided. In all her twenty-eight years of being a member of her Grandfather and Heavenly Father's house of worship, never had she felt so much like an orphan.

Chapter 8

There was nothing quite like the rich smell of coffee brewing in the morning. Dream entered Treehouse Coffee Shop as if she were dying, and a cup of coffee was her only lifeline.

"How can I help you today?" The hipster young woman wore a colorful knit hat and a grin as wide as the Delaware River.

"Yes. Does your coffee come in IV Drip or just cups?"

Baffled, the cashier, whom Dream believed looked like she should be named Pepper, turned to the Barista unsure how to reply. "I'm only kidding."

Pepper laughed, her shoulders dropping an inch, her relief evident. Ordering her usual regular coffee, Dream waited as the cashier rang her up. Looking around for a table she spotted Nicole already seated at a round table in the corner, studying her cell as she sipped, presumably, her Chai Latte. After adding an obscene amount of sugar to her cup, Dream joined her, pulling out one of the color coordinated yet mismatched chairs she found so endearing.

"Hey. You made it." Nicole sent her phone to sleep before welcoming her friend with a kiss on her cheek.

"I have to admit that this is all too foreign for me. I feel like I'm ditching class." Taking the seat opposite Nicole, she sat and sipped from her cup.

Nicole's featured softened. "Still not used to being unemployed?"

"Among other things," Dream added. She had yet to share the latest of her woes to her friends. The news of being fired from ministry could wait until Sunday. That way she'd only need to recount the ordeal once more.

Dream had spent the better part of Tuesday explaining all of her misfortunes to her mother. Her retelling entailed so much detail it could have been mistaken for programming in HD. Yet, in all she'd shared with Suzi Collins, church gossip had worried her mother the most, not surprisingly. At least, Suzi hadn't suggested Dream move back home as a solution to her many issues.

Taking another sip from her cup, Nicole crossed her legs, positioning herself for a proper chat. "How's the business planning going?" Dream recognized Nicole's attempt to lift her spirits, not having the slightest clue, she'd just grabbed a shovel, dug a whole, and kicked them in.

Avoiding drowning in disappointment, Dream had not allowed herself to think of her grand business plan; the one she could no longer afford to launch. The guilt of the missing church money had gnawed at her day and night. Two days had passed since it disappeared and all hopes to find it had vanished with it.

When it came down to it, the blame was justly placed at her feet for its disappearance. Therefore, the restitution should come from the toil of her hands. She stayed up late pouring over her financial records, thinking of how best to pay back every missing cent. In the end, her only solution came at the expense of her dreams. No startup fund meant no starting a business.

Not wanting to grieve over the death of her future, Dream steered the conversation away from admitting she failed before she even began. "I'd rather talk about you. How's work?"

Raising a brow, Nicole set down her cup before taking her intended sip. "Me? Aren't you the same person who banned me from Sunday dinner, for talking about work?"

Dream shrugged. "I was crabby that day."

"How is that different from any other day?" Nicole giggled.

"You and Tami are getting a little too comfortable saying exactly how you really feel," she teased.

"Did I hear my name?" Tami laid a hand on Dream's shoulder before bending forward and kissing her check. She circled the table toward Nicole and repeated the gesture.

"Good morning. Glad you could make it." Nicole reciprocated.

"Almost thought I wouldn't." Tami took a seat and exhaled. "Did you know morning sickness is a bold faced lie?"

Nicole laughed.

"Oh! Don't laugh sweetheart. I'm sure you're next and let me tell you that from sunup to sundown, I am battling waves of nausea that not even the stomach bug can contend with."

"Sounds pleasant," Nicole teased. "I'm looking forward to it."

"You only say that because you don't know how much I suffer."

"Touché. Yet, I still wouldn't count on me being next in line. I need to get married first and that seems to be far off."

Dream interrupted. "Didn't you guys decide to set a date?"

Nicole shrugged. "It's been nearly a week and we are still dateless. Haven't even spoken about it."

Drew had a serious issue and Dream would be just the person to remedy his ailment of cowardice. It's not as if she had anything else better to do. Just because her life was at a complete halt, didn't mean, her loved ones needed to suffer the same fate.

"As soon as the Summer League Tournament is over, I'm sure Drew and I will have time to get it all settled."

Dream wouldn't bank on that, but for now, she'd keep her thoughts to herself.

"I think so too." Tami sipped from her cup and winced. "Peppermint tea," she said answering their bewildered expressions. "Its gross, but vomiting is worse."

Great. They were back to discussing puke. Nicole began to apprise them of a woman who came in with a severe case of food poisoning. Tuning out the conversation, Dream prayed for God to save her from anything more that would turn her stomach.

"Good morning ladies. What brings you to my neck of the woods?" David held a cup of coffee and small bag, most likely containing some baked good.

It was now abundantly clear that God hated her and her stomach. Ok, that was overdramatic. Pulling the reigns back, she reassessed. God didn't hate her, but her prayers had definitely been hitting a glass ceiling. Choosing to remain quiet while her friends offered their greetings, Dream took more interest in the baked goods bag, than the man holding it.

"You live near here?" Tami asked, wincing again as she sipped her abominable tea.

"Yeah, but it's not so bad."

She chuckled and offered her apologies. "It's the tea. I'm sure your neighborhood is great."

As gracious as always, Nicole invited David to join them. Restraining the conniption ready to burst, Dream hugged her coffee, burning holes in Nicole who responded with a smile, ignoring the death stare.

"If you're sure." Not waiting for a response, David pulled out the seat beside Dream's, blinding her with his manufactured grin, the twinkle in his eye meant to entice but instead repulsed.

Petitioning God with an emergency prayer, Dream asked for saving. *Not to sound unappreciative God, because You know that I am most grateful for eternal life, but I need a different kind of saving right about now.*

"So Dream? Did you get your tail light fixed? I'd hate to have to pull you over again."

Hearing David's fabricated amusement at his own tasteless joke was the exact opposite of what Dream had considered salvation. *Is it because I didn't say Amen? My bad. Amen. Amen, and again, Amen.*

When David made no effort to leave, she knew she was on her own. Being that as it may, there was no sense wasting a perfectly good opportunity to wipe the smug smile from Ken's face. "Actually Officer. I got fired for being late for work." Back now against the white ladder back chair, Dream picked up her cup of coffee and took a satisfying gulp. The look on David's face was sweeter than her coffee.

Looking to her friends, who had suddenly developed a keen interest at a chalkboard and the floor, David questioned her sincerity. Nicole's nose wrinkled as she nodded. His shoulders slumped. "I'm sorry Dream, I was just-"

"Doing your job? I know. Don't worry about it. I don't blame you."

While everyone else seemed awkward in the silence that followed, Dream found herself at ease. She met Tami's widened eyes, chastising her for having the audacity to be so blunt. Dream raised a shoulder. Tami couldn't honestly blame her for knocking him down a peg. Like a charm, it worked. Never before had she seen David so sheepish. It was quite a marvel. One that she found she could appreciate.

Placing her forearms on the table and leaning forward, Nicole pasted an easy smile in place. "Any plans for the weekend David?"

The vibration of Dream's phone was a welcome sensation. Before pulling the cell from her pocket, she excused herself not caring who in particular God had sent to rescue her from a conversation she'd found lacking before it began. For goodness sakes, she'd rather discuss disease and vomit, as opposed to David's flavor of the week.

The screech of the chair gliding across the floor echoed throughout the coffee shop. Several patrons turned toward the offending noise before returning quickly to their conversations and hot beverages.

Checking her cell and seeing her FauxPa's name glowing on the screen, her feet ushered her outdoors quickly. For two long days, she'd waited anxiously to hear her fate. Now that the call had come, two days hadn't seemed nearly long enough.

Leveling her voice, she answered coolly. Not overly chipper, lest he think she didn't take the situation seriously. Yet, not too melancholy leading him to believe he needed to be fragile with her. "Good morning, Gramps."

"Every morning God wakes me up, most certainly is good," his response equally cool.

He was careful not to address her. Had he used a nickname, she'd assume he was in good spirits and could deduce she was in the clear. The opposite could be assumed, had he used her given name, which he'd use more often to chastise her. Instead, he bested her, and chose to praise God.

How many years had she studied him with people? From the tender age of four, she recalled watching him interact with young and old alike. The way he could be soft and strong, like quality toilet tissue, had always enraptured her. As a Pastor, he was well versed in being cool, calm, and collected, whenever the situation called for it, and he was ever so accomplished at it.

In all her years of marveling at his ability, never would she think she'd be the recipient of his methods. On the other end of the phone line, he'd given nothing away with his words or tone, which only served to increase her anxiety.

However, while having lacked FauxPa's social graces, she'd picked up a pointer or two from her unofficial mentor. Sometimes a situation, like this one, called for a little strategy in order to ferret out the information she sought and she had the perfect plan. The mere idea, that she'd have to leave her coffee date early, not only served as confirmation that her plan was God sent, but that He'd heard her prayer after all.

"To what do I owe a phone call so early in the morning?" As if she hadn't already known the answer to that question. Gramps had finally come to a decision.

"At the risk of sounding like an old fuddy-duddy, I prefer conversing face to face. All of this new fan dangled technology can't hold a candle to some good ol' fashioned human interaction. If it's no bother, could you stop by the church today? Whenever you get a chance, that is."

The corner of her mouth tilted north a fraction. Little did he know she'd already stepped in line behind a woman in running attire, waiting to purchase him a coffee and muffin, planning to deliver them in person. "I think I can break away," she replied. "I'll be there in a bit."

"Ok. See you then." Not even his departing greeting offered any hints.

Fitting her cup in the carton carry as well as the cup she'd purchased for Gramps, she rolled in the top of the to go bag essentially sealing the muffin inside, and placed it between the cups. Balancing the coffee carrier in one hand, Dream returned to the table and made her excuses.

"I'll walk you out." David stood and offered his goodbyes as well, the suggestive grins on her friend's faces making her cringe. The idea of anything happening with David, on any level other than mere acquaintances made her stomach sour.

He held the door open for her, just as a woman carrying a baby strapped to her front, entered, giving her gleeful thanks. He followed her with his eyes, until she reached the counter. Shaking her head, Dream exited quickly hoping the woman would keep his attention long enough for her to get to her car parked nearby.

Sidestepping a dog, and its cell phone chatty owner, Dream hurried her feet. Only two more cars down and she could get in her car and pretend she didn't see David as she pulled into traffic. The beep alerting her the car doors where unlocked were music to her ears. Stepping off the curb, she rounded the SUV and pulled opened the door.

"Let me help you." David pulled the door open wider and divested her of the coffee.

Startled, she jumped out of her skin and into the car. "Did you have to sneak up on me?"

Grin wider than Merchant Street, he held the door open as she leaned over to grab ahold of it to pull it closed.

"Sneak up on you? Now darling, I offered to walk you to your car. How could you possibly think I'd renege on that promise?"

"Can't a girl hope?" Dream smiled mirthlessly. "Besides, I figured you were probably busy rolling your tongue up off the floor, and stuffing your eyeballs back in their sockets."

His outright chuckle fell over her like a burlap dress. Dream scratched her arm subconsciously.

"There's no need to be jealous, *Mami*. My eyes lost focus for just a second, but I assure you that my heart is at your feet."

"Great. That makes it easier to kick clear across the street. And don't call me *Mami*."

He placed his manicured hand to his chest, feigning heartbreak, as he laughed heartily again. Using the distraction, she took the opportunity to yank the door from his grasp. His speed and strength proved too much for her weaker arms, and he recovered swiftly. "Wait a second there, darling. I wanted to make sure we're ok."

"Don't call me darling. And yep, we're good. No hard feelings." She tried the door again but it didn't budge.

"Dream, let me make it up to you. Let me take you to out."

How did he think that spending additional time in his presence was restitution for her losing her job? "David, I appreciate your tenacity. Like a bulldog with his jowls locked on an intruder's arm, you just won't let it go, but I can't go out with you. Remember? I told you this last week. And the week before that. And before that," she sighed.

"What?" David pulled his head back as if he'd been sucker punched. "Did you think I meant on a date?" He huffed. "I heard you loud and clear. We're just friends. I was thinking more of a group thing." He shrugged. "A bunch of us are going to a summer concert at the park next weekend. Thought you'd like to tag along."

Dream considered his invitation for what was considered an appropriate timeframe, as to not seem rude. "I'll think about it" Code for, no thanks, but I don't want to hurt your feelings.

If Officer Escobar were proficient in any kind of investigative work, he would have no trouble decoding the not so cryptic message of being politely turned down.

Unclear if he'd gotten a clue, he nodded.

"Don't forget your coffee."

What kind of plan did she have without her bribe? After carefully handing over the carton, David closed the door before stepping back up on the curb, waving as she rode past him.

Group outing her foot. Yeah, and she'd stolen the missing church money to purchase a diamond engagement ring for herself. How gullible did he think she was? Well that was obvious, now that she'd thought about it. If David thought for one second, she'd fall for his manipulations, he done himself the bigger disservice.

Dream stopped at the stop sign, looking in both directions, before making a right. The ticking of her turning signal echoed in the quiet car then stopped, leaving only her thoughts to fill the silence.

In the span of two minutes, the brute of a man had blatantly ogled another woman with no regards to her presence, proceeded to come to her car directly afterward to ask her out, as if he hadn't just completely disrespected her, and then looked her dead in the eyes and attempted to hoodwink her.

The Casanova had chosen the wrong victim. If she cared one iota about David, she would have happily put in enough effort to teach him a lesson. Nevertheless, she didn't care and frankly, she had bigger fish to fry. Namely, the whale of a problem awaiting her at church. This one, on the other hand, she cared for deeply.

"You do know that the speed limit isn't a suggestion, but a law," Pastor Collins said, not looking to the door from where she waited.

The smile tugging in her heart manifested itself on her face. "You do know that keeping your only grandchild in suspense is also against the law?"

"I must have missed that one." Removing his glasses, he folded in each temple before slipping them into a black case. "Besides, you aren't my biological granddaughter, so technically that rule doesn't apply to me." He tried hard to keep his amusement at bay but she could see the twinkle in his eye.

"Did someone forget their fiber this morning?" She approached, kissing him on his wrinkled cheek. "No worries. I brought you nourishment." Moving aside spectacles, she placed the coffee and bag before him.

"Perhaps, I like intrigue. For all you know, I was a spy in a previous life." Closing the study Bible, he laughed, and placed it on the shelf beside his desk.

"Have you been staying up late again watching old movies?"

"I'll have you know, missy, that I would have made a terrific James Bond if I didn't disapprove of lying, manipulation, and cavorting with a different woman every night. And no, I have not."

"Gramps that pretty much leaves drinking Martini's stirred not shaken, and further proves that you would have made a terrible spy, since the strongest thing to touch your lips is mouth wash."

"Your tongue's as sharp as your multiplication skills, young lady. For your information, you are forgetting the most important part of a spy's job. Ascertaining information by using these, these and this." Pastor Collins pointed to his eyes, ears and the side of his head, signifying the organ within.

Dream took the upholstered seat facing his desk and crossed her feet at the ankles. "Don't forget your fists and guns," she joked.

"You're enough of a pistol." Unraveling the to-go bag she'd brought, he looked in and inhaled the scent of the muffin. "Now what are you trying to bribe me with?"

"Can't a granddaughter be nice without it being a bribe?" Her mock outrage made him smile.

"Of course she could. Just not my granddaughter."

Resting her elbows on the arms of the seat, she sat back comfortably in the chair. "Now, I'm your granddaughter again?"

Pastor Collins rolled up the bag and set aside, interlocking his hands then resting them before him on the desk. He'd morphed from playful Gramps to authoritarian clergyman faster than Clark Kent to Superman.

"I thank you for being patient regarding the issue of the missing money." All hopes that the deposit had miraculously been found had just disappeared like a puff of smoke. "I can imagine you've been anxious."

Dream nodded, a slight smile acknowledging his gratitude. As if, she'd make a fuss over having this conversation sooner. She'd rather anywhere than here for the reason she had been.

"During the few days since you were here last, I haven't just been praying. I've been actively trying to figure out what happened. I do want to share some information with you. Not because I am obligated to, but because I want you to know everything that weighed my decision."

The dread that filled her midsection, clutched to her internal organs and squeezed.

"First, I wanted you to know that several of the umm... concerned," he finally said, content with the word, "yes, concerned members of the church have offered their condolences for the loss of your employment."

Since she'd sat down, Gramps eyes hadn't left hers, until that moment, but only briefly, before his tenacity reappeared once again.

Their condolences? More like a poor attempt to fill him in on the gossip about his granddaughter. But, what could she say? Her unemployment followed her around like a ball and chain. It wasn't exactly a secret.

"Second, as you may have guessed, the money has not been found. I spent a day in that office myself and searched for it."

At least someone had searched again. Only to honor her grandfather's wish to stay away, had she not come back to tear the office apart in search of it.

"Lastly, I had to apprise the board of the situation. Understandably, there are some major concerns. Some of them have asked me to remove you. Others have fought on your behalf."

"And you?" No matter what everyone else believed, it was her Gramps opinion that mattered most to her.

"I believe you are distracted with all that's going on in your life. Including Max Davidson. I can't help but wonder why he was here in the first place, and what was so important that you rushed from here shirking your responsibility."

Dream thought about how to answer his question without validating his assumption. Burned scarves, unreturned kisses in Max's apartment, and hightailing it out of a mall parking lot, wouldn't exactly paint her as a focused and responsible adult.

"You are right. I have no valid excuse."

Pastor Collins raised an eyebrow. "That's it? You aren't going to regale me with a story that would be too hard to believe if I didn't know you personally?"

Well she had one. She just wasn't going to share it. "No. I was irresponsible. There is no story that will change that."

He considered her for a moment, before exhaling deeply. "I'm sorry to hear that. I guess you leave me with no choice but to remove you as treasurer."

She expected his decision to be as such, but it hurt hearing it nevertheless. Dipping her chin, she nodded, ashamed to look into her Gramps eyes and seeing his disappointment. It had been ten years since she'd last seen that same disappointment in his eyes, when she'd broken curfew and returned with a passion mark on her neck.

At twenty-eight years old, she'd come a long way from an emotionally unstable teen, unable to understand the ramifications of her decisions, let alone make amends for them. However, she wasn't eighteen years old anymore. She couldn't hide behind youth and naiveté as excuses to be held unaccountable.

"I understand your decision." Ignoring the surprise registered on Gramps face, she continued. "I plan to pay back every missing cent."

"Did you inherit a fortune from a dead relative I don't know of?" His skepticism was wealthier than any relative she knew dead or alive.

Rather than divulging any details of recompense, she rose to her feet. "I'll be away for the weekend, but I'll stop by next week to drop it off." She circled the desk and pecked his cheek before he started asking questions she had no desire to answer. "Love you, Gramps."

"I love you back, Twinkle."

She walked out of his office simultaneously relieved it was over, and crushed that it was over on a completely different level.

Chapter 9

It had been too long since Dream had had a proper vacation. It mattered not that she was on a permanent vacation, she needed to get away from life, as she knew it. Perhaps some time away could help aide in hearing what God wanted her to do for employment.

Pleading for direction in her career only led her to the bottom of the staircase that led to the beach house in Ocean City. That, and avoiding her mother like the plague. Since learning of Dream's dismissal as Church Treasurer, Suzi had appointed herself Dream's personal cheerleader and confidant. She appreciated her mother's support, but she drew the line when her mother offered to stay over a few nights.

A day early and more than ready to forget all of her troubles for a while, she looked up at the beautiful staircase that led to the equally beautiful house. A white balustrade railing lined a wrap-around porch. Instead of windows, French doors anchored each side of the rounded double doors. Atypical to most Ocean City dwellings, the house didn't have a second level porch, but was a beauty nevertheless.

Perspiration trickled down her back as she hoisted her luggage up the steps in the brutal summer heat. Her bladder's unfortunate timing reminded her she'd indulged in too much water during the long trip. What should have taken an hour, took twice as long with the bumper-to-bumper traffic to the shore. Panting, she knocked on the door trying desperately not to resort to potty training dancing. Cool air whooshed out as the front door opened, the relief only lasting briefly. Max stood at the door in shorts and a sleeveless tee, brows bunched. "What are you doing here?"

"Accepting your invitation." When he made no move to invite her in, she crossed her legs and locked her knees.

"I just meant... I just assumed you'd be coming with Tami. I wasn't expecting anyone today." The struggle playing across his features rattled her. With all that had happened, she hadn't even thought to ask when everyone else was arriving. Was she not welcome now?

"I just assumed everyone would already be here." Looking over his shoulder, she peeked into the foyer for a toilet, as if it would be waiting for her by the stairs. Turning back to the street, she searched for a bush. Max hadn't budged from the entrance and she needed an emergency plan. Maybe there was a local place to stay, and find a restroom if he was rescinding his invitation.

She needed to be careful with her savings. Unexpected hotel stays weren't how she planned to spend her reserves, especially since she's handed over a healthy stack of cash for the pink scarf. Right now, she just needed a bathroom, and she'd rather pee in a bush than a public restroom. Surely, he wouldn't refuse her the decency of a respectable bathroom. "Can I just use your bathroom?"

Understanding registering, he quickly moved aside, pointing her in the right direction. She thanked him and rushed in not taking the time to appreciate the interior. Returning from the restroom, she took advantage of being alone in the bright main room. Another large picture window on the back wall framed a view of a neatly trimmed green lawn that led to a long dock with a boat resting by it. No beach, but the view of the ocean was breathtaking. The sun beat down on the waves creating a polished effect on the surface of the dark waters.

Walking back toward the door, she surveyed the walls and tables for photos, but found none. On the other side of the French door she'd admired from outside, she could see the porch begging someone to take advantage of the chairs in the shade.

Beyond a nearby opened entrance, Max's voice carried. The breaks between his speaking confirmed he was on the phone. Walking towards the sound of his voice, Dream found her luggage situated against the wall by the door. She entered the kitchen just as his conversation ended. The scent of bacon stirred her appetite. Max preparing lunch stirred her heart. She loved bacon almost as much as pizza, but neither nearly as much as Max. What would it be like to enter into this scene for the rest of her days?

"Hey. Have you eaten? I made some turkey club sandwiches." He plated the sandwiches and carried them to a round wooden kitchen table tucked into a corner with cushioned benched seating, a slightly different view of the ocean water than of the large room she had just vacated.

"Yeah, thanks. Bacon makes everything better." Stepping further into the room, she noted the tall white cabinets and stainless steel appliances reflecting the sunlight filtering in through the window above the large sink.

Nodding, he pulled out a bottled water, and a can of pop from the large refrigerator, offering her a choice. She opted for the soda. She'd practically drowned herself with the amount of water she drank on the trip.

"Sorry to break the news, but its turkey bacon." A twitch in his lips, Max sat at the table, after grabbing a bag of baked chips, and proceeded to say grace.

Scrunching her nose, she lifted the lightly toasted bread to get a peek at this 'turkey bacon'. Why did people insist on changing the natural order of things? Bacon came from pigs not turkeys. Chips were fried not baked. Only to appease her growling stomach, but mostly for not wanting to pass up the chance to eat a meal prepared by Max, she decided to try the fake bacon.

Max eyed her as he bit into his sandwich. Was he waiting for her to eat? Picking up her sandwich, she took a bite. Not real bacon, but also not too bad. The chips were actually a pleasant surprise, evident by the large portion she harpooned. Gulping her Coke, she placed a hand over her mouth to hold in the belch that was rising quickly. An indiscernible burp escaped although, Max seemed none the wiser.

"Like the chips?" Sitting back against the upholstered kitchen chair, his gaze twinkled with delight.

"More than I thought I would." Dream slid the bag to the far end of the table afraid she'd eat the whole bag if it were within arm's reach for a minute longer. Max followed the bag's trajectory before returning his gaze to her. Resisting the urge to suck the cheddar chip residue from her fingers, she walked over to the sink and washed her hands.

"Want to finish this later?" Peeking over her shoulder, she eyed Max collecting the dishes, her half eaten sandwich on the plate he picked up.

Hope sprung up. "As in to go or come back later for it?"

Placing the plate on the island, he reached the sink, just as she stepped away drying her hands with a paper towel. Adding dish detergent to the sponge, he kept his back to her not providing a response. That didn't bode well.

"Does that mean I can stay?" *Come on. Say yes.*

"I spoke to Tami. She won't be here until tomorrow."

"Guess that just leaves you and me." Dream leaned on the island watching in fascination, a domesticated Max as he dried the dish he'd used. He turned immediately, his eyes pried open as if she'd just announced she was an alien from outer space.

"What? Did I say something wrong?"

"When don't you?" Turning back, he placed the dish in the cupboard. "I'm sorry, you can't stay."

"Because? Am I missing something?" Swallowing the last of her soda, she tossed the can in the recycling can as cool as an ice cube. Attempting to be inconspicuous, she searched for the bag of chips. A few more wouldn't hurt, would they? They were baked after all.

Huffing, Max placed his hands on his waist stealing her attention. "It's not appropriate for you and me to sleep under the same roof, alone." Leveling her a gaze, he waited expectantly for her to understand his meaning. Not that it took a genius to figure out what he meant. She hadn't thought about that, but now that he looked extremely uncomfortable about the situation, she had no choice but to amplify his embarrassment. There was really nothing else to do about it.

"Why not?"

Scrubbing his face with both hands, he took a breath. "You know why."

Softly at first before bubbling over, her laughter filled the professionally decorated kitchen. "Don't you trust me Mr. Davidson?" Stepping around the island, Dream arched a brow and served up her wickedest smile.

Max stood his ground, crossing his arms over his chest, raising a brow of his own. "Not even one strand on your head."

Walking away, she turned at the door. "Don't worry, your reputation is intact. I'm as dangerous as turkey bacon and baked chips." She winked and exited the kitchen.

With the sound of her sandals on the tile floor fading, Max allowed his lips to turn up. The recollection of her inhaling the baked chips broadened his grin. She was a junk food junkie and seeing her squirm at anything remotely healthier than pepperoni pizza nearly had him losing his composure. He'd make sure to hide the bag of chips. He couldn't be sure, but her eyes seemed to be roaming where the bag had unintentionally landed. She'd finish off the bag by nightfall, if given the chance.

Straightening, he composed himself, thinking of the problem at hand. She wouldn't be around by nightfall. She had to go. Opening the door to find Dream on the doorstep threw him for a rollercoaster loop. The sun behind her made her appear angelic, not that she needed sunrays to make her a remarkable sight.

Nevertheless, his blood pressure spiked wondering what to do. As soon as she disappeared into the half bathroom, he dialed Tami and insisted that she and Jonah get there tonight. Tongues would be wagging if the two of them spent the night in the same house, alone. Blessedly, Tami agreed but in essence couldn't help resolve the sticky situation in which he found himself.

Tami's muffled giggles on the other side of phone line sparked his irritation. She denied being involved in any scheme that Dream had cooked up in being there alone. With no reinforcements, he girded his strength. Stashing the chips in the highest cupboard in the kitchen, he went in search of his unwanted guest. Finding Dream standing half way up the stairs, her luggage wedged between her leg and the step, he ran up to offer assistance in carting her luggage back down and into her gas guzzler.

The sudden flash of her camera phone blinded him sending him careening down the stairs. Her gasps and shouts, intermingled with the thudding of his head on the floor. Her warm hands lifted his head, the pain searing in his head exploding with each movement.

"Max! Max! Can you hear me?" The shouts blared in his ear magnifying his pain.

"Please stop yelling." With hesitation, he opened his eyes only to find Dream's face a mere inches from his, her breath tickling his nose.

"Are you alright?" The panic in her eyes made him want to wrap her in his arms and chase away all her fears. He must have really hit his head hard.

"I'd be better, if you could give me a little room to breathe?" Immediately complying with his breathless reply, she sat back on her haunches, placing a hand to his back, aiding him in sitting up.

"Let's get you to a hospital." Getting to her feet, Dream held out a hand expecting he'd purposefully grasp any part of her.

"I'm fine. I don't need to go to a hospital." Proving as much, he stood with little effort. Squeezing his eyes shut he fought to gain control of the ringing in his ears or was that Dream talking?

"You are the most stubborn man on the planet. Sometimes, I wonder why I'm wait-"

His attention snapped to her. A faint pink hue colored her cheeks. Dream blushing was a rarity. What was she going to say to cause such a reaction? "Why you are waiting for what?"

"I've been trying to talk you into going to the emergency for the better of five minutes and all you hear is that? Of course." Murmuring, she dug through her purse. Snatching a bottle of Tylenol from her purse, she met his gaze agitated, handing him the bottle.

"Dream," his bellowing voice issuing a warning. She'd not dodge this. Was she scheming again? He'd not fall prey to her hair-brained ideas.

"Take two of these," she demanded.

Opening the childproof bottle with ease, he fixed his gaze on her. "Waiting for what?" He pushed.

"Fine." Clasping her hands in front of her, she straightened, as he removed the cotton from the bottle and opened his palm to capture the capsules. "For you to propose."

White pills cascaded to the tile floor, scattering like glass marbles. Dropping to the floor quickly, Dream placed her arm on the floor in an attempt to cordon off their escape into the floor vent. Gathering up the pills in a pile before examining the floor in search of any strays, she walked into the kitchen in search of a broom and dustpan.

She was getting better at recognizing her faults and perhaps, just maybe, blurting out that she was awaiting a proposal from a man that had barely acknowledged her existence was a tad extreme, but what else could she do? She'd made God a promise to be a better Dream, and she was certain that lying outright to her future husband wasn't what God would consider an improvement.

Opening the third pantry door, she found what she sought and headed back to clean up the mess. Max was no longer in a state of shock where she'd left him. In fact, he wasn't even where she'd left him. Where had he gone? Probably passing out somewhere. Dream huffed and continued toward the mess, the opened front door pulling her attention. Outside, she eyed Max carrying her luggage to her car.

Abandoning the broom by the door, she rushed down the steps toward Max, who'd already deposited her suitcase by the backdoor of her truck. Determined, he approached the house, scowling. Always scowling. She'd need not see his face to know he was. "What are you doing?" She asked as he reached the bottom of the porch stairs.

"You can't stay here." He marched up the steps, not bothering to acknowledge her as he walked by.

"I can't leave you alone," she said exasperated as she motioned to his head. Did he really expect to be ok immediately after falling down the stairs? Men were so senseless when they hadn't just slammed their ahead against a hard surface. It was only reasonable they'd be more so, after having done so.

Exhaling deeply, he whined. "Oh, how I wish you would."

"Don't be foolish. You just fell down a flight of stairs. I can't just leave you. You could have a concussion. And since you're refusing to go to the hospital, it falls on my shoulders to make sure you don't die until Tami gets here." Eyeing her suitcase, she looked back at him as she descended the stairs. "Just wait for me so I can examine your head. I'll need to grab my suitcase first."

"It was four steps," he spat. Lightning fast he turned to her. "What were you doing on the stairs anyhow?"

"I was taking a selfie." Rolling her lips inward, she imprisoned them with her teeth to keep her amusement at bay.

Shaking his head, not bothering to comment, Max stormed into the house, slamming the door then locking it for good measure.

The nerve of the man! Talk about overreacting. It's not as if she expected a proposal right then, and there. Some serious wooing needed to take place first. Flowers. Dinner dates. A couple of good night kisses. The idea of kissing Max distracted her for a second, making her giddy. The sun overheating her skin woke her from her trance. Right now, he just needed time to gather his thoughts.

In the meantime, she just wanted to be settled in her bedroom, secretly keeping an eye on him in case he was feeling woozy. A concussion wasn't to be taken lightly.

That just left the matter of a locked front door. At her attention to the French door, a shadow quickly ducked out of sight. Max was watching her, the sneak. Two could play that game. Getting back into the coolness of the indoors would require some stealth maneuvering.

A house this airy had to have multiple ways to go out and enjoy the outdoors. A living room view of a dock meant a back entrance. The backyard was sure to have a patio door of some kind. At the least, a window to a lower level. That was her best bet.

Pushing her suitcase into her backseat, she waved goodbye to the man hiding behind the sheer curtain that quickly jerked closed, not that it helped. Men really were clueless. "It's sheer!" She shouted, pointing at the curtain. "I can still see you!" Tossing him a thumbs-up, she could only imagine his embarrassment. He was so cute when his face flushed.

When his guard was down, and with the cover of darkness shielding her, she'd be back and with any luck, Max wouldn't have finished off the baked chips.

Chapter 10

Only the flickering light from the television illuminated the darkened house. Removing her sandals, Dream inched closer to the patio door. Turning the knob, she slowly inched the back door open. A loud squeak forced her to shut the door. In her panic, it slipped from her grasp closing with a discernible clap. Shushing the door quiet, she ran down the stairs, skipping several before turning and crashing into a large rosebush.

Sudden light cascaded down the stairs followed by footsteps. "Is someone out there?" Max's booming voice filled the night's sky.

Slapping a hand over her mouth, she held in her distress. Thorns pierced her right side, tearing flesh. Closing her eyes tightly, she tried not to focus on the pain.

After a minute of quiet, the patio door closed, the clicking of the lock echoing in the dark. Satisfied that only the lapping waves of the shore were her company, she disengaged from the bush, her mission becoming that much more difficult now that she was wounded. Unable to see the damage to her upper body, she winced at the stinging on her shoulder blade and arm. Stupid rosebush. "I need a little help here God," she whispered, contemplating how to proceed.

No use in fretting about her battle scars now. Sitting out back, under the moon wasn't going to help either. She could clean up any scrapes once she was inside. Scouring the darkened backyard, she searched for an alternative means of entry. The kitchen window illuminated, a curtain moving slightly with the ocean breeze. It was open slightly. "Thanks, God. I knew I could count on you." Dismissing the crazy thought that Max was wasting electricity keeping a window open when the air conditioner was on, she surveyed the yard ensuring she was alone.

Rising carefully to keep from adding to her injuries, she could see a shadow moving across the curtain. Quietly heading back up the steps, Dream walked to the balcony's end, being careful to duck below the kitchen window.

Edging up slowly, she spied Max behind an opened refrigerator door. Footing the fridge door closed, he poured juice into a glass. Setting it on the island, he reached for the cabinet above the fridge, pulling out a bag of chips after a quick peek to the kitchen's entrance. Not just any bag of chips. *Her* bag of chips. Of all the sneaky things, she'd ever seen. How she knew he'd hidden them from her, she was unsure, but she had no doubt that was exactly what he'd done. After taking a hand full, he clipped the bag closed and sat it on the counter. Grabbing his drink, he exited the kitchen, flicking the light switch off on his way out.

Slipping her hands under the window, she pushed as it easily glided open. Taking a deep breath at the burning pain from extending her flesh, she sat on the windowsill until the pain subsided a little. Slipping her feet in first with ease, she then carefully slid in her upper body, contorting her limbs antagonizing her open scars. Lowering the window to its former state, she allowed herself to breathe.

An excitement coursed through her every tense muscle. She'd done it. She was in.

Although, the original purpose of sitting in the dark wasn't to calm him, it had done just that. Praying helped too. Of all the hair-brained things Dream had ever said, admitting that she was awaiting a marriage proposal topped the list. She was crazier than a wet cat. Sorting through the archive of memories, he couldn't remember one instance where he'd done anything to encourage such an expectation since returning from California. In fact, an abundant recollection of safe distances, little conversation, and no eye contact assaulted him. He'd even rejected her kiss. All done on purpose to avoid any misunderstandings, and all for naught.

Soundlessly, he set his glass down on the floor and stepped into the shadows of the kitchen, leaning against the doorjamb. She'd waited longer than he'd anticipated; he'd give her that. The sun had set over an hour ago. Nevertheless, as expected, he could now add unlawful entry to her growing rap sheet. Looking too pleased with herself, she crept to the island on tiptoe gingerly opening the bag of chips, catching her bottom lip between her teeth as the crunching noise of plastic unraveled. Pulling a man-full, handful out of the bag, she stuffed her mouth with the baked chips he'd purposefully left on the island. Rolling her eyes back in ecstasy, she moaned delighting at the salty treat.

Stopping short of palm slapping his front, Max settled his hand over his mouth unable to grasp the fact that this was actually occurring. Another crunching noise as she slid the bag away from her. Cat burglar, she was not. She had as much focus as a Midwest tornado, and as much stealth as a panda wearing jingle bells. Apparently, the appetite of one too. Taking a few steps, she returned to the bag and took another helping. Dusting her hands of the crumbs, she tiptoed pass the island heading right toward him unsuspectingly lurking in the dark.

Two steps before reaching him, Max flicked the switch, the stunning brightness of the overhead lights capturing her unchecked expression of surprise. "Going somewhere?"

A muffled croak was her only reply. Whether looking for a place to hide or escape, she whirled around first to the window, then island, and back toward the kitchen entrance before settling her eyes on him, her flailing limbs following suit, her eyes closing tightly as if he'd experienced physical pain at being found out.

As much as he appreciated seeing her frazzled state, this was ending, now. Pushing off the doorjamb, he neared her. Rather than be alarmed, the woman chewed her mouthful of chips, a twinkle in her eye, as her shoulders relaxed.

"Care to explain?"

Holding up a finger, she gestured to her mouth as she chomped, exaggerating the motion. Swallowing a big gulp, her finger still at attention, she moved to the refrigerator. Smacking her lips for emphasis, she pulled a can from the fridge, cracked it open, downing it sugary contents.

Lifting a brow, he awaited a response. The cogs were turning in that maze of her brain and he was liable to pick her up, toss her over his shoulder, and put her on a bus to Canada, when whatever concocted nonsense she was thinking up, passed her lips.

"Well, I was breaking in so that I could go take a long shower before going to bed, after I made sure you weren't unconscious somewhere." Her unexpected honesty nearly knocked him over. What was he supposed to do with that? "Do *you* care to explain why you were hiding the chips?" Expression fierce, she was genuinely galled.

Well, the surprise of Dream speaking sanity didn't last long. Served him right for knowing the absurdity was coming and letting his guard down anyway. It didn't matter. It changed nothing. "You can't stay here." Why couldn't she see the danger in that?

"Kicking a woman out in the dead of night, for her own good. How chivalrous?" Clapping a hand over her mouth, she peered at him, lightning sparks from eyes. "Do you see what've you done? I used sarcasm. You know how much I loathe sarcasm."

Pinching the bridge of his nose, he braced himself. The absurdity had apparently only just begun.

"What I meant to say, and very clearly I might add, is that while you are very sweet to worry over my reputation-"

"You couldn't pay me to care less about your reputation." Honestly, he worried of his own. A Christian man of character was how he managed to build rapports with those who could help him help others less fortunate. He had to be trustworthy.

"Don't interrupt. It's rude. You are, in turn, tossing me out into the street in the middle of the night, which is worse." She presented her summation like a lawyer would closing arguments. "Do you know what happens to innocent women roaming the streets at night?"

"Innocent is a bit of a stretch, and I am not asking you to roam anywhere. I'm telling you, like I did while it was still daylight out, to go home." Brushing past her, he headed for the opened window with the intention of locking it. Her wince grabbed his attention. *Join the club, toots. Touching you is torture for me too, even if only accidental.*

The grimace on Dream's face was genuine enough, as she contorted to get a better look at her shoulder blade. Red, angry gashes marred her fair skin. Upon closer inspection, the scrapes ran the length of her shoulder and arm, dried blood caking her skin, where it had once trickled.

Cautiously drawing nearer, he examined her scrapes. "What happened to you?" The unusual tenderness in his tone surprised him.

"I fell into the rosebush in the backyard." Attempting to hide her pain, she lowered her arm giving up the task of assessing the damage.

"Sit," he motioned for the stool. Returning a minute later with the first aid kit, he opened the plastic case, taking inventory. Setting aside alcohol wipes, ointment, and bandages, he closed the case pushing it aside.

"I have to clean the gashes. This may sting a bit." With a nod, she gave him silent permission to continue. Tearing the packaging, he removed the moist towel and cleaned the gashes on her arm. Tensing, she pulled her arm forward, fanning the area with her hand. "Sorry."

"It's ok." The gentleness of her voice struck him down to the core. There had only been a few times, he'd seen Dream vulnerable, and it was in those times, he fought hardest to not love her. The summer she lost her great grandmother, had secretly been hard on him. The gleam in her wide smile and dark eyes dulled, although she'd try to put on a happy face. This was very different from losing a loved one, but the effect on his heart was still the same. This time around he was close by, lending a helping hand. Too close, in fact.

Swallowing, he squeezed a small bit of ointment onto the tip of his finger and lightly covered her scrapes. It was wrong to feel a pull when he touched her. She needed medical attention for goodness sakes, not his pulse spiking at an innocent touch.

Tearing open a second alcohol towelette wipe, he paused when it was time to tend to her shoulder. Her long dark tresses cascaded down, blanketing her back. Brushing her hair aside seemed too intimate a gesture, but some insane urge warred within to reach out and let her shiny hair run through his fingers. Just once. Starting by her neck, he palmed her hair and gently pulled it aside, letting it fall through his grasp just so he could attempt it again. Setting it over her opposite shoulder, she reached for the strays, bunching them with the bulk of the silky hair he'd already pushed aside.

The slope of her neck, now exposed, taunted him. He forced down the lump in his throat, wondering what it would be like to place just the tenderest of kisses there. Stuck on stupid, he forgot why he sat there mouth gaped opened like an idiot who'd never made it to first base.

Oblivious to his torture, and thinking of her own pain, she turned slightly toward him. "This time could you fan the area after you clean it? These, sting more than the ones on my arm."

Closing his mouth, his glands went into overdrive salivating like a Saint Bernard. This was ridiculous. The quicker he patched her up, the faster he could put some much-needed distance between them.

The smaller scrapes barely elicited a response, aiding in getting them bandaged up easily. Her biggest gash, closest to the top of her shoulder, had swelled and still had traces of fresh blood. Taking care, he gently wiped the cut as she cried out in pain. With nothing to fan away the sting of the disinfectant, he leaned in close and blew.

Her face mostly hidden by her shoulder, she turned and watched as he attempted to minimize the pain, his eyes locking on hers. He held her gaze, as a fire ignited in her eyes that matched the one he was having trouble containing. Dream swiveled in her stool facing him, her eyes darting between his eyes and mouth. For what felt like an agonizing minute, she did nothing, torturing him. The slightest fear seeped into her expression, and she broke eye contact, lowering her chin. It was all he needed to not let this moment slip.

Throwing caution into the ocean breeze, he gently placed a finger beneath her chin lifting it before leaning in capturing her lips.

Her kiss was heaven. Soft lips explored his and when she stood, settling her warm hands on his shoulders, he couldn't contain the fireworks going off inside. Standing so abruptly, he sent the stool careening back as he increased the urgency in his kiss. She met it with equal fervor. Years of pent up desire poured from him, into that kiss. It needed to end, but he couldn't bring himself to pull away knowing this pure bliss was never to be felt again. Her hands snaked around to his back and settled there, as she closed the gap between them. Warning signals exploded to back away, but his lips wouldn't comply, instead continuing its pilgrimage of her lips as his hands locked into the tresses at the nape of her neck.

A woman's voice echoed in the quiet kitchen, "No wire hangers, ever!" Startled, Max pulled away from Dream, all sense rushing into him furiously like white water rapids. Turning away, he wiped his mouth as if it would extinguish the electric currents that had it ablaze. He'd kissed her. Although, ravished, was a more accurate description of what he'd just done. The stab of his conscience punctured deep. Eyelids slowly slid closed as he recognized his folly. "I should have known you'd know where to find the boys." The woman's menacing voice woke him from his stupor.

Despite Faye Dunaway's voice crawling over his skin, he turned needing to apologize, no matter that the woman had the craziest ringtone. It wasn't the time to question why lines from *Mommie Dearest* echoed in the kitchen.

Dream didn't answer her phone, but slid it back in her pocket before gazing upon him. "That was my mom." Her breathless explanation smeared lipstick served as a reminder that he'd not just stepped over the line, like an Olympic Athlete, he'd Long Jumped it.

Dream already had a preconceived notion of marriage before the kiss. What would her hopes be now? It wouldn't surprise him one iota, if she were planning a shotgun wedding as she studied the granite countertop. Was that blushing? The rare pink tinging her cheeks, warmed something inside…no! Walking over to the freezer, he snatched up an ice cube, popped it into his mouth hoping to extinguish the source of his reaction. Groaning, he picked up the stool and set it back in place.

The woman had completely undone him with just a look. This was exactly why they couldn't be alone for one night.

Stepping away from her, he checked his thinking. This wasn't her fault. Since returning from two years in California, she'd hinted constantly about wanting more, though why she'd changed her mind he hadn't a clue or a care. She'd chosen New York. He pushed away the bitterness, having moved on with life. This entire mess was his fault.

For years before and since their falling out, he'd been the one to make sure they never crossed the line and today he'd failed. Now, since he was responsible for the mess, he'd be the one responsible to fix it.

Settling his face into his hands, he girded himself for an uncomfortable conversation.

"Max." Stiffening, at her warm hands lightly placed on his back, he jerked when she began to caress it. "You ok?"

Gently pulling her hands from his person, he looked into her eyes, stepping away again. "Dream, I'm sorry. I shouldn't have kissed you."

"Don't apologize. I wanted you to kiss me." Stepping in closer, her features softened, uttering reassurances that the kiss wasn't unwelcomed.

"That doesn't make it ok. You and I are only friends." Moving another pace away, he added space between them hoping she would understand his meaning, without the need to voice it. A frenzy of confusion consumed him. His heart, mind, and body, all fighting to reign over him.

"It does, when two people wanted to do it." Grinning, she drummed her fingernails on the island.

He couldn't deny that there had been many times when he desperately wanted to kiss her. For more years than he cared to admit, he wanted to kiss her. Seeing her walk down her mother's staircase on prom night sent his heart for a loop. Dream in that red gown had turned his brain to oatmeal. That was too many moons ago. Too much hurt had he felt since then.

"It won't ever happen again. Again, I am sorry for overstepping." Not allowing her to argue, he continued. "It's getting too late for you to drive back alone. I have you sharing a room with Nicole. It's the second door to the right once you get to the top of the stairs. I'm staying elsewhere for the night." Without another word, he grabbed his keys and left the house. A long night in his car was what awaited him because the alternative was equivalent to real bacon and fried chips. Neither was good for his heart.

Chapter 11

Dark blue waves did their dance flowing into each other rhythmically. Legs hanging freely above the water, Max lay back, arms folded behind him as a makeshift pillow, feeling the warmth of the morning sun on his face. He snatched a precious few moments of sleep, dozing off sporadically only to be awakened by the innate sense of being vulnerable while asleep out in the open. Yet, he wouldn't complain. He needed the time alone with God under the stars. A warm bed would have only hindered his desire to forego sleep in lieu of prayer and communion, although his back wasn't in accord.

Sitting up, he stretched, working the kinks from his stiffened body. His phone, now dead, offered no answer to the time. He looked up to the sky for a clue, as if he'd had any knowledge of time based on the placement of the sun. Laughing to himself for the wasted effort, he was left without a reasonable answer.

That seemed to be a common thread in his life lately. Despite his nightlong vigil, his heart and mind continued to war over Dream's place in his life. Too many times, he recalled the look that brought him to his knees and gave into her. Each time, he knew that had he been given a chance to relive that he'd kiss her all over again. Therein was the problem, because each and every time he thought he'd give in, he also felt shame for feeling the pull.

How did a man choose what was best for him? How many times had he not asked God to take the desire for Dream away? Hundreds? Thousands? Could that be a sign that she was for him? Of course not. Temptation wasn't from God. But He didn't remove it either. He told us how to overcome it.

Now his heart and mind were aligning itself. Relief began to trickle in. He'd had a plan. Shame filled him at how quickly he'd forgotten he intended to offer a marriage proposal, but he'd make up for it. There'd be no man more loyal than he was. Starting today, that is. The heaviness that had weighed him down had lightened thinking of his bride to be.

In fact, his salvation from the wrecked he caused was already in motion. In fact, she was probably already on her way to the house.

Startled awake, Max popped up from the couch. The pounding on the door more distinct now that he was fully awake, he rose to answer it. Another knock, had his feet moving again. Rubbing his eyes, he opened the door. Fully irritated, Emily Serrano stood at the threshold, looking like she hadn't slept in days. His savior needed a shower. That was nothing to fret over and could be remedied easily.

"Finally!" Bulldozing past him, a laptop in hand, she searched the nearby walls, crouching low. "I need an outlet. Now."

Perhaps sooner than later he could convince her that water was her friend.

"Hey Em. Glad you made it. How are you? Good. I'm glad to hear it. Me? Well, I'm an idiot."

"What else is new? Can we save your counseling session for later? Like after I plug in my laptop. I'm having a writing breakthrough and I'm only on seven percent."

"Kitchen, by the table. Mine was charging, but feel free to disconnect it." Walking out to grab Emily's luggage from the porch, Dream's SUV had been inexplicably missing since he'd come back after a long night out. Equally relieved and dismayed, he pulled the rolling suitcase into the house, leaving it by the staircase, before following Emily into the kitchen. Hope sprung up. Perhaps last night had all been a dream and hadn't just broken the promise he made to himself twelve years ago, ruining his future in the process.

Sitting atop the island, a plate of prepared breakfast sent that notion crashing, her stay clearly palpable. Slowly closing his eyes, Max reeled within, the seed of hope dying a painful death. For the tenth time he questioned his failure at resisting her one day longer?

"What time is it?"

"Almost one. I've been sitting outside for nearly two hours. I walked around back trying to find another way in and stepped in something's very smelly and soft business. You owe me a new pair of shoes." Slipping them off, she looked intently into her screen, typing away, mostly ignoring him after a swift scolding. At least, the smell hadn't derived from her.

He wasn't offended. Max knew better than to interrupt a writer, when creative juices were flowing and dropped her worn shoes into a garbage bag. Leaving Emily to her task, he took a minute to clear the fog in his head due to his unexpected nap as he took the offending bag to the garbage can on the side of the house

He'd managed to get three hours of sleep, although it felt like he'd only blinked before Emily threatened to rip the door off its hinges. What had Dream done with herself all day, other than make breakfast? He needed to talk to her and draw the line back in the sand before she read more into the kiss than there actually was.

All of his guests would be arriving soon and it'd be best they untangle themselves before they had an audience. Dragging a hand down his face, he let out an agitated breath. It was careless, crossing the line of friendship. Further proof that he could never have a life with Dream Collins. She only spurred emotions that led to decisions that would never lead him to the life he needed. Wrenching his train of thought from his mixed up emotions, Max returned his focus to solving his problems rather than wallowing in them.

Upon Tami's request, the gang would be having Sunday dinner tonight rather than on Sunday when they'd all be traveling back home and unable to keep the tradition going. The woman probably wouldn't be able to tolerate the smell of food, let alone enjoy eating it, but he'd indulge his sister nevertheless.

If anything, Sunday dinner on a Friday was sure to be anything but traditional. Other than Tyler, his best friend from high school or Abbi, the fourth musketeer of girlfriends, who lived in Chicago, there was rarely an outsider at their dinners. He and Emily had been friends since high school, but their friendship never seeped into his friendship with the others.

In reality, the gang, as they affectionately referred to the collection of friends, were originally Tami's friends, not his own. Not that he didn't care for them. It wasn't until he was an adult and finally resettled back into his hometown, nearly over two years ago, that he was officially adopted into the close-knit friendships.

It was now three years since he made a mistake that altered the course of his future. Although not as he imagined, he found he wasn't sorry for the path God had led him on. Granted, he was anxious to get started on being a family man, he couldn't help but wonder if he was destined to never have either as a fitting penance for his sins.

His hunger pangs directed him back into the kitchen. The plate of breakfast was like a beacon, calling out to him. He inspected the plate discreetly. French Toast with melted whip cream and strawberries, encompassed most of the plate leaving little room for a few strips of bacon and scrambled eggs, all of it cold to the touch. It must have been sitting for hours, not exactly appetizing now.

Rising from the chair, Emily approached grinning. "Go on." Leaning on the island, she waited. Spotting the plate, she scrutinized it, her eyebrow hiking. "Did you make this?"

"Weren't you just in crazed, don't-bother-me, writer mode?"

"I'm conducting research." Rummaging through drawers, she found a fork. She pierced a strawberry, the soggy fruit sliding from the fork, landed on the gray speckled granite countertop with a light splat.

"What kind of research?"

"Of the romantic variety." She eyed him as she continued to toy with the breakfast fare.

Was she flirting? The thought made his heart slow its rhythmic beating. Not exactly the reaction a man should have toward the woman he planned to marry. Flirting or not, he was being ridiculous.

Steeling his resolve, he aimed to grab ahold the wheel of life with an iron grip and get it back on track. He'd planned to be engaged to Emily before the weekend ended and he would see it through. There was no time like the present.

***

"What do you mean, no? I just asked you to marry me?" The woman sat at the kitchen island crunching on baked chips as if he'd ask her if she wanted anchovies on her pizza.

"It's not difficult to understand Max. No." She sipped from her can of pop, swallowing before continuing. "I don't love you in that way. Where is all of this coming from?" Emily pushed back her stool, eyeing the soggy French toast with disgust. Pointing to it, Max gave her the nod to toss it in the garbage. She walked over to the can, aided the food off the plate with the fork before placing the plate in the sink.

"We're best friends. Isn't that half way to love anyway? We'd be good together. How about you just take some time and think about it?" Circling the island, Max closed the lid to the receptacle.

"Because there isn't anything to think about. I am not, nor have I ever been, or ever will be, in love with you. Besides you're in love with-"

Don't remind him. "That's a non-issue. I don't want to marry Dream. If I did, I'd would have proposed to her but, I didn't. I'm here asking *you* to marry me. Besides, you were just flirting with me. That has to mean something."

"First, I never mentioned Dream. You did. Which just further tells me you are head over heels for her. Second, even if you weren't in love with Dream, which I know you are, but even if you weren't, I still wouldn't marry you. Third. I wasn't flirting. I was trying to get you to give me some tidbits of your night with Dream as inspiration for my book, but obviously you are out of practice being that you don't even know when a woman is flirting or not.

"And lastly, please listen carefully since this is the most important one, I, Emily Serrano, am not in love with you, Max Davidson. You, Max Davidson, are more like a brother, than future lover. Besides, do you remember we kissed once right after graduation? It felt…wrong. I went home and brushed me teeth."

"You did not," Max commented incredulously.

"Maybe I didn't. But I thought about it."

"And I will have you know, Em, that I make those dudes in your books look like chumps. I can sweep a woman off of her feet so well, she'd be up making me breakfast the next morning." The smug smile and saucy wink lasted but a second seeing the reaction in Emily's features.

"Wait! It's not what you think."

"And what do I think?"

"That I made the same mistake twice. I promise you I didn't. Nothing happened. I slept on the deck and she slept upstairs."

"You're right. You're an idiot."

"For sleeping on the deck?"

"Well yeah that too, but mostly for this self-denial you agonize over. Why do you torture yourself like this? It's not healthy."

"Maybe you can fix me. Marry me."

Emily grabbed Max by the arms and faced him. "Look at me and tell me your madly in love with me. That I am the one your mind wanders to and makes your heart full with want. Tell me I'm the one you picture on your honeymoon."

The idea of honeymooning with Emily made him feel shameful. She was a lovely woman for sure. Funny, bright and talented, but if he were honest, he couldn't picture himself performing all of his husbandly duties with her. She didn't ignite the desire to kiss her endlessly and lock himself out of a house to keep his desires in check.

Nope. Em definitely didn't invoke that. Maybe they could just agree to not fulfill that part of marriage. Shaking his head, he discarded that idea. Who was he kidding? He wanted a nice quiet life, but he also wanted a true wife. He was a full fledge red-blooded man that longed for that as much as children, family and companionship.

"Wonderful! The look of shame and disgust on your face is all the proof I need."

Quickly seeing this idea going up in flames, he set out to explain. "I'm ready to settle down and start a family life. Do you know that if I get married and father a baby by next year, I'll be the same age my dad was when Tami was born?"

"What made you think of that Slink?" Emily crossed her arms. Her quirky nickname didn't make much sense to him, but she insisted he looked like his nickname ought to be Slink.

"I've been thinking about my dad a lot lately." He felt like he was in another place, other than a rented kitchen. He lowered into the stool, flashes of memories fading in and out of his mind.

"Anything specific?"

"My dad died young, but he always said that his faith and family were his biggest accomplishments. I used to be good at what I did Em. Photography was my world. My photos have been featured all over the world." Max rested against the island. "Don't get me wrong. I know photos of beautiful women in barely there swimwear sells itself, but it still felt great to be successful at something. I made a lot of money then." She didn't need to know even more so now. "But by my dad's standards, I'm failing."

"You aren't your dad. Besides, you have a solid relationship with Jesus. Your faith would be an accomplishment in his eyes."

"It's not enough. I've traveled the world. I've rubbed elbows with the elite in the industry. I dated a model. Seen and done many things, some of which I wish I hadn't yet, it all feels meaningless. My heart desires companionship. Maybe even a pretty, little girl I can call Princess and she squeals when Daddy's gets home." Max tuned back into current space and time and focused on his confidant. "Is that crazy?"

"Of course not, but Max, God will send the right woman. Don't go off making Ishmaels when God wants to bless you with Isaacs. I hope that you have gotten this marrying me business out of your warped brain. And just so you know, I want my future husband to want to me for me, not for a dream he wants to fulfill with anybody that's willing." Emily playfully punched him in the arm.

"I'm sorry. It was completely selfish of me to ask you to marry me."

"Yep."

"How about I treat you to the ultimate Boardwalk experience. All the pizza, hot dogs, games, and rides you can handle."

Grinning, she aimed to take advantage. "Well, Mr. I've-Made-Lots-Of-Money I love to play the arcade game with the claw so don't forget your wallet."

His heart felt light and unburdened at least for the moment. Emily was a true friend and he was blessed to have her. She'd make some guy really happy one day. She'd also leave him broke if he weren't careful.

"By the way, next time you want to propose, get on one knee and at least produce a ring of some kind. You really do stink at this you know."

"I can't believe I forgot that part." The touch of red colored his face. "I actually do have a ring. I'm not that clueless."

Eyes wide like saucers, Emily took a step forward practically salivating.

"I'm taking it back as soon as we get back." The warning in his tone brokered no argument.

"Definitely." She nodded. Her agreement coming too quickly. "Could I at least take a look?"

Max pulled the ring from his pocket knowing she'd pester him until he caved. She gasped at the sight. It was a bit ostentatious, but she fawned over it, as he knew she would. Emily had never been one to care too much about fashion and shoes, but diamonds were her weakness. She simply adored her birthstone too much.

"This is gorgeous!" Was it his imagination or had she just teared up?

"Are you crying?"

"No. I can't believe I just turned down this ring."

"You didn't. You turned me down." Were all women prone to hysterics? Max stuffed his hands in pockets and shook his head in disbelief.

"Can I wear it? Just for the weekend? Being that I saved you from a terrible marriage. It can be your way of showing your gratitude." Emily slid the ring onto her finger, her lower lip clenched between her teeth as if holding back the adoration from bursting forth.

"Isn't overdosing on claw arcade games enough compensation?"

Her narrowed gaze met his. "You wanted me to birth a brood of little Maxes and Maxines. The suggestion alone is at least worth a carat of compensation."

Pink colored his cheeks. He'd actually said that aloud. "Fine. Just for tonight. I don't want you getting attached."

Giddy, she jumped into his arms and laid it on him. The smooch to his lips fell flat. It was worse than their first kiss. "Wow. Nothing. It's like kissing a doll." Still admiring the ring, she headed back to her laptop, taking the large diamond chip on her finger and the bag of the baked ones with her. "You want my advice? Stop running away and just tell that woman you are in love with her." Still enamored she cooed at the ring as she brought a chip to her mouth.

Tell Dream he loved her. Not going to happen. If only Em knew how much he felt like a cad right now. There was no use in telling his best friend he'd kissed Dream. She'd only insist she was right and the last thing he needed to do was encourage Emily believing she was always right.

Oblivious to his inner torment, she continued. "I know Dream can be a bit nutty, but she'll keep you guessing. You know, keep the mystery alive."

"I don't want mystery. I want a woman that will be a good mother to my children. One that will preferably not teach them how to break into a home by climbing into opened windows. Or one that wouldn't have me crossing state lines in a panic. You know what would be fantastic? A wife that wouldn't embarrass me in public or get me escorted out of sports arenas. And if it's not too much to ask, one that will cook a meal once and while and not feed her family pepperoni pizza every day. Is it wrong to want a simple life? Dream is anything but."

"Max."

Tami, face drained of color despite her olive skin, diced him with her glare. Her husband Jonah, standing beside her, holding a bag, scratched his brow uncomfortably. They'd heard his rant. Stepping forward toward his sister, movement behind Tami stole his attention. Face ashen, he met Dream's gaze. Eyes, filled with unshed tears, she stormed into the kitchen, snatched the bag of baked chips from Emily, turned, and stalked out the opened front door, not bothering to close it behind her. Tami trailed behind her calling out to her.

"Good going bro," Jonah slapped a hand on Max's shoulder.

Max let his head slump back and his shoulders fall. How did he always find himself in trouble when it involved Dream?

Chapter 12

Stuffing the bag of chips into the midsection of the man walking opposite her as if he were a football player, Dream ignored his protest and kept heading away from the house. Of all the things she heard, and saw in the forsaken kitchen where Max had kissed her, rescuing the bag of chips was the only thing that made any sense. Emily could keep the man, but she would not sit idly by and let the woman steal her chips. Not that she could eat a bite of her new favorite vice, that reminded her of the buffoon who'd introduced her to them.

Ignoring Tami's shouts to return, Dream picked up her pace and ducked down a street and onto the Boardwalk. Her best friend meant well, but she just needed time alone to process what had just happened. How could he kiss her as if he'd been born to do only that, one night, and then completely decimate her character the following? The realization slapped her in the face. It was a very common occurrence. Hadn't her parents warned her about the fickleness of men? She'd never imagine Max to be one of them.

Spotting the sands of the beach, Dream headed toward it. The volume of people frolicking would help her blend in. She'd be the most clothed, but at least she was among the masses. Walking a good ways, she rested in the shade under the pier, the cold sand a relief from the dry, hot sand. Giggles filtered from behind one of the wooden pier columns that held up the fishing dock.

"Just one more Stacy," the young voice pleaded.

Giggling, a young feminine voice replied, "You said that three kisses ago. We have to go before my father flips."

A redheaded teen girl pulled a lanky blonde boy from their hideout. Spotting Dream, Stacy gasped, startled still, her beau following suit.

"Be careful Stacy. Boys like to kiss you, and then stomp on your heart." Bitterness washed over Dream more thoroughly than any Atlantic Ocean wave ever could. If she could save someone else from the same fate, she'd take up the cause.

"You're crazy lady," the blonde boy retorted pulling Stacy along.

"Hey kid. Is your name Max?" Dream asked.

Stacy shook her head in response. "It's Donnie."

"Don't talk to homeless people, Stacy." Allowing herself to be dragged, Stacy's anxious eyes fixed on Dream, offering a sad smile before disappearing amidst the sea of beachgoers.

In less than one minute she'd been referred to as crazy, but that was nothing new. Homeless, not that she could blame Donnie. Sitting under a pier alone looking like something the ocean washed ashore, could make a person look destitute. But how dare he call her lady? That was a blatant insult. She could be no more than five years his senior. Possibly, maybe ten if she was generous. Nevertheless, that hardly qualified her as a lady, at least not in the way the walking hormone implied.

It seemed the more she aimed to please God, the more He took from her. At least that's what her heartache wanted her to believe, but she'd loved God too long to give into that notion just yet.

Dream sat in the same spot contemplating her life until her innards protested. Of all the times to crave a pepperoni pizza, this was the worst. "You shouldn't be hungry," Dream scolded her tummy. "I'm heartbroken here. Can't you band together with the rest of me?"

She looked up to find Donnie walking by alone, witnessing her conversation. "I knew you were crazy."

She shrugged. She couldn't argue with him there.

Walking back slowly, she prayed that everyone would be otherwise occupied and she could slip in undetected. Her tired limbs craved a warm shower and cool pillow. Her stomach ached for nourishment. Come morning, she'd head home and wallow in the comfort of her own home before she picked up the pieces of her shattered life.

Reaching the house, she trudged up the stairs and through the door. Shutting it quietly, she headed directly for the stairs, passing go, and wishing she could collect two hundred dollars now that her nest egg had been scrambled.

No such luck, unless Nicole was handing out cold hard cash at the top of the stairs. "Just in time. Dinner should be ready by now." Primly she descended, greeting Dream with a kiss on the cheek.

"I'm not hungry." Continuing to be defiant, Dream's stomach announced otherwise, the pangs intolerably insistent.

"That's physically impossible," Nicole joked. "Besides, it's Sunday Dinner. You have to come."

"Actually, it's Friday, so there ya go." Sidestepping Nicole, she began her ascent once more.

"Tami asked to switch it to today. So there *you* go. Hurry and clean yourself up. I'm famished."

When was Tami given the authority to change the days of the week? More importantly, why wasn't she given some special privilege too? The ability to hear people's private thoughts was a good one. Perhaps being unable to smell bad, even after running and bicycling around town all day. That would come in handy right about now. Although her breath probably smelled fantastic from all of the Shriver's saltwater Taffy she'd consumed. Dream took her time making it to her bedroom, and for good measure, she showered before changing.

Not typically spiteful, she found she wasn't a bit remorseful, but perhaps a little dim-witted. Remaining foul smelling would have been a far better way to liven up the festivities. Too late. She was springtime fresh now.

Thinking it through a bit more as she rummaged through Nicole's bag for perfume, she wasn't about to let Max see her torn apart. He'd never see that along with sticks, stones, and rosebushes, his words did indeed hurt her.

Instead, she'd lift herself up and take it like a woman. Max wanted distance. He'd get it in spades. Ironically, her declaration held as much weight as a feather. What would really change? Nothing. For years, Max had kept his distance. It made no difference anymore. It was time to move on. She found herself doing that in abundance lately. What was one more task to add to the dreary list?

Slipping on her sandals, Dream made her way to the dining room, head held high, and stomach having a tantrum.

If he looked down, Max was sure he could see the bottom of the cliff of which he found himself at its edge. In twenty-four hours, he'd kissed the woman he swore he'd never admit he had feelings for again, been denied by the woman he wanted to have feelings for but couldn't, made his pregnant sister cry, and managed to make all three scarce for the better part of the day.

To add to the heaping load, Drew's evil eye burned a hole through him from the other end of the table. And because life wasn't already complicated enough, David Escobar grinned as he took the seat in the middle of the table, leaving the seat between them vacant.

"Thank you for inviting me Tami. I'm usually a Cape May kind of guy, but Ocean City works too."

"You invited him?" Max and Drew spoke in unison, both glaring at Tami as she brushed them off.

"I love Cape May. Unfortunately, I don't get down there as much as I'd like to."

"The trip is a little longer, but I don't mind it."

David and Tami continued with their polite conversation, excluding him and Drew as if they weren't seated at the table. Which begged the question, why *was* David sitting at this table? He'd certainly hadn't invited him.

Nicole entered the dining room carrying a bowl of mashed potatoes and took the seat to the left of Drew and beside Tami. She joined in their conversation with ease like ingredients being folded into one another. Drew's brow creased as he took notice. Nicole placed her hand over his and served up a big smile, softening his grimace. Before long, he was pulled into her trance, panting like a dog getting a belly rub.

Jonah walked in carrying a few side dishes of vegetables and placed on table. He rubbed his hands together and took the seat to Tami's left and beside Max.

He didn't know why he was suddenly so aware that David sat alone on one side of the table with two empty chairs anchoring him. Two women had yet to enter, both of whom couldn't stand the sight of him now, and one would be dismayed to sit beside him.

Admittedly, he had a preference who sat beside him, but it didn't really matter what he wanted. As if God were playing some colossal joke, Dream and Emily arrived at the dining room at the same time. Dream gestured for Emily to enter first, as she had a large tray of fried chicken in her hands.

Emily volunteered to fry it all up once Tami refused his request. Nicole didn't eat meat, and was therefore not going to mutilate it in hot grease either.

With frustration, Emily banned him from the kitchen and took over the task. She removed the ring and slid it in her back pocket, much to his relief. He couldn't very well take it back with raw chicken embedded in its crevices. Not that he'd risk telling her that.

The smell of the chicken wafted through the room and Emily nodded to Dream, entering first. David stood and helped her set down the large dish. Without thinking about it, she sat beside David to Drew's right.

Max's heart leapt at an answered prayer. Dream would have to take the only seat left available, beside him. He watched her with curious eyes as she took in the scene, the realization now settling in. Lips tight, she took in David and the seat beside him. She exhaled loudly, but made her way to the chair without objection, without as much as a glance at him.

"Thank you Dream for making it. We had to reheat the food," Tami said before sending her best friend a wink.

Dream tightened her lips suppressing the grin. Too bad. She had a great smile. Max shook away the thought. He just wanted to apologize, not get caught up in more trouble. This was probably the only chance he'd get to express his sorrow and he wouldn't ruin it with more selfish desires.

"I'm glad you could make it David. Nicole and I are so happy you took us up on our offer." Nicole nodded gleefully, Drew's affectionate gaze slipping behind a stern look, although Nicole seemed not to notice or care.

They carried on about a coffee shop and coincidences when Max leaned into Dream. "Can we talk after dinner?" He whispered.

She poured herself a glass of water. "You've said enough."

He deserved that, but he wouldn't give up on making things right. Perhaps he could salvage the remainder of the weekend. Sitting upright, he tried to tune into anything but the nearness of her.

"And Em, I can't believe you've never been to one of our Sunday dinners. How have you managed to avoid us for so long?" Tami sipped some concoction Nicole recommended.

"Technically, I still haven't been, since it's Friday. I guess I've just been lucky." Good-natured laughter cocooned Max, although the same couldn't be said for Dream, offering only a polite smile.

"We'll have to change that and thank you for cooking the chicken. It smells delicious and believe me, that is a rare comment from me these days."

"Congratulations, by the way." Emily looked between the couple as they gushed. "When are you due?"

"The spring," Tami replied.

"I hope it's a girl born in April. Every girl's birthstone ought to be a diamond."

"I see you wear them well." Tami's brow creased. "Are you engaged?"

"Ummm." Panic filling her eyes, Emily turned to Max in search of rescuing.

Sneaking a peek at Dream, Max paid everyone else little attention, as Dream picked up her glass of water and began to sip. "It's mine," he admitted lowly.

Unintentionally being showered with the spray of Dream's drink did little to cool him from the hot seat he found himself. The blank stares around the table bore into him like arrows at a target.

Covering her mouth, Dream reached for a napkin just as Max did. Clumsy hands knocked into each other, hers shaking slightly. Was his admission the cause of her tremble? He sneaked a peak as she finally managed to wrestle away a napkin, making work of cleaning the dribble on her chin in slow purposeful motions. When her eyes finally met his, he didn't know what to make of the unreadable expression.

Facing the gawking crowd he reigned in the dread that had momentarily seized him. No longer giving into odd circumstances wreaking havoc, he refused to fall victim to misunderstandings and general foolishness, mostly a result of his own hand. It stopped now. "How about we eat before we begin share time?" The rustling of everyone settling into their seats was the only affirmation he received to his request. "If everyone can join hands, I'll pray over our bounty."

The confused looks around the table didn't surprise him. Joining hands wasn't their normal routine, but getting Dream's intertwined with his as they prayed weighed on his heart. Slowly everyone slipped a hand into their neighbor's. David faced both palms up awaiting the two women anchoring him to take ahold.

Max huffed. Focused on his own wants, he'd overlooked the fact that Dream would have her other hand imprisoned in David's. It wouldn't matter. His eyes would be closed during the prayer, and he'd not have to witness it.

In an unladylike manner, Emily slapped her hand into David's without a care. Dream kept both hands on her lap, fiddling with her napkin. At the clearing of his throat, Dream raised her eyes to Max, her glare, Medusa sealed and approved. Extending his hand a bit closer, he waited for her to accept it.

The spark that lit her eyes, sent his pride soaring. She brought her napkin to her mouth and sneezed loudly into it. A fake one, if he'd ever heard one.

"Actually, I think I'm coming down with something. I really shouldn't. I wouldn't want to make anyone sick."

Well played Dream.

"In that case, let us pray." He turned his empty hand flush to the polished tabletop.

"Don't break the circle on my account," she said motioning to the hands of each man beside her.

He should have known she wouldn't leave well enough alone. Rather than making a big deal out of nothing, he closed the circle, and prayed over the food, including a petition to heal Dream from any malady real or imaginary, though he kept that thought to himself.

She sneezed again for good measure, feminine snickers intermingled with a few quiet God bless yous. Max ended the prayer more determined to make things right with the little troublemaker. Suppressing his smile, he served himself a heaping load of peas before passing the plate.

Clearing the table Max, reached for Dream's plate knowing she'd neither, ask for his assistance, nor thank him for offering it. Lifting the plate, he wasn't surprised finding she hadn't finished her peas. Unable to eat another bite, she'd patted her stomach for effect, until three minutes later, Drew carried in a few pies. Sitting up ramrod straight, she looked over David in search of an option she liked, instead settling for a variety.

Max shook his head as she used her fork to scrape up then eat, the offending apple pie filling that had the audacity to escape the crust and settle on the plate.

"Done?" He waited, her dinner plate in hand, lowering it an invitation to add the dessert plate to it. Had he not seen the plate being used, he would have mistaken it for a clean one. Dismissing his hospitality, she piled the plate atop the larger one chock full of peas.

Why bother serving the peas, if you aren't going to eat them? She was worse than a child. He cracked a smile seeing a miniature version of Dream seated at his dinner table pleading with Daddy to forego the vegetables for a bowl of ice cream.

The vision, so clear and warming, rocked his core off its axis. Gathering the plates, he hustled into the kitchen in need of a minute alone. Of all the crazy and foolhardy things to imagine, a domesticated life with Dream was at the top of the list. Clutching the edge of the counter, he dipped his chin taking a moment to gather sane thoughts, combating the ones sure to drive him to distraction.

"You alright?" Drew placed a few dishes in the sink, planting his hands on his sides.

"Yep."

"I don't know what's going on, but I know I don't like it." Drew's brow creased in concern. "How did David manage to coerce an invitation from your sister?"

"Ask your fiancée," Max replied, crossing his arms across his chest. "It wasn't my idea. I'm just as surprised as you are."

"You know as well as I do, that guy is trouble."

Max huffed. "He's not such a bad guy."

"Yeah? Will Dream think that once she falls for his charms then goes and replaces her like yesterday's trash once the chase is over?"

A kick to the stomach wouldn't have felt more real than the current state of his clenched gut. There was no way on God's green earth Dream would fall for David's recycled pick-up lines, was there?

After a few seconds, the tightening in his midsection loosened. Of course, Dream wasn't interested in David. She refused to take his hand as she had his. His ego fell a notch at being placed on the same playing level as David, but he couldn't worry over that now.

While, he sat in the kitchen moping like a sap, David currently sat beside Dream, doing what he did whenever he was around women.

"We should get back." Max brushed past Drew and into the lion's den without haste.

Chapter 13

Apparently, a formal complaint would need to be lodged in order to keep Share Time from descending into the pits of sappy feelings and blooming tears. *Steel Magnolias* met *Sisterhood of the Traveling Pants*, and any minute someone was going to suggest group hugs and singing Kumbaya around a campfire. To keep her mind from spiraling slowly into madness, Dream mentally drafted her complaint.

Nicole, with her ailing patient stories, was accused of inciting tears and snot. A repeat offender, with no chance of reform. Her fiancée, Drew, was being charged with bludgeoning a topic to an inch within its life, before moving onto the next predictable one. Bible study, basketball, and Nicole. The man needed to expand his horizons.

While some needed to move on, others needed to bring it back a notch. Twelve subscribers hardly qualified as internet sensation, especially when six of the subscribers were seated at that very table and two more were Jonah's mother and his mother-in-law. But you couldn't tell Jonah Scorch-sese otherwise. It wouldn't surprise her in the least if he was preparing a speech for winning a YouTube award.

If Tami weren't careful, she'd be implicated as well. There were only so many ways one could describe morning sickness, and frankly, the first go around had been sufficient and this second offense couldn't go unpunished.

A tinge of guilt penetrated seeing Tami sip her ginger ale. At just a few months pregnant, Tami had transformed into a walking, over-emotional, vomit box. That deserved a little mercy on her part. After all, what were best friends for if not to listen to the very explicit details of a pregnant friend's bodily fluids?

Tami finished her latest account of being sick all night and looked to David. "Your turn."

Taken aback, he widened his eyes. "Me? Well, I wasn't expecting to share, but I guess I could. My highlight of the week," David scratched his chin in contemplation. "I arrested a vandal that had damaged some downtown businesses with graffiti."

Congratulations were offered peppered with a few questions. Inquiring minds wanted to know. It was noble but the last thing David needed was an ego boost. After satisfying everyone's curiosity, he continued. "My low. Being turned down for a date…again." He chuckled. "I don't know why, but she keeps turning me down."

Heart plummeting like a failing elevator, Dream ceased her thoughts from wandering suddenly keenly aware of every word and every person. Drew was scowling, his eyes darting between Max and David. Something was amiss there, but she had neither the time nor inclination to solve that mystery. She'd had too much on her plate already, and their problems equated to the peas she'd left behind.

Emily, on the other hand, took a fervent interest in David's misfortune, pulling out a notepad she began scribbling with haste. Everyone seated opposite her, gifted David his or her undivided attention. As if he were a movie screen during its climatic scene, they were sucked into the women problems always associated with David.

"Why don't you record a few YouTube videos highlighting all of your dramatics? Your life is like a *telenovela* anyway." Dream shook her head, immune to the charm that usually rendered others helpless.

"Only if you'll be my leading lady?" Flashing an easy grin, he hooded eyes. Those must be his dreamy eyes, she supposed. Thankfully, she wasn't sleepy.

"I can be the lady that leads you to your car." Her tight smile was anything but friendly. Would he ever get a clue?

"That's one of the things I like about you, Dream," he said, aiming a finger at her, his shoulders relaxed. "You aren't afraid to say what's on your mind."

Did he really think his very accurate assessment of her character could butter her up? He could keep his compliments, because she didn't need anyone to confirm what she already knew about herself. "I prefer music to television, but good luck with that."

"I thought you were part of the drama club in high school?" Jonah asked. "You even convinced Ethan to audition. Remember?"

Jonah's big blues blinked as he awaited a response, not an inkling how running his trap about the past was not the least bit helpful or appropriate.

"Who's Ethan?" David asked, scanning the room in search of a loose tongue.

"Some loser," Max replied into the clasped hand shielding his cough.

Dream whipped her head round and seared him with a questioning gaze.

"Ethan is my best friend." Jonah offered. "He and Dream dated in high school." Pulling Tami in closer, he put an arm around her shoulders. "They starred in *Beauty and The Beast* together. It was actually pretty good."

Max raised an eyebrow and let out a humorless laugh. Max disapproved? Yeah? Well, what else was new? What did he know? She was fantastic as Belle, and from what she could remember, he'd been sick and didn't bother attending.

"I think we are moving off topic." Nicole commanded everyone's attention. "Is there anything you want to share?" She asked politely.

"Let's not overwhelm our guests Nicky?" Drew pulled her chair closer to his. "Besides, we still have three more confessions to go before we can go out back and start a bonfire."

Nicole eyed him suspiciously. "Right," she said. "Who wants to go next?"

"I will." Dream spoke up. "She would have preferred to keep her confession to the immediate gang but there was no way she was going to carry this heavy load around for another week. "My highlight." Instantly her thoughts returned to being swept up in a kiss with Max, her face flaming. It was best to leave well enough alone and keep it to herself. "Since the week isn't over yet, I reserve the right to announce one on Sunday before we all leave."

"You sure you didn't already have one? That's a pretty shade of pink in your cheeks." Tami chuckled, her shoulders shaking as a snort escaped.

She wasn't sure, but pregnancy hormones must include some sort of courage booster. Tami's usually tame tongue was buying her some expensive trouble, she couldn't afford. However, Dream wasn't unreasonable. If, for some reason, Tami were unable to control her outbursts due to medical reasons, she'd only need to provide a note stating so rather than paying the piper. Otherwise, she was just cast in David's *telenovela* in a minor storyline, and her name was officially added to the complaint.

"Something I need to share..." This was tougher than she'd imagined. "As much as I would love to start my own business, I'm going to hold off on branching out on my own for now." Bombarded with questions and her friends pushing her to try, she inhaled deeply then let it out slowly. She could do this. "Guys, this was difficult to come to terms with. Just know that I haven't given up on it. It's just on the backburner for a while longer."

They continued the assault, questions, and suggestions tangled up like Christmas lights, she didn't know where one began and the other ended.

"Enough!" Drew yelled. "She's made peace with it for now. Let's not make an already difficult decision that much harder on her."

When had he become her designated big brother, she was unsure, but for now, she appreciated the benefit of having an older brother to look out for her. She sent him a sly wink coaxing a twitch in his lips, although working extra hard to keep up the grimace.

Looking around the table, she didn't let her gaze linger too long on Max as he focused on her. His steepled hands lowered, collapsing into themselves as he leaned forward on the table. "Are you sure you don't want to talk about it?" The determination in his eyes, made her want to spill every secret hurt if it meant he would lend his ear.

David slid his chair back, its legs scraping the floor pulling her from the trance. Under the table, the cold touch of his hand upon hers startled her. She yanked her hand free and placed atop the table. Wishing he'd move on and find another victim, her heart jerked at the revelation that Max felt that way about her.

That truth fired a hole in her so deep, she'd jump in the ocean just to stop the burn. It was imperative to get the admission done and over with. Maybe then, she could begin to move on with all she'd lost in life. Shedding the skin of her current life stung, but sometimes it was necessary to start fresh. She was crossing the Jordan River to new beginnings. Bringing along old baggage was pointless and only weighed her down.

"No. I'm done with that subject and many others. I'm letting go and moving on." Her statement hung in the air, their eyes locked into each other's. Max broke contact first and nodded his understanding.

Lifting her shoulders, she turned from him and continued shedding the dead weight holding her down. "My low is that I've been removed as CCCs treasurer."

The gasps and questions were quiet then gaining momentum as everyone spoke at the same time.

"Why?" Drew asked concerned.

"I don't think I'm at liberty to discuss that," she answered truthfully, though she'd never thought that deep enough about it.

"Honey! When did they let you go?" Nicole pushed her seat back and faced Dream, hands on her lap.

"Monday."

She could feel Max studying her profile, but chose to ignore it. "Does this have anything to do with our trip to Delaware?"

Of course, he'd make it impossible to tune him out, but she continued trying and didn't reply.

"What trip to Delaware?" Tami asked, eyes darting between the two of them.

"Long story," Max answered turning back to Dream. "Does it?" The tenderness in his voice betrayed her hurt again. He had no right easing her reeling emotions toward him. She was determined to remain detached no matter how his voice pleaded for cooperation.

"Not really." Not directly anyway.

"That sounds like a polite yes." Max leaned in closer. "You can tell me."

"You've been busy buddy," David interrupted. "Engagement rings with one woman and trips to Delaware with another." The sparks in his eyes betrayed his grin.

Emily, red as a tomato, removed the ring from her finger, a look of shame washing over her.

"Emily, you don't have to take it off." Max assured her.

A dagger to her heart would be no less painful than Max's words piercing her. Her stomach churned hearing the love of her life plead with another woman to wear his engagement ring, a day after she'd kissed him. One of the most perfect moments in her life was tarnished by infidelity, lies, and deceit. She hadn't asked God for confirmation to move on from Max Davidson, but He provided it nevertheless. His infinite wisdom and all that good stuff.

Being flanked by two men that caused such angst in the past few weeks, felt like being imprisoned and suffocating. "Excuse me," she stood regally holding hand to her middle to keep it from roiling. She'd not let them see her effected. So many warring emotions dueled for her attention. Anger, jealousy, pain, betrayal. In the end, she chose to what she'd never done. Remain calm.

Max jumped to his feet, placing a hand to Dream's arm keeping her rooted to the floor. "Dream, wait. I need to clear this mess up."

"It's the least you could do," David continued.

Max wasn't a violent man but his friend was pushing him to his limit. He fixed David with a glare that quieted the man for the moment.

"I'm not engaged. We're not engaged." He motioned between him and his best friend. Emily chimed in confirming his declaration.

Dream moved away from him, standing at the threshold of the opened French doors that led to the front porch. Dusk was fast approaching, the evening heat not so brutal. The quiet street was peaceful in contradiction to all she was feeling within. It mattered not whether they were or weren't now because eventually he would be. This was just the revelation she needed to pull up her skirts to trudge ahead.

With her back to the dinner party, Dream crossed her arms and listened.

"I'll start with my low," Max spoke. "I failed a friend. I'll leave it at that."

Dream's eyes slid closed. Did he think that helped? His admission was so vague, it was practically torture having to speculate his meaning. Did he regret the kiss? The candid words spoken to a friend in confidence? Both? Neither? Was she even the friend he referred to?

"My highlight was being mistaken for the next Bachelor." The chorus of laughter lightened her mood.

"My brother on TV. You know what's crazy? I just read that he was spotted in at a local mall buying a scarf."

"You? I'd qualify to be the next Bachelor before you," David added.

Laughter bubbled up from the pit of Dream's stomach and bellowed out into the warm air. This was the most ridiculous conversation.

"Moving on," Max added quickly, intensifying her amusement. He was probably beet red, the image kept her laughter going.

"I do want to share something," Max interjected subduing her enjoyment. "But before you jump to conclusions, please let me say all I have to say first." After a few murmurs of agreement, he pressed on. "I asked Emily to marry me, but she said no."

Dream walked out of the French doors not needing to hear any of the particulars. It changed nothing. The fact remained that he had indeed asked someone else to share his life for the rest of hers, no matter the response.

Chapter 14

It was quite clear that Nicole wasn't attempting to be quiet during her morning routine. Slamming the bathroom door, she opened it several minutes later, the loud hiss of her hairdryer barely masking her boisterous singing. Did she suspect that Dream had been up for an hour and feigned sleep? Probably. That hadn't stopped Dream from continuing the charade.

"This is so stupid. Dream Marcela Collins! Get up this instant. I know you're awake. You're not even snoring." Nicole stood somewhere close behind her.

"I don't snore." And shame on Nicole for saying so aloud.

"Tell it to my ears in the middle of the night. You can't stay up here all day." Wrapping the blanket around her arms as if it were yarn, Nicole tugged Dream's blanket free.

"I can sleep without it." Dream's groggy voice was muffled further by her pillow.

"*Levantate.* You can't stay in bed all day. Its vacation." The pulling of legs, Dream's eyes shot open, arms grasping for something to hold onto. "Get up, or I get you up my way."

"Fine," Dream shouted. "But isn't the point of vacation to sleep in and lounge all day?" She felt the release of her legs and sat up. "You're nothing but a bully."

Dressed in a swimsuit and cover up, Nicole held out Dream's bathing suit. "We're going to the beach," she said grinning.

Great. Because she hadn't spent enough time at the beach already. Huffing, she mentally shook herself. This entire disastrous vacation now had her thinking sarcastically to herself.

"You can't hide my car keys forever. I will find them and when I do, guess who I'm going to run over first?"

Nicole cracked up. "I'd say with the month you've had, even you don't know the answer to that."

"Don't be so sure about that Dr. McBully."

Continuing to find amusement in the situation, Nicole tossed the swimsuit at Dream and plopped onto her bed, as Dream rose to her feet.

"I apologize in advance because I'm about to be completely selfish."

Dream faced her with an exaggerated frown. "You are the last person on the planet that could ever be selfish. It's as if selflessness is embedded in your DNA. It gets irritating."

Nicole crossed her leg, fidgeting with her fingernails. "I need advice."

"Financial or spiritual?" Sitting on her bed, she removed the stretchy hair tie from her wrist and twisted her hair up into a mess bun.

"Love."

Laughter filled the room. There was no one on earth less qualified to give advice on love. "Has Pastor Pretty boy forgotten to put the moon in his eyes along with the stars?"

Red settled on Nicole's cheeks. "Drew has gotten a little cold in our relationship."

Brows furrowed she cut Nicole a glare. "Cold as in verbally or emotionally abusive?" She had his cold alright. Dream rose from the bed in search of some clothes and Vaseline, battle ready.

Giggling interrupted her focus. "Not if he values life as he knows it."

Dream chuckled. Nicole was often so prim and proper she'd forgotten that hot lava Latina flowed under the surface.

"I meant that he hasn't been very affectionate and every time I try and sneak a kiss, he finds an excuse to leave or not be alone."

The man was finally cracking. "Have you guys chosen a wedding date yet?"

"No. Why?"

"I think Pastor Pretty Boy is afraid to be alone with you. Maybe you should find a way to make him rush the wedding date if you know what I mean."

"Dream! Are you suggesting I seduce him?"

Waving her hand, Dream shook her head. "No. What do I know about seducing anyone?" Her one attempt was a miserable failure. "You could fall into a rosebush." That had yielded some unexpectedly blissful results.

"What?" Nicole asked confused.

"Never mind. Why don't you plan a romantic date tonight? Just the two of you. What excuse could he have to be busy here?"

Covering her grin with her manicured nails, Nicole was doing a poor job at hiding her excitement. "Thanks," she finally said. "Now get dressed." She rose and walked to the door.

Fisted hands were shoved to Dreams sides. "I just gave you great advice and your back to being Dr. McBully?"

"That's all you've got? I expected something a little more vicious."

"Actually, I planned on introducing Dr. McPretty, but you loss that honor and I didn't have time to think of anything cleverer. It's not my best, but it will work for now. She turned on her heel and into the bathroom.

Feeling like the quintessential idiot, Dream settled herself a good ways away from the group. They'd all ended up on her formal complaint that had graduated from mental notes to actually being drafted in her phone, after hiding her car keys and holding her hostage.

Lathering up on sunblock, she donned her sunglasses and soaked up the sun. She wondered how long before her best friends would seek her out. Funny enough, she hadn't even finished the thought before Nicole stabbed a beach umbrella into the sand and opened it as Tami smoothed out her towel near Dream's.

"So." Nicole looked over to Tami and shrugged. Tami opening her eyes, perplexed, shrugged in return.

"You two really do stink at this."

"We are just trying to tread softly." Tami warned. "Besides, we aren't used to seeing you like this."

"By this, do you mean quiet and subdued?" Dream grinned.

Nicole grimaced. "Drew thinks you are going to go postal any minute."

Sitting up, Dream hugged her knees. "You make me sound psychotic. After things settle down, please regale me with that bit of information again. Drew being afraid of me is something I should be enjoying, but I'm just not up for it now."

Grinning, Nicole nodded. "You got it."

"So if you aren't psychotic, what's going in there?"

"I'm just trying to move on with life."

"How's that working out?" Nicole asked rubbing Dream's back.

"Jury's still out."

"Oh, Dream. I'm so sorry. I don't know what Max was thinking." Tami, Dream's favorite jellyfish was back and looked ready to cry. Tears begat tears and the one thing she would not give Max Davidson was seeing her cry. Those were reserved for God alone.

"I'm sure he was thinking about his happiness." Dream pulled Tami's hands into hers. She could see the turmoil she faced caught between her best friend and brother. "You can't blame him for it. He has that right."

Laying her head on Dream's shoulder, Nicole moved her arm up around Dream's shoulder and squeezed. "And you have every right to feel too. You just trust us to be rational for you ok?"

Dream laughed. "Are you offering to babysit me because I'm, irrational?"

"Well when you put it that way, its sounds like you are ready to be committed, and we are carrying the straitjacket." Tami scrunched her nose offended.

"I calls 'em, as I sees 'em, honey. And I can assume that Pastor Drew put you up initiating this pow-wow." Directing her question to Nicole, she faced her. "Did he send over some scripture too," Dream joked. Nicole's face flushed. "He did!" Dream laughed harder. "That fiancée of yours sure likes to Bible beat me. "

"He's just trying to help. We all are."

"I know and I appreciate it. I really do. How about you text me the verses, and I'll look at them later." Something to occupy her thoughts later. "Now if you just be kind enough to return my car keys, I can go home and begin renewing my life. You keeping here against my will isn't going to help."

"Maybe, but neither is sulking at home alone. Besides, David is here."

Slowly intertwining her hands, Dream straightened her lengthy legs before her and rested her hands on her lap demurely, her movements methodical and calculating. "I'm going to say this just once, so listen carefully McPretty and McPrego."

"But she's not a doc-" Nicole began to interrupt before Dream's glare cut off her correction.

"I have no interest in David as a human let alone a boyfriend. God bless his heart. Kindly remove the horrific idea from your heads and bury it deep in the sand. Please and thank you."

Eyeing each other, her friends headed off in different directions without a word leaving her to what should have been relaxing under the sun, but instead worry now consumed her at whatever they had gotten her involved in. After a half hour of the sky not falling in, she could only assume, they'd performed some damage control much to her delight.

It was amazing to see how much life was lived if one could sit and observe. Dream observed the beach goers closely. She learned that the mom with the two children was more patient that humanly possible. The mom beside her, not so much. More than once, Dream held back her chuckle when the Mom threatened to run away.

The elderly couple wearing scarves during a heat wave yelled at each other just to be heard, but shared comfortable silences. When his wife fell asleep, he rose from his chair to cover her with a towel, although they were both under the shade of two umbrellas. Turning away from the private moment that made her yearn for companionship like lungs did air, she checked the tears that threatened.

"Hey, Dream."

Shielding the sun from her vision, she looked up to see Max hovering. "Tami asked me to bring back the sunblock she borrowed."

"She didn't borrow any." She pointed out looking out over to the ocean.

"Then why would she...never mind. Now that I'm here, I was hoping we could talk."

"Haven't you said enough?" The last thing on earth, she wanted was to talk to Max Davidson.

"I'd like to explain. Can I sit?" Max gestured to the sand beside her.

Her heart screamed no, yet longed for any words to soothe the rejection. One that would take away all the pain. The chances of that were nil, therefore hearing an explanation pointless. Whether she wanted to hear it or not, she knew, she wasn't ready to speak to him. Lord only knew what would fly out of her mouth. She'd not give him any more reasons to deem her unworthy.

"I don't own the beach. You are free to sit wherever you like." As soon as he did, she stood, gathering her towel and bag. "Luckily, I can too." Leisurely she walked away. If he had any logical cells in his brain, he'd give her some space.

Taking a giant step over an abandoned sand castle, Dream stumbled into a young woman. "Stacy."

"Homeless lady. You look…different."

Cracking a smile, Dream supposed she looked less crazy, but apparently still *lady* like. "I'm not homeless. I was just having a bad day. So where's Don Juan?" Glancing around the area, Dream searched for the blonde hormone in shorts.

Brows pinching, Stacy looked confused. "His name is Donnie, not Don Juan."

Stifling a laugh, Dream dipped her chin. "Right. Sorry."

"Doesn't matter anyway. You were right about him."

"My name is Dream." Extending her hand, she waited for Stacy to accept it.

"Come again?" Stacy looked caught between bolting and crying but slipped her hand in reluctantly.

Dream chuckled. "That's my name."

"Like when we sleep?" Intrigue twitched in her smile. "Yep."

"That's different. Well, Dream. I found Donnie kissing another girl under the same pier an hour ago."

"Dream." A hand touched her shoulder stealing her attention. Max, jaw set, looked ready to square off. Seeing Stacy, he sobered. "Hi."

"Hi," Stacy replied apprehensively.

"I'm Max," he extended a hand.

Narrowing her gaze at his hand, she looked between Dream and Max. Dream could see all the questions and emotions roiling under the mass of red hair appearing to be set ablaze from the intensity of the sunlight beating down on them.

"*Thee* Max?" She asked Dream, horrified. Tilting her head and arching her brows quickly, Dream said nothing more. Nothing else needed to be communicated for Stacy heard her loud and clear. "Jerk." Storming away, she looked back once, scowl firmly in place. How refreshing. Dream couldn't be more proud. The girl managed to sum it all up in one word. Bravo, Stacy. If she ever saw Donnie, she'd be sure to repay the favor.

Not bothering to address Max, she continued her walk. Not getting the picture, Max tugged her hand with his own. "Wait."

"What? I don't want to do this."

"Why does that girl think you are homeless?"

Now, he was eavesdropping? The shine was fading from this man faster than toddler's plastic toy jewelry. "Not that I need to explain anything to you, but if it means you'll leave me alone, it was a simple misunderstanding."

"Not good enough."

"You've already made that abundantly clear. Now if you'll let go, I can too."

"What's that supposed to mean?"

"I'm sure you'll figure it out soon enough."

"Stop acting like a spoiled brat and talk to me."

Oh. No. He. Didn't. Before she could tongue lash him thoroughly, he yanked her belongings from her hands, tossed them in the sand, and tossed her over his shoulders.

He was running into the ocean as she pounded on his back, to no avail. Saltwater swallowed her whole before she could to cry out from the cold. Afraid to open her eyes under water, she sank while being pushed and pulled by the current. Strong hands pulled her up as she gasped for air.

"Why didn't you swim up?"

"Because I can't swim," she said breathless. "Why would you do that?" She panted too spent to thrash him.

"I just assumed you knew how to swim. You could have drowned. I'm so sorry." Exerted he drew in one lungful of air after another. His shoulders rose up and down as his breathing matched hers. It was only then she took in the sight before her.

Glistening in the sun, rivulets of water treaded down Max's distressed face as he held her. His olive skin appeared golden as the sunlight bounced off him. Her hands rested on his defined shoulders to help keep her afloat, the only part of his upper body visible other than his muscular arms in the tank top he wore. She swallowed. She was drowning within, at the sight of him, but this time there was nothing he could do to save her.

Dream wiped the ocean water from her face, in hopes the attraction she felt would somehow be expelled as well. Quickly she realized it was pointless as the hands that wiped away saltwater, were also covered in the same saltwater and her attraction ran deeper than Max's physical beauty.

Not just attraction, but love that was as deep and wide as the Atlantic. Boy, oh boy, was she in bigger trouble than sinking to the ocean floor.

Chapter 15

It seemed like a good idea at the time, before he'd found out the hard way, she couldn't swim. In retrospect, every memory of her in a body of water was on a float or in shallow water. That was too close for comfort, even if the result was Dream latching onto him for dear life as they bobbed in the water together like a buoy.

In that moment, he couldn't remember what insane reasons he'd fed himself to keep from loving her openly. Not one single reason came to mind. He pulled her closer and held her tighter, all the reasons he'd tossed her into the water forgotten.

Lulled by the motion of the waves, serenity filled her countenance, simultaneously capturing and breaking his heart. She trusted him, but she shouldn't. He'd barely trusted himself in her presence.

Closing her eyes slowly, she tilted her head back, face to the sun, and basked in it. Never had she looked so beautiful. Wet stringy hair and no make-up only added to his appreciation. Sunrays bounced off the expanse of her slender neck, before she lowered her chin.

Like his conflicting emotions, the coolness of the water by his swaying feet, contrasted with the warmer water on the surface. Lips trembling, she held fast to him, the warmth of her hands seeping into his shoulders despite the frigid waters.

"Are you cold?"

Her nod was lazy. "A little."

As much as he hated their own little world coming to an end, he'd never want to leave it if he endured it much longer. "Don't let go." He meant it in every way imaginable.

"I won't," she replied.

How he wished he had the gall to ask more of her, but how dare he? Like a dam being emptied, his shortcomings, and how he had projected them onto the one woman who'd stripped away the façade he'd worked so hard to erect, burst forth from the confines he'd sealed them in and pushed to the back of his mind and heart. Stored away like old clothes in an attic.

Loving Dream meant betraying himself. Not having her was an empty existence. A double-edged sword that had sliced his heart in pieces. *God what are you doing to me?*

I know the plans I have for you...

Floating there in the Atlantic Ocean, holding this crazy beautiful woman, he heard the words, the scripture resounded in every part of his being.

Dream closed her eyes and whispered, "I know the plans I have for you." Tranquility enveloping her, as she held tight.

"What'd you say?" Heart beating like a drum, he could hardly believe what he'd heard.

Sheepish, she shook her head dismissively. "Something God just spoke to me. Don't mind me."

Had he said the words aloud too? No, he hadn't. He was sure of that. Was it even possible he was imagining it? It couldn't be. Perhaps they'd both swallowed too much saltwater.

"I better get you back to shore."

She nodded, her grip tightening. "Hold on, ok?"

"Until God says otherwise," she replied.

Max, dared not read too much into the reply and swam to shore, Dream holding onto his back as if her life depended on it, because it had.

The remainder of the day at the beach was spent amicably between them. Other than the heat of the sun, things had cooled since wading in the water together. Sporadic thoughts of floating with Dream sneaked into his conscience. Something happened between them out there in the ocean. It was inexplicable and profound. It was also scary despite the wonder of it all.

Max couldn't shake the feeling that God was bonding them together. That rattled him to his bones. Many years ago, he'd let the idea of a life with Dream die a painful death. Moving on from Dream was one of the hardest things he'd ever done, and he wasn't ready to jump at the chance to have to relive it all over again.

California was his destination. Shooting covers for Emily's first novels during college had been nothing more than a bit of fun while helping a friend. Never would he have thought it would have ballooned into a career that would move him across the country at the time he most wanted to escape.

God had been moving in his life, or so he thought. One opportunity after another sprung up like weeds in an unkempt garden. He'd moved up the career ladder so fast, he'd developed aeroplane ears. Before he knew it, he was listed as a regular photographer for a major modeling agency in LA.

Then came Ava. An up and coming model, sweet when she wanted to be. Not so much, when she needed to be. Other than her long dark hair, she and Dream were nothing alike, except his desire to want to kiss her.

Unlike with Dream, it hadn't taken years. Not even months. Ava wasn't timid about what she wanted in life, including Max.

At first, he'd resisted her feminine charms, his Christian upbringing solid. However, it wasn't long before visiting local churches on Sunday morning was replaced by hanging out at bars and clubs on Saturday nights, in the name of his career. Connections were important if he wanted to make it in this business.

The explosion of work he'd gotten from Ava's recommendations had been proof enough of that. Bible time gave way to editing women into perfection and prayer into building his freelance business.

Max laid back onto his towel, his arm slung over his face, to shield his eyes from the blaze of the sun, as his past threatened to burn him within. He continued down the path down memory lane knowing he'd regret it.

Ava floated into his view. He wouldn't have called it love, but he had been content with her. They'd become close and it wasn't long before their relationship became physical. The first and only woman he'd been with.

He'd worked hard to keep the guilt of his sin buried. Recognizing it, would prove to be inconvenient with his new lifestyle of freedom. Unable to outrun it, he set out to bandage the bleed, offering Ava his fidelity and a monogamous relationship. It wasn't marriage, but it had to be better than casual intimacy.

Rather than feel dejected when Ava outright laughed at him, relief consumed him. Although, he had been with no other woman and had no desire to be, the idea of a commitment to Ava felt like he was killing a piece of himself. Nevertheless, he'd made a go of living right.

Alone at night, the thought brought him little comfort. He grew to hate being alone for his heart betrayed him in the quiet. Most nights he'd spend in Ava's bed or in the companied of acquaintances, drinking his guilt into oblivion.

The day he'd received the invitation to his only sister's wedding, had sent him reeling. The ache for his family and friends consumed him like gasoline lit on fire.

He hated himself for missing that life. He'd worked so hard to leave it all behind. To leave Dream behind. He hadn't thought about her in months, and then one small envelope exhumed all he thought was dead and buried.

What was South Jersey compared to LA? Nothing. The closest major city was Philadelphia. It was laughable. There was nothing to miss about South Jersey, other than his loved one. He didn't miss Dream. He wouldn't allow himself to miss her. She'd made her choice and he'd made his.

Ringing the doorbell to Ava's condo, he longed to get lost in her kisses and fully stocked bar. Anything to take away the hurt bombarding him. She answered the door in sweats and a tee, her eyes red from crying. She couldn't meet his eyes and left him standing at the door.

Following her in, he closed the door behind him, the sun filtering in through the wall-to-wall windows.

"Hey. What's wrong?" He set down the bag of Chinese food she loved and pulled her into a hug. She sobbed on his shoulder before pulling away to sit on patterned club chair. Hugging the throw pillow, she steadied her voice.

"I need to tell you something. You should probably sit down."

His stomach bottomed out, but he complied, giving her his full attention.

"Max, I went to a clinic today."

A myriad of horrible diagnoses' rushed into his brain. Was she sick?

"I had an abortion today," she said her voice weak and broken

His heart stopped beating and his brain slowed as he took in the significance of her words. Sitting back with a thump, he realized he was speechless. She stood quickly and walked over to the bar, pouring herself a drink. She probably shouldn't be drinking, but he was too stunned to chastise her about it.

"Was the baby…" He could scarcely say the words. "Was the baby mine?"

Her laughter was almost evil. "Yes. *It* was yours."

Never before had he felt so sick in all of his life. "Why didn't you tell me you were pregnant? He sat forward trying to reign in all he was feeling. Hurt. Betrayal. Cheated.

"Because I knew you would want me to keep it."

His heart broke at how Ava continued to refer to the baby as 'it'. The ice in her cup clinked as she paced, and sipped the drink in hand.

"I had a right to know." The words escaped in a breathless whisper. He couldn't gather himself enough to speak all he was feeling.

"And I've told you." She sniffled, as she held the glass cup with amber liquid inside.

Behind him, he heard her pour another drink. She brought it to him, and sat on the single chair again. She sipped her drink and wiped away the moisture escaping her nose courtesy of her previous breakdown.

Max placed the glass on the table and paced. This was all too much to take in, and he needed to be sober to process it.

"Max, I've already told you that my career means everything to me. A baby would have ruined everything."

The words meant to pacify her decision cut him deeply. Up until ten minutes prior he hadn't even contemplated fatherhood and now he'd felt as if he'd been robbed of the opportunity. An inexplicable ache of yearning and missing what he had never known, consumed him.

"I've been thinking, and I believe it's for the best that we don't see each other anymore."

He heard the words, but they meant little in comparison to what she had already shared. He nodded and left her condo without a backward glance.

Parking his car across from his apartment building, the idea of purposefully entering solitude kept him rooted to his seat. For an hour, he sat in silence allowing the voices in his head to beat him down. Guilt and shame for his part in his pain.

Max flicked on the radio, turning up the volume to deafening levels in hopes to drown out his own thoughts.

Immediately he recognized the song that played. Daughtry's raspy melodic voice crooned on. Home. Max had heard the song numerous times, but unlike before, they resonated on a deeper level. An understanding. Every lyric reverberated deep in his spirit. He wanted to go home. Not just to South Jersey, but to Jesus.

For the first time in nearly two years, and right in his car, Max cried out to God, pouring himself out until empty. He'd stayed up for hours asking for forgiveness for every sin he could remember. The desire to wipe the slate clean and begin anew, consumed him.

A tap to his leg brought him back to the present. "You ok?" Jonah towered over him, tossing up a beach ball.

"Yeah, why?"

"A bunch of locals challenged us to a game of volleyball. You in?"

Max jumped to his feet, more than willing to be distracted from reminiscing about his past. "Lead the way."

A few yards from where they were camped, a net already setup. A few men he hadn't recognized were warming up on the opposite side of the net.

Drew and David carried over a few chairs and situated them by the other spectators. Jonah rushed over to his wife and helped her with her belongings.

Dream dragged a cooler behind her, brushing David off with a wave at his attempt to be chivalrous. Max couldn't help the grin as wide as the volleyball net, at her rejection.

Fifteen minutes in, sweat poured off them like a waterfall. During the break, Max rushed over to the cooler, where Dream had been using it as a makeshift ottoman as she slept.

He lifted her feet and nearly laughed aloud at the sight of her feet. Perfectly polished nails did little to mask two of the ugliest big toes he'd ever seen. They'd looked like malformed lightbulbs.

The movement woke her and she buried her feet in the sand as he lifted the lid and dug dig deep for the coldest bottle of water he could find. She eyed him suspiciously, as he gulped from the plastic bottle. Finishing it, he winked before rushing back to the court where the game resumed and they'd taken a beaten.

"I'm exhausted," Drew let out as he collapsed at Nicole's feet. She kissed the top of his head and kneaded his shoulders. "You played well."

He huffed and closed his eyes sinking into her treatment. "We just got murdered. I'll stick to basketball."

"It wasn't that bad," Tami chimed in. "So they spiked on Jonah, a lot."

"Babe," Jonah protested.

Tami continued her assessment of the game, turning a deaf ear to Jonah's gripe. "But you all did a good job, for never having played together. Especially a sport you hardly ever play. Job well done guys."

David looked around the group brow pinched, before Nicole answered the question he hadn't voiced. "She's a middle school teacher."

He nodded his understanding and relaxed beside Dream, resting his arms on his upturned knees. "What did you think?"

"I fell asleep. That's what I thought."

Nicole covered her mouth to hide her chuckle as Tami raised an eyebrow, sporting a crooked grin. "Sports isn't really Dream's thing."

Dream spoke up quickly. "That is not true. I like sports just fine, so long as I am watching real athletes."

The chorus of grunts and bellyaching from the men didn't seem to bother her. Max didn't complain, however. They'd gotten creamed out there and if she hadn't witnessed it, to God be the glory.

"I don't know about you all, but I'm ready for some dinner." Jonah began folding up his chair and stuffing into the travel case, as Tami followed suit and folded two towels, dropping them in her beach bag.

"Actually," Nicole interrupted, "I wanted to have a date night with Drew. Alone."

Her fiancée gave her a sidelong glance before clearing his throat and hesitantly agreeing.

"That sounds like fun. Jonah, let's have a date night too."

Halting his struggle with the portable chair, Jonah sent his wife a doubtful look. "You can't hold anything down. Don't you think we should get some take out, and eat it back at the house, in case you get sick?"

The perfectly sound plan had failed somewhere in its delivery. Watery eyes peered back at Jonah and before he could take a step forward. Crocodile sized tears ran the length of Tami's face. "I guess that makes sense. I understand." She swiped away the tears that wouldn't cease and got busy doing anything to take the attention away from her breakdown.

Jonah encapsulated her in his arms and apologized. "That was just one idea. The other is if you want to spend the night on the town, we could do that too."

She shook her head, a mix of snot and tears surely being absorbed into his brother-in-law's shirt. It was odd seeing his sister break down often and usually without good cause. Without warning, the memory of holding Ava the way Jonah held Tami now surfaced.

Had hormones been the reason for Ava's tears all those years ago? Guilt? He'd never know. He'd only seen Ava once since that day. Almost a year later he'd flown to LA to tie up some loose ends on his last photo assignment. Ava walked into the modeling agency with a man twice her age. Never acknowledging his presence, despite having brushed past him.

Being seen in public holding someone's hands had meant she finally, on some level, committed to someone. Funny enough, her moving onto someone else, hadn't hurt him. Unbeknownst to her, he wondered what they would say to one another had they ever run into each other, and now he knew. Nothing. It was as if God had orchestrated the closure he needed, all in one fell swoop. No muss. No fuss and for the best. Teetering between betrayal and peace of mind, he'd not known what he would have escaped once he began speaking.

"You know what? I'm going to just call this one." Jonah said still consoling his hormonal wife. "We need a date night. Soon we won't be able to go out whenever we want. This is a good opportunity to take advantage of it being just the two of us."

Tami's tears multiplied. "Well excuse us for being a burden!" She rubbed her belly. "If you didn't want to have a baby then-"

"Whoa there, honey," Jonah peeled her from his chest and looked into her eyes. "I love you and our baby. Just tell me the right words to say that will allow us to get something to eat and not put me in the doghouse. I'm striking out here."

Looking up into her husband's face, Tami smiled. "I'm a mess aren't I?"

David circled a finger near his temple and laughed as he mouthed Cuckoo, Cuckoo. Max fixed him a stern look in warning. David waved him off and approached Dream, whispering something in her ear that made her face light up like the sun. Grabbing her bag, she followed David out of sight. As much as something inside warned him to pull her back, something bigger urged him to let her go. He didn't know why, but it felt right, even if his flesh rebelled.

Chapter 16

It was pizza heaven or better known by locals as Piccini's. Dream sat at the square speckled table and opened the menu. Columns of pizza options made her want to cry. There had to be at least fifty options. She took in the site of the pizzeria and fell in love. Her favorite was the brick oven pizza facing you from the order counter.

David sat opposite her and perused his menu. When a waitress approached the table, he put in an order for drinks and an appetizer.

"What are you doing? We aren't staying. You said we'd get a few pies to take back with us."

"And we will. This place has been on the Food Network. I just wanted to get the full experience."

Dream raised an eyebrow. "I'm ordering a pizza to go. You can stay if you want to. And you are paying for my pizza."

David tossed up his hands in surrender. "Anything the lady wants."

"Don't call me that."

"So I can't call you *Mami* or Lady?"

"You can call me a cab so my pizza doesn't get cold by the time I make it back to the house."

David laughed aloud. "You never hold back do you?"

Dream exhaled an exasperated breath. Nothing she ever said turned this man off. The more she resisted, the more he insisted. Perhaps that was the problem. And just like that, an idea popped in her head sounding a bell.

Actually, the bell signified an order was up, but the timing was perfect, nevertheless. Dream applied some lip-gloss, and got ready to put on the show of a lifetime. Her high school performance as Belle wouldn't hold a candle to this depiction.

Two hours later, she'd walked up the front steps to the house, weary from her efforts. David had taken to the sweet version of Dream like a doughnut to milk, and if she didn't get a minute to break from character, she'd lose her mind.

"That wasn't so bad, was it?" David held two fresh hot boxes of pizza in both hands.

Bad, no. Excruciating was a more accurate description. She remembered she was aiming to be a better Dream and chose her words carefully. "The pizza was fantastic." By far, it was the only complete truth she could offer at the moment.

"Of all the choices on the menu, you still choose pepperoni. We'll have to come back again, so you can try something new."

The idea felt like a weight tied to her feet. "Sure will." *Without you.*

"How about when we get back I take you out on a proper date?"

"You know, I'm really exhausted. I should get to bed."

Dream turned the knob, anxious to get inside. "Wait." David set the pizzas down on a porch chair and stepped into her personal space. "I know what you're doing and it won't work."

"What is that exactly?"

"You're trying to be nice to me so that I will stop pursuing you."

Busted.

"You figured I'm only chasing because you are running and if you stop running, I'd lose interest."

"Drats!" Dream had no intention of denying it.

Rather than be upset, he laughed. "I admit that was the case at first, but now I really like you. I'd like a real chance."

Before she could tell him even one reason, she'd never give him a chance, he closed the distance between them and pressed his lips to hers holding her tight as she struggled in his grasp. At the sudden light that cascaded over them, David pulled away and cleared his throat.

"I'm sorry, I didn't mean to interrupt." Emily closed the door, the swift slap from Dream's hand to David's face sounding in accord. Entering before him, she hurried up the steps ignoring his call out to her.

After scrubbing off sunblock and ocean water from her skin, and rinsing away sand in crevices it had no business being gathered, Dream collapsed into bed, sleep taking her almost immediately. She'd slept for a few undisturbed hours before she awoke. The moon still hung high, its light mirrored on the dark waters.

She dressed and slipped downstairs to the darkened kitchen. The light above the stove illuminated a small area of the kitchen. Once her eyes adjusted, she was able to move around well enough without having to flip on any light switches. With any luck, she could see well enough, and wouldn't send any dishes crashing to the floor.

Minutes later, light spilled from the door adjacent to the kitchen as Emily trudged through, a mug in hand as she headed for the Keurig. She jumped back, her free hand flying to her chest, at the sight of Dream sitting on an island stool eating a slice of cold pizza.

"Goodness gracious. You scared the fatigue right out of me. I almost threw my mug at you."

Dream placed her slice on the plate and chewed, not bothering to respond despite being tickled by Emily's confession.

"Do you usually eat cold pizza at four in the morning?" Emily continued to the coffee maker waiting for it to refill the cup and presumably refuel the woman.

"Do you usually drink coffee at four in the morning?"

"When I have a deadline I do."

Her answer peaked an interest Dream wish it hadn't. Sitting up in her stool, she kept her anticipation below the surface. "New novel?"

Emily looked taken aback. "Yeah. It's the first in a new series."

It took all she had to keep the excitement from bubbling over. She was still waiting for the last book in Emily's series. Masking her elation, she nodded nonchalantly not daring enough to ask for specifics.

"Dream?"

"Yeah?" She stuffed the last of the crust into her mouth, hoping she didn't seem too eager to hear whatever Emily was ready to divulge, her expression severe.

"About earlier. It's none of my business, but Max is my best friend and I will always do what is best for him. Including not staying quiet."

While that could have been interpreted as a threat, Dream didn't see it that way. It was no less than she would have done for her friends. "I understand, and while I don't need to explain myself, I will because I respect you for being a good friend to Max. I didn't kiss David. He kissed me and then I slapped him."

"I know. I saw it all. I've been secretly studying him for a character I'm working on. I opened the door in hopes to get him to back off."

Dream bit the inside of her cheek, her lips twitching. "Thank you."

"I did it for Max."

"And why is that?"

"Max is in love with you, even if he won't admit it."

Dream laughed. It was the most preposterous thing she'd ever heard at four in the morning, and she'd seen some awfully preposterous infomercials at that hour, promising the world for only nineteen-ninety-nine, plus shipping and handling.

"I think you don't know your best friend as well as you think you do."

She grabbed her mug from the coffee machine and stepped forward. "You can think that if you like, but trust me on this one."

"Why are you telling me this?" Rattled, Dream's voice cracked.

"Like I said. I will always do what is best for him, including not staying quiet."

Emily disappeared into the office, effectively ending their conversation with the click of a closed door.

The early morning sun rising was a welcomed companion. With only a few other sun-rising enthusiasts, the beach was blissfully vacant.

Finding a spot closer to the dunes, Dream unfolded her towel and sat facing the horizon. The waves of the ocean crashing against the shore weren't competing with the noise, pollution beachgoers packed along with their coolers and umbrellas.

Wrapping her arms around her knees, she rested her chin there. A sudden burst of pink filled the sky behind the clouds, running across the expanse of the horizon. The color, so unexpected, filled Dream with awe. No sooner had she marveled over the magnificence of it, did a surge of fiery orange blend so perfectly with the pink, she couldn't take her eyes away. When the bright light of the actual sun had finally broken the horizon and risen above it, it was hard to grasp that this miraculous phenomenon occurred daily.

Never before had she felt so close to God. Seeing His creation so vividly, in all its splendor, resurrected a love for Him she hadn't realized had gone stale. Rather than pray quickly, just to be able to scratch it off her Christian duty's daily checklist, she opened up her heart to God, allowing it all to burst forth as the sun just had.

She laid down the confusion of losing her job, the jealousy toward a woman who had never been anything but kind, the lust for Max that wasn't her husband, the resentment to her Gramps for removing her from ministry, and the undeserved anger toward God for allowing the torrent of catastrophes that knocked her down over, and over again.

And because it was such fresh confusion, she told God about the bomb Emily dropped on her lap.

"God. What if Emily is wrong? Or worse. What if he does love me, but we just don't work as a couple?"

Only silence answered her questions.

"God, I know you can hear me. Tell me what to do."

Gulls soared above, their cries her only reply. Long ago, she'd thought God told her that Max was the one, now she wasn't so sure. Had she wasted so many years for nothing? God's silence frightened her. Surely, He wouldn't abandon her.

Dream shook away the fear. Her thoughts were running away from her again. They pushed and pulled like waves on the shore. Love wasn't supposed to be this hard. Neither God's, nor Max's. What was she fighting for? What was she waiting for?

Max? He was as confused as she was. He'd asked her not to let go, and in that moment alone in the ocean with him, she dared hoped it meant more. How long was she to hold on? Until she was old and gray, like Sarah. That was a tall order to ask of her and one she wasn't sure she wanted to fulfill.

It seemed as if she wasn't waiting on Max, she was waiting on God. Never in all her years, had she ever experienced such turmoil. Was God's answer a test? In retrospect, she'd never really needed to show her faith in action. She was born and raised in the church, and somehow that had qualified her as a Christian.

She finally understood why people could doubt there was a God, or at least one that cared. She felt so tiny in such a big universe. Although she'd believe what her Bible study classes had told her about God loving her and never leaving her, she had a hard time accepting that as absolute truth in the midst of her current circumstances.

These thoughts were lies. Hadn't God just shown Himself to her in the sunrise? Guilt finally grabbed ahold of her. God's love for her had to be true. He would never leave her.

Even if He chose to be silent from this moment forth, she needed to trust in the God that didn't change even when her circumstances had. With crystal-clear clarity, she finally understood firsthand the importance of faith.

Refusing to brush away the tears she finally set free, she laid back allowing the ocean breeze to dry them, as if God Himself were wiping them from her face, as the crashing waves lulled her into a peaceful slumber.

Either she was on fire or she had died and gone to hell. The heat on her back caused the scrapes on her shoulder to ache fiercely. Her skin felt stretched tight, reminding her of the rotisserie chicken, its skin golden and crispy. Voices whispering near her confused her even more. Was hell a community you shared with equal offenders? If only she'd not blamed God for all of her maladies, perhaps she'd be walking on a golden road rather than burning up. Images of Dorothy and a yellow brick road swam in her imagination.

Shaking her head free of the nonsensical images that plagued her, she fought against the invisible chains that bound her. Was there a way to free one's self from eternal damnation? She had to try. Sitting up she opened her eyes, immediately shielding them from the sun that now sat higher in the sky than it had a few minutes ago.

The heat was bouncing off the sand like a sizzling hot plate. Wincing, she felt the pain on her back, recognizing the effects of sunburn. How long had she been asleep? Turning to sit on her bottom, she canvased the beach now blanketed with bright umbrellas and a myriad of swimsuit-clad folk, frolicking in the ocean just as they had the day prior.

Teasing her, the sun blinded her from straight above. Good grief, it had to be near noon. No wonder her back felt as if it had been set under a broiler. She been out in the sun all morning with no sunblock or umbrella. A quick peek at her shoulders and she grimaced at her red shoulders. Of all the days to wear the open back top, she chose this one.

Gathering her towel, she draped it over her shoulders to ward off the sun until she could get indoors. She looked utterly ridiculous.

Lifting the gate latch, Dream stepped off the Boardwalk and into the backyard of the rental. Climbing the steps onto the back porch, she yearned to get indoors and out of the blazing heat. The patio door opened, the air-conditioned air blasting her briefly. It felt fantastic.

As tempted as she was to head up the nearby stairwell, her parched mouth protested. Once in the kitchen, her stomach felt queasy. A voice carried from the office as she checked the cabinets for some pain medication. A headache had begun by her temples and had moved toward the middle of her forehead.

Finding the bottle in the back of the cabinet, she reached on tiptoes and winced when she stretched to reach it. A burst of pain radiated throughout her burned skin.

Not wanting to risk feeling that pain again, she slid a kitchen chair across the floor to the cabinet and climbed upon it. Shoving the pill bottle in her bra, she used both hands to steady herself as reached for the unseen floor, careful not to contort lest she feel the discomfort on her burned skin.

"No pockets in SuperGirl's costume?"

The chair below her wobbled at her startled jump, sending it crashing to the floor, and her, into Max's arms. Fire shot up her exposed skin as he held her tight. "Let go," she pleaded.

Red faced, he released her and moved a safe distance away. "I wasn't..." Scratching his stubble he stopped then started again. "You were falling and I reacted. I wasn't trying anything."

She could clear up the misunderstanding, but that would mean spending more time in the kitchen, when her back craved cool water. "Sorry. I didn't mean to be rude." Leaving the chair where it collided with the hardwood floor, she grabbed the bottled waters and eased around the island.

"Why are you wearing a beach towel like a cape?"

Not bothering to reply or slow down, she reached the bottom of the stairs only to be stopped short of climbing the first step, when her towel caught behind her, pulling her back.

"Are you just coming back from the beach?" There was an accusation somewhere in between the lines. Max held the towel.

"Could you please let go of the towel?" Lifting a flip-flopped foot, she tried forging ahead, only to be pulled back once again. "Yes. I was at the beach. Now I am here, and I just want to go and take a shower."

Ignoring her plea, he held tight to the towel. "You don't look so good."

"I assure you I feel worse." Dream reached up and untied the towel from around her neck to keep from choking, setting herself free, as trudged up the stairs.

Opening the door to her bedroom, she could hear the shower calling. Footing the door closed, she waited for the slam that never came.

"That's a nasty sunburn."

She didn't address him, but instead uncapped the pain pills, popped a few into her palm, then gulped them down with a swig of water. If she ignored him, maybe he'd go away.

Shuffling through the bureau, she searched Nicole's drawers for a loose fitting tee, knowing she'd only packed tanks and summer dresses. Finding one, she opened it up, and then stuffed back into the drawer. What was loose fitting on Nicole was sure to be form fitting on her more curvaceous build.

"I have a t-shirt you can borrow, if you want."

Anything to get into the shower faster, worked for her. "That would be great. Thanks."

Peeling himself from the doorjamb, he was gone but a minute before returning with options.

Grabbing the folded tee on the top of the pile, she thanked him and asked him to close the door after him. No sense in beating around the bush.

She was still plenty upset with him, even if she choose to be civil about it. Yet, there he was still standing there, her request falling on deaf ears. "Is there anything else?"

Shaking his head, he placed the other tees on the bed before vacating the room. Finally.

After her shower, she tried as best as she could to apply lotion on her burns before slipping on the loose fitting tee. She'd need to get burn ointment after resting for a bit.

She lay on her tummy allowing her back the cool air. The scent of Max's tee drove her to distraction. Not even the lotion could mask his smell. More than once she found her nose buried in the tee inhaling deeply as if her brain had gone haywire, forgetting that all the parts of her body, cohesively, were supposed to temporarily dislike him. Before she knew it, she was dozing off again, the scent of Max drifting her off to sleep.

Chapter 17

Traffic hadn't delayed them too much on the way back home. Granted a conscious person would have made a better travel companion, but at least he'd gotten the chance to drive Dream's SUV. Since this afternoon, she'd been dead to the world, only her snores proof she was still alive. That's what a few nighttime pain meds did when you took them in the middle of the day. He'd bet anything she didn't bother reading the label to the pill bottle.

Even with Drew's help, getting her to the car had been a chore, but they'd managed the feat. At least she had been asleep when she slipped from their grasp and landed on the floor. With any luck, the pain meds were still busy at work, and she wouldn't feel a thing when, she finally awoke.

Max parked the car in an open spot closest to her condo, and grabbed her bag, tossing it over his shoulder. After trying several keys, he finally found the one that opened her front door, it sticking a little in the corner. He left her bag by the door and flicked the switch that illuminated the staircase. Nicole and Drew should be arriving shortly, and he'd leave Nicole to situate Dream in her bedroom.

Returning to the car, he opened the back door and chuckled. Only the seatbelt kept Dream from falling forward, as her head wobbled from side to side. Had he known better he would have guessed she had had a few drinks too many.

"Dream." Max nudged her shoulder. "Dream." Her head plopped back, her face now visible. His attempts at waking her elicited no reaction.

He pushed aside the hair from her face and studied her. Never had such a rare moment presented itself. The opportunity to admire her openly. Not even was she aware to his painstaking appraisal of her. His heart hitched watching her sleep. He'd promised himself he'd move on from her, although the reasons he'd told himself no longer seemed to hold water. Probably never had.

Dream sighed, bringing his attention to her lips, slightly parted, and tormenting him. When they weren't speaking nonsense, he had found a more useful occupation for them. That kiss still monopolized a significant amount of his daily thoughts. Snapping out of his daydreaming, Max tried waking her again.

Leaning in close to her ear, he whispered, "Dream. Wake up honey." He could feel the warmth of each exhale on his neck. "Wake up for me baby."

"Max," Dream finally said, her voice a fraction of its usually full quality. He backed away only to be pulled forward as her hands captured his face and pressed his lips to hers. Responding tenderly, he softened her rough kiss. It was all he remembered. He pulled away, lest he get too lost to get back.

Lifting his lids, he looked to her soft skin and pink tinged lips. The urge to caress her cheek trumped the desire to kiss her again, odd as it was. Pushing away from her, he brought his hand nearer, running the back of his hand down her cheek. It was softer than he anticipated.

Dream exhaled, a smile emerging, followed by a light snore. Max pulled his hand back slowly. Had she knowingly kissed him or had she been sleep kissing?

There was no doubt it was the latter. Did that mean she was dreaming of him?

He unstrapped her seatbelt and lifted her into his arms at the sight of Drew's truck pulling up beside hers, his car following suit. Drew waited for Nicole to exit Max's car before following Max into the condo.

Dream cuddled up to Max's chest, inhaling deeply. His heart began to pound with a love so strong, he'd nearly dropped her. Nicole followed him up the stairs, hot on his heels.

"The last door," She instructed from behind him.

Dream's bedroom was everything he expected it to be. Frilly and feminine. There was no way their bedroom together would be so girly. The thought smacked him upside the head, coupled with a punch to the gut.

With all the tenderness he could manage, he lowered Dream onto her bed and high tailed it out of her domain, snatching his keys from Nicole with all the calm he could muster. Making it home in short order, he refused to acknowledge the crazy ideas that had infiltrated his thinking.   Dream was a friend and nothing more. Yes, he responded to her beauty and couldn't deny the chemistry between them, but he'd already been down that road. Physical attraction may ignite a relationship but wasn't enough to sustain one and when it came down to it, they had been as opposite as up and down.

Then why did he feel an inexplicable love for her deep down in his core where long, glorious hair and perfectly pout lips didn't matter? It was the same question he'd asked himself since the summer before Dream left for college. Twelve years later, he still didn't have the answer.

It had been a few years since his last drink, but the urge to pour one surprised him. Never had he been more grateful for never keeping any in stock. It had never solved any of his problems before. Well not this particular problem anyway.

Like being saturated in skunk spray, his love for Dream was seeped from every pore and no matter how hard he tried, he couldn't rid himself of it. True, he'd succeeded in evading it for a while, but like a bounty hunter, it had eventually caught up to him.

Crossing the dark eat-in kitchen into the living room, Max slammed into the side table, sending his Bible careening to the floor. Flicking on the lamp, he looked down upon his Bible lying open on the floor almost purposefully, as if someone had been sitting there reading it.

He crouched to gather it and didn't have to read the pages to know what scripture was found on the page in the book of Jeremiah.

I know the plans I have for you.

Max sat on the couch, bringing the Bible to his lap, leaving it open. "What plans are those God? I gotta say it feels like you left me out of the loop."

My ways are higher than your ways.

Silence followed as it usually had when it came to praying about Dream. One would think that after twelve years, he'd get a clue. Max reached for his iPad and fired up his email. Photography had always occupied his mind and now helping others had filled that gap.

He'd received two more inquiries from the local Pastors apprising him of possible worthy causes to donate to. The only thing in his life he felt he had a firm grasp on. Giving his money away.

Opening his growing list of potential benefactors, he added covering the medical bills of a family at the church on the other side of town. It was bad enough they'd lost the patriarch of the family. They shouldn't have to suffer further by going into debt for trying to bring him healing. Max added a side note to add some extra funds for other bills and a mortgage payment or two, if he found their claim legitimate.

Before he forgot, he included new gear for the Summer Basketball League Drew headed up. He'd secretly donated what was needed to fund the Championship Tournament. Now that it was under way, he couldn't have the home team playing in rags and shoddy equipment. Lastly, he highlighted Dream's name. A request from Pastor Collins with only her name as the recipient in need and a request to chat about it.

Max's love life was a complete disaster but his secret ministry had an anointing that could only come from God. If there was one thing he was confident about, this was it. Helping those in need and the discernment to choose who received the blessings. Studying her name, he'd huffed. "Ok God. Someone needs your help. Tell me what to do." This time, he knew God would not be silent at this request.

Chapter 18

A full week of hydrating inside and out, then peeling like a slimy snake, and she'd had just about enough of sunburn running her life. She had things she needed to do to get her life back on track and they weren't going to happen while she peeled her skin as if it were dried glue. It was repulsive but she couldn't help herself.

Tucking a check into her back pocket, Dream slipped on her sandals and tied up her hair. Grabbing her purse and keys, she peeked at the mirror hung by the front door, checking for any lumps and seeing none. Satisfied she looked presentable, she opened her door ready to ride the train to the next stage of life where she had decided it was time to let go and move on.

Before she could step foot onto the platform, her train derailed. Max Davidson standing at her door was bound to make that happen.

"Hey. What are you doing here?"

Max stepped back from the door. "Are you on your way out?"

"Actually I was, but I have a few minutes, I guess."

"I was on my way to your church, but wanted to stop by and give you some news. It can wait if you're in a rush."

Dream struggled with how to respond. "I'm on my way to church too."

Max perked up. "Have you been reinstated?"

Ouch. "No. I just needed to drop something off to my Gramps."

"I can save you the trip if you want."

As tempting as the offer was, she missed the church and wanted to be there for a few minutes, despite the reason for her visit. Besides, it was still her home church. Nothing would change that.

"I wanted to see Gramps while I was there, but thanks. Were you going to speak with Gramps too?" Dream closed her front door then locked it.

"Yes, but I needed to drop off a donation for a colleague. Some new equipment for the Summer Basketball League."

"That was really nice. Anyone I know?" The short trek to her car came to a swift end. She unlocked her door, and waited for Max to find his tongue.

"Probably not."

"What's his name?"

"I promised I wouldn't tell."

"Well why not?" His dodgy answers only heightened her curiosity.

"Can't a person get some privacy when requested?"

"Of course he can, but he should know that a gesture like that is going to make others curious. Naturally, people will want to know who cared enough to give so much. Perhaps the boys will want to write thank you notes or something."

"Thank you notes?"

"Yep. Now who was it?"

"Can we move on from this conversation please?" Max crossed his toned arms across his chest. Dream looked everywhere but where his muscles bulged. She's already had plenty of breakfast and didn't need to feast on anything else, even if only with her eyes. Besides, she decided again to move on. At least until lunch when she'd probably change it back.

"Fine. I take it you didn't come over here to discuss an enigmatic philanthropist."

"As a matter of fact, I did."

Intrigued, Dream leaned against her hot car before pulling away quickly.

Max took a step forward. "Are you alright?"

What was with her and the sun? One morning, she basked in its glory, and now it seemed intent on making her miserable at every turn.

"Yeah, I'm fine."

Scrutinizing her, he waited until she insisted, before he backed away. "How's your sunburn?"

"It's better. Thanks for that. Tami told me what happened. I guess I didn't pay much attention to the label."

Max coughed into his closed fist hiding a smirk. She ignored whatever that was and wondered if he could fill in the blanks.

She'd awoken in her bedroom unsure how she'd gotten there, only bits and pieces floating in her memory, none of which made any sense. She must have been dreaming about Max because somewhere in her consciousness she felt wrapped in his scent and felt his warm lips on hers. Dream cleared her throat as it would clear away the blurry visions. The tee she borrowed from him had surely done a number on her.

Which reminded her. "I have your t-shirt upstairs. I just have to wash it and then I'll return it to you."

"No worries. I have plenty."

Good. She wasn't in a rush to make good on that promise. "So what did you come over for again?"

"An opportunity. Enigmatic Philanthropist is in search of someone to help keep their spending accounts in order. A large amount of money has been set aside to donate to worthy causes and the finances have gotten a little messy."

A job literally landing on her doorstep. That was unexpected and most likely too good to be true. Borderline sinister even. "How did you say you know this man?"

"I didn't, and I never said it was a man."

"Oh, it's a man alright. Thanks, but he sounds pretty creepy, and the last thing I need is to be kidnapped on top of everything else."

Dream opened her car door and turned to get in. The check in her pocket burned into her soul every minute she had it in her possession. The only remedy was donating it as soon as she could.

"Actually, you'd be working with me." Max faced the ground and cleared his throat. "In an office, I mean. I'd be your supervisor."

Dream turned slowly. "Come again?"

"I am overseeing the project. You'd report to me, so no need to worry about stealing you away."

Only my heart and sanity.

"I'll give you some time to think about it. If you have any questions, just reach out. The salary is competitive."

The perks weren't so bad either. She surveyed his build as he headed back to his car then stopped and faced her. Snapping her attention back north, she straightened.

"This is a great opportunity Dream. I hope you consider it."

Dream watched his car until it disappeared down the road then pinched herself. "Ouch." Yep she was awake. Her cell phone vibrated in her purse confirming so. She jumped in and checked the screen before sliding a finger across the screen to answer. "Hey, Gramps."

"It's your mother."

"Hey Mom." Trouble was on the horizon, mostly because she'd ignored the last three calls from her overbearing mother.

"Is Gramps ok?"

"He's fine, but I've just about lost my mind."

Yep, trouble. "Because?" Dream asked though not really interested.

"Well, daring daughter, my only child."

So *she* was in trouble. Just great.

Suzi continued. "I've called you three times in the past two days with no answer, and you answer after just two rings when Gramps calls." She tsked.

Oh that.

"Anyway," she continued. "I have some fantastic news."

She was in double trouble.

"Are you home? I'll stop by."

"No! I mean no." Dream soothed away the panic rising up. "I'm on my way to the church." Dream slid her key into the ignition and turned it.

"Wonderful. I'm already here. I'll wait for you."

Dream palm slapped her forehead. "Okie dokie. See you in a bit."

Ten minutes later, she drove into the church parking lot relieved Max's car was absent. Her mother's, on the other hand, shone in the bright sunlight. She'd never seen anything more ridiculous. Her mother needed a sports car as much as she needed a rash.

As usual, the quietude of the church during the week reached out and pulled her to the sanctuary. Gramps and Mom could wait a few minutes while she took advantage of being able to pray at the altar alone. Her feet rushed to where she planned to quietly remind God of all her troubles and plead for his intervention. When she knelt and closed her eyes, she couldn't bring herself to go there again. Every week she begged God, and every week a new calamity came upon her. She was done begging.

"I'm done God. I'm just going to thank you for what I have. An overbearing mother that loves me more than I can imagine. A grandfather who didn't have to take on the role but did so lovingly. He is a wonderful Pastor. Fair to a fault. For my odd assortment of friends. They are a family to a woman with little family. Thank you for placing them in my life even though they all think I'm the insane one. For a safe place to worship you. No church is perfect and good luck finding one without a gossip or two, but this one is perfect for me because I find you here."

That felt good and freeing. A good old honest prayer. On the surface, it may have appeared as if she were complaining, but God knew her heart. Everything she loved and was thankful for was flawed. Always would be. That was life wasn't it? A bunch of flawed people living flawed lives in need of a flawless Savior. All the time she'd spent waiting for God to just magically fix things. Then doubting Him when she didn't think he would.

How ridiculous for her flawed thinking to dictate His perfect purpose. Somewhere along the line, she'd learn the purpose of all she had been enduring lately. Until then, there was no use fretting over it. God would work it out. She just needed to put her best foot forward even when life seemed to be pushing against her with all its might.

Dream huffed and sat back on her haunches. "I do need to ask you for one thing. Mom is waiting for me. Help me. Please." She marched over to Gramps office and dove right into the barracuda infested waters.

"Good morning." Entering the opened door, she interrupted the discussion of a women's luncheon her mom was helping organize.

"Twinkle! What brings you by?" He rose and returned the kiss she offered.

"I would have thought mom told you I was coming." Dream offered her mother the same greeting before sitting beside her.

"No. She didn't." He sat and checked his cell phone when a buzz alerted him of a text, his mouth upturned at the corner after quickly reading it. He reverted his attention back to them quickly.

"Funny, since she called me from your phone." Dream eyed her mother, her accusation unmistakable.

Gramps shook his head. "Two peas in a pod, I tell you."

"We are nothing alike," Suzi, laughed. She adjusted her position in the seat, tucking one foot behind the other as she smoothed her skirt.

"Nothing." Dream agreed.

Gramps looked between the two and laughed. "You could be twins for crying out loud. Both quick to offer an opinion whether anyone's asked for it or not. Act first, think later. Wouldn't recognize a boundary if it jumped up and bit you. And for some unknown reason, both drive a car neither have any business driving. Now if both of you stubborn, no nonsense women, would all enlighten me as to why you are really here, perhaps I could get back to writing my sermon."

Mouths gaped open they stared at Gramps. Suzi spoke first. "I needed to get in touch with Dream. I'm sorry I borrowed your phone without your permission."

He nodded. "You are forgiven. Twinkle?"

She reached into her back pocket and placed the check on his desk. "I came to make up for my error."

He unfolded the check, looked it over, then peered at her stunned. "You sure?"

"More than anything."

He nodded and offered her a sad smile. "Ok you two. Scat. I got work to do. And if a young man comes in, please send him in. He's my next appointment."

Dream kissed her Gramps goodbye and walked alongside her mother, they popped in to say hello to Rosita before making it into the foyer.

"Come on. Spit it out. I know you are just chomping at the bit to give me your news."

Suzi schooled her features. "I am not."

"Yeah you are. Go on," Dream insisted.

Suzi smiled wide. "I found you a job."

Dream could feel her heart free falling, landing somewhere on the floor between her feet. "Umm...what?"

"Mrs. Sanderson needs a cashier at the store, and I told her that you would be interested."

"And why would you do that? Mom, Mrs. Sanderson, and I use that term loosely, is two years younger than I am and sells selfie sticks at the mall."

"Are you implying that you are too good for an honest living?"

"Of course not." Dream had to stop and think before speaking. A foreign concept she'd need to navigate carefully. She was coming up blank. The urge to tell her mother she was a college graduate who could probably find a job not meant for a teenage girl, clobbered her upside the head.

Before she could say what she couldn't hold back a second longer, footsteps reigned in her tongue. "Good morning ladies." Max walked in looking more handsome than he had half hour .ago. Perhaps it was he smile fixed on his face. "Mrs. Collins, how are you? You look lovely."

Max fell into her embrace as she offered her gratitude. "Max, darling. How are you? How's your mom?"

"We're both well. Thanks."

"Splendid. I must say that you get more handsome every time I see you."

He beamed that smile again and Dream could just about vomit. Where was this charmer when they were alone? The phoniness was truly sickening. This was what morning sickness must feel like. She made a mental note to never tease Tami again. Not even in her own head.

"Thank you Mrs. Collins."

"When are you settling down? Hasn't a woman caught your eye yet? I'm sure your mom is dying for a grandbaby. You aren't getting any younger." Suzi pressed.

The comment seemed to dull the light in his eyes. "Well Tami is expecting. I think my mom has already gone bankrupt." He put on an even phonier smile than before. One that betrayed him for it hadn't been nearly as bright.

"Yes, but a child needs a cousin to play with. Cousins are a child's first best friend."

"I suppose you're right." Max listened as Suzi went on about a friend's daughter carrying twins or some such business.

"Mom, can we please get back to me and my problems."

Max widened his eyes a fraction.

"Honestly, Dream. Must you be so rude? I'm sorry Max. But then again, you know how she can be."

He nodded and let out a small chuckle. Dream winked and continued with her tantrum.

"Mother, we need to finish discussing this dilemma you have dragged me into."

"I better get going. Pastor Collins is expecting me."

"Yes, go on ahead," Suzi, answered grimacing at her only offspring.

"Thanks." A few steps away and he turned to Dream, a smug smile situated on his handsome face. "Oh and Dream. Don't be late for work Monday morning. Mr. E.P. is anxious to have you on the team." He winked and disappeared down the hall.

She smiled at the reference. Mr. E.P. was her Godsend? Dream shook her head. Why God chose to send her help via the top of the crazy pile, she'd never know, but she supposed beggars couldn't be choosers.

Chapter 19

Dream entered the small office space, observing the space as she spun in a complete circle. Max sat at his desk pretending he hadn't noticed her, despite electricity shooting through him, jolting his heart. A nuisance he'd be working hard to get under control.

So long as they'd be working together, there would be no room for anything other than a business relationship in and out of the office. Ignoring his flesh, Max wondered what she thought of their new office space.

It had taken him a few days to secure the perfect location, but once he set his eyes on the small one room office that would fit two desks, a few chairs for clients, and a filing cabinet, he knew it would be enough to get them started.

Eventually, the space would transition into her office and he'd move on to his next project. He'd failed to mention that the position he offered was a temporary one, but he'd cross that bridge when he got to it. In the meantime, he had a very real account that was in some serious need of organizing before he could approach her about starting her own business.

As crazy as the idea seemed, he couldn't help feel that the arrangement would somehow work. After all, it was God's plan, not his. There was no way he could ever think up something so out of his line of thinking. In exchange for helping properly maintain financial records of his charitable endeavors, Dream would receive a paycheck, and he'd have the opportunity to sow into her future.

Max sat back in his chair pondering again why Dream had written a check for over eight thousand dollars to her home church, not that it was any of his concern. After seeing the check billow to the floor from the edge of Pastor Collins's desk to his feet, his eyes traveled across its front, Dream's name, and the check amount scorching his vision. If she could afford to donate such a lofty amount, why was he here, going through such extremes? He didn't know the answer to that, but the Holy Spirit had spoken to his heart and he'd have to trust that if not her.

"So this is it?" Dream turned to him, her purse and laptop bag by her side.

"I know it's not much, but Mr. E.P. prefers putting the money into those who truly need it, rather than operating expenses. If it proves to be more affordable and a sound investment, he is going to purchase this building. We'd keep this office and he'd lease the others."

"You won't hear a complaint from me. Even if we could use some fresh flowers or some art on the walls."

He figured she'd say as much. If he decided to buy the building, she could decorate however, she saw fit. He'd probably regret that idea, having seen her dainty bedroom. Heat crawled up his neck. He meant her dainty living room. He had no business recalling anything about her bedroom. Standing to his feet, he moved toward the desk parallel to his own.

"This is your desk. You don't need to bring your own laptop. One is provided for you. Some accounting software is already uploaded, along with the bookkeeping software Mr. E.P. prefers. You'll find office supplies in your desk and at the bottom of the filing cabinet, but if anything is missing, make out a list, and once I approve it, you can order it."

Dream moved to the other side of the desk and sat.

"The bathroom is down the hall. We share it with the other two offices on this floor."

She winced then put on a polite smile as she listened intently. Recognition set in. So much for finding the perfect office. Then again, her dislike of public bathrooms would have made the search for suitable office space with a private restroom that much harder and most definitely out of the price range he'd planned for this endeavor. It was already to be his costliest thus far.

He could imagine she'd be going home for lunch breaks for the unforeseeable future. It was probably for the best. Having lunch together would only further blur the lines between them, he'd need to bring back into focus.

"I'd love to know how a photographer, slash, graphic artist, landed this job." She sat forward, hands intertwined as her arms lay out in front of her.

He'd known she'd have questions. Probably lots of them, but he would rather evade them, than create a string of lies that could circle the earth.

"I'd love to know that I can trust you to get started."

Max removed a manila folder from his desk, and walked it over to her nearly empty desk.

"These are some of the charities and people, Mr. E.P. has blessed in the past several months and receipts for what he has purchased or donated. Use your expertise to organize them as best as you can. I'd like to see what has been spent monthly and on average, per charity and individual. From there, we can create a budget and streamline the spending. Mr. E.P. wants to help as much as he can, but we need to have proper record keeping for taxes."

Dream nodded and reached for the folder. He pulled it back before she could grasp it. "Dream, a large part of this job is discretion. The names and charities you see in this folder aren't to be discussed outside of these four walls."

"Yes, Mr. Davidson."

He waited for a teasing smile or a twinkle in her eye but found none. Was she baiting him? He continued, pretending her address hadn't caught him off guard. If he didn't pay it any mind, she'd lose interest in her taunting. At least that was the advice his mother game him when a sixth grade bully tormented his life in a new school.

Come to think of it, Dream returning the boy's teasing tenfold, had been what saved him from a miserable year. Nevertheless, nothing in life was free and he supposed he was now paying the piper.

"FYI, you may find some individuals are labeled using a code word. Only Mr. E.P. knows their true identity, so you will have to file it using the code word."

She took the file from him and nodded. "Who decides on the chosen charities or individuals? Is there a specific criteria? Can anyone suggest a cause, or person in need?"

Max swooped his dark gray dress jacket from the back of his chair and slipped his arms into the sleeves. "Mr. E.P. has a method he believes is reliable. If word got out that a wealthy man was giving away money, could you imagine the outpouring of people that would flood this office in search of handouts?"

"That would probably be a hot mess." Dream sat up immediately. "I meant it would probably result in chaos.

I'll get started right away." She fired up her laptop and opened the drawers taking stock of her supplies.

"One more thing. There will be some days that I will be out of the office for most of the day. I meet with the clients that reach out to Mr. E.P. and-"

Interrupting him, she waved a hand. "Are we going to keep referring to him as Mr. E.P.? It seems foolish when we both know it isn't his real name, yet continue to call him so."

"Do you have a different name you prefer?" Max walked over to his desk to check his agenda book before sliding open a top drawer and removing a set of keys.

"Yeah. How about his real one?"

"I already told you that he wants to remain anonymous. And what does it matter so long as you are getting paid?"

"Speaking of which, will this anonymous employer of mine be signing my checks weekly or biweekly?"

"Twice a month, *I* will be signing a check. Which reminds me. You will be paid as a freelancer, which means you are responsible for reporting your own income." Dream raised an eyebrow, a smirk on her face. "I guess you already know that." He pointed to the computer. "Be sure to add yourself as a business expense."

"Will do," she said politely, her smile warming the room.

Max walked out of the office and breathed a sigh of relief. The air conditioner had done little to cool him down when she smiled at him like that. Perhaps, this wasn't God's doing at all. Working with a woman he was attracted to had only led him into trouble. How could he have forgotten that?

Vowing right then and there, no matter what, this time would be different. He had already learned his lesson. True, his feelings for Dream ran deeper than attraction, but that was all the more reason to keep his distance. He had no plans on marrying her, and therefore nothing else could come from their relationship other than friendship and now business.

Max buttoned his jacket at the waist, tucked his hands in the pockets of his modern suit pants, and walked down two blocks to the diner. Sitting at a back table, Emily sat sipping coffee and looking over a laminated menu.

"I see my party." Max pointed to Emily when the hostess approached with a greeting and a menu. She nodded and went back to her station behind a counter, sorting through receipts.

"You're late Slink." Her gaze never leaving the menu, she took another sip of coffee.

Unbuttoning his jacket, he removed it and hung on the coat rack nearby before sitting across from Emily. "I'm here now."

His favorite waitress in the whole wide world approached, a carafe in hand. "You're late. Coffee?"

"Yes, thank you." He unbuttoned his cuffs and rolled up his sleeves, as Marley flipped over the empty mug.

Emily finally placed the menu faced down. "Would you mind warming mine up a bit, Marley?" She slid her mug a little closer to the apron-clad server who only smiled as she poured the hot dark brew in one cup, then the other.

"Are you all ready to order?" Nodding, Emily rushed to finish her sip. Emily's usual fare of a grapefruit and oatmeal with raisins, paired with Max's request for an omelet with toast, rounded off their order. "I don't know why I even bother asking," Marley said, slipping the pencil in her apron pocket.

The fifty-something waitress was a safe distance away before Emily pounced. "What's with the suit?"

"I have a meeting right after." Attention focused on his task, Max poured a bit of sugar into his coffee and stirred. The well-worn spoon clicked against the rim of the mug before he set it on the saucer.

She nodded, tugging her lip and watching him quizzically. "A meeting with who? You don't work."

He grinned before sipping his coffee. Returning it to the table, he added a dab more of sugar. "You of all people should know that just because you don't have an employer doesn't mean you don't work. Coffee is stronger than it usually is, but pretty good."

She jolted forward. "You're giddy. You're never giddy. The coffee here is never good. What gives?"

Was he giddy? He hadn't noticed. A normal Monday from what he could tell. Other than the woman, he'd crushed on for as long as he could remember sat in an office secretly helping him with a ministry that had materialized from seemingly nowhere. Nope. No reason to be giddy at all.

"Your eyes are twinkling," Emily, teased.

Only one other person had accused his eyes of twinkling. Max schooled his features and peered out the window, elbows propped on the table as he clasped his hands.

The main street, only a few blocks from his apartment, was a ghost town in comparison to LA, but he found better suited him. His life in LA had come about often lately. Was God in any of it?

"Anybody home?" Waving a hand in his face, Emily widened his eyes.

"Sorry. I was somewhere else?"

"I'd say. You went from giddy to frowning, like the face on one of those melted ice cream pops. You know. The character ones the ice cream trucks sell in the summer."

She hadn't been trying, but she'd lightened his mood. "Those were my dad's favorite," he laughed. "He'd always said that if the face was still smiling, that meant it was happy to be eaten. Whenever Tami's would melt to frowning, she'd feel guilty and stop eating it."

"And you?"

Raising a brow, he pinned her with a look. "Me? I'd hurry and eat mine, so hers wouldn't melt entirely before I could enjoy it."

"Why am I not surprised?" Emily sipped again. "Was today Dream's first day?"

Max choked in the hot brew that now burned his throat. "How did you know that?" He coughed as he spoke.

Pulling a few napkins from the dispenser, she set them on the coffee that splattered out of his cup and onto the wooden surface. "Tami called to invite me to Sunday dinner. It came up."

News traveled fast in these parts. "Yeah. She's organizing a few things with my bank accounts."

"I thought some philanthropist hired her-" She paused, not moving a muscle as her gaze traveled up from the coffee stained napkins to his eyes. "You're the philanthropist. Slink, what are you up to?" She stopped sopping up the coffee, shoulders slumped.

"I can't believe I just said that." He could palm slap his front. "Obviously, Emily, you can't tell anyone."

"Since you asked I won't, but do you really think she isn't going to figure this out sooner or later?"

"I know what I'm doing." Max sat back at the arrival of Marley with her large round tray carrying their breakfast. She placed each plate on the steadiest table in the diner, Max sending her off with a wink. "Em?" He picked up a fork, wiping it clean it with a napkin and began cutting into his omelet. "Since when do I need to ask you to keep things private and does that mean that every conversation we've ever had where I didn't ask, is now public knowledge?"

Emily dumped her raisins into her oatmeal, stirring them in. "Are you seriously asking me that?"

Closing his eyes, he let his head fall back in disbelief. Straightening, he raised a brow.

"What?" She asked taking in spoonful of oatmeal.

"Whenever you answer with a question you're either lying or hiding something. Which is it?"

A family, with two toddlers were seated beside them raising the noise level up in that part of the diner. He watched them settle in, the dad pressing a kiss to the toddler's forehead as he slid her in a child seat. The bouncy girl babbled what only her parents could understand. She reached the spoon and pretended to feed herself much to her parents delight. Yearning filled him.

"I may have told Dream that you were in love with her." Digging a spoon into the oatmeal once again, Emily stuffed her mouth.

Breaking away from the scene beside him, the desire for family free falling like a kite without wind, Max turned to Emily flabbergasted. "Have you lost your mind?"

Cheeks filled to the brim, she shook her head in response to his question.

"Then why else would you do that?"

She made no attempt to swallow her oatmeal. With her fingers, she pretended to widen her mouth into a grin and pointed to him."

"I've already told you that she can't make me happy."

Emily slammed her hand on the table, her brow creased deep. Hurrying to get all the oatmeal down, he waited to hear whatever had gotten her all fired up.

Appalled she gaped at him. "You are like a bi-polar Mr. Darcy." Shaking her head, she scowled. "With all of this, I love you, but I don't want to love you, nonsense."

"What?"

"Mr. Darcy," she said enunciating each symbol. "Pride and Prejudice? Jane Austen?"

Did she expect him to know what, on earth she was talking about? Shaking his head, he widened his eyes, not understanding a lick of what she was referring.

"Boy, did I dodge a bullet." Releasing an agitated breath, she dug into her oatmeal once more.

"And why's that?" Fully frustrated he wish she'd stop talking in riddles.

She didn't reply but continued eating as she glared at him.

"What do you want me to say Em? Am I attracted to her? Yes. Do I want to be in a relationship with her? No. I can't go down that road again."

Her silence prompted him to continue.

We're just too different. What happens once the fire dies down and we have nothing left in common? I'll tell you. Both of us trapped into a marriage neither of us wants. Secretly miserable. Why can't you see that?"

Emily pushed her empty bowl aside and brought her napkin to the corners of her mouth.

"Not every woman you are attracted to is Ava. Why do you continue to allow her to make the decisions in your life?"

Dream wasn't Ava? Was that where his trepidation stemmed from? It couldn't. He'd left Jersey to nurse a broken heart long before he'd met Ava.

"Dream molded my opinion of her long before I knew Ava."

"She was nineteen years old Max and getting ready to go off to college. She'd just broken up with her high school sweetheart. What did you expect her to do? Put her life on hold to date a guy she had no idea had an interest in her?"

Max swallowed. "Of course not, but I waited for her Em. She chose to stay in New York for another year to see what it had to offer. What I had to offer wasn't appealing enough. What was I supposed to do with that?"

Emily wrinkled her nose, a sympathetic expression. "I think she was scared Max. There was always something between you. Even while she was dating Ethan in high school. It would charge the air whenever you were together. To be away at school for a few years and come back to a relationship with you must have been overwhelming. It's not as if you are a go with the flow kind of guy. You have two speeds. Parked or full throttle."

Max pushed his omelet aside. "I do not."

"I'm just saying. You didn't even talk to her about her decision. You just up and left for California for two years. That's the full throttle I was referring to. "

Emily had a point there.

"What did she say when you told her I loved her?"

"Is that an admission?"

He fixed her with a glare.

"Fine. I'll let it go. She laughed at me," Emily admitted sheepishly. "Didn't believe a word."

Max didn't know what to make of that.

"But if it's any consolation, she looked like she desperately wanted to believe it."

Before he could think about it, the truth escaped his lips. "We kissed. At the beach house the night before you got there."

Emily's brows creased in a sympathetic expression. "Is that why you rushed me to come over?"

Max nodded.

"And then she heard you say all those things." Understanding dawned on her. "No wonder she was fuming." Emily huffed. "Well, I gotta go." She tossed a few dollars on the table. "Thanks for breakfast. Don't forget to tip Marley." Before he knew it and just like that, she was out the door leaving him to stew on the big fat slab of truth they'd birthed and set on the table.

A million thoughts surfaced yet none of them would bring him back to the peace he'd felt before having met with Emily. Women really were from Venus or some other place that wasn't Earth.

Chapter 20

Summer had given way to late fall and Dream had settled into a comfortable rhythm in the office over the last three months. A knock on the door pulled her attention from the laptop screen.

"Good morning Maria with an h." Dream sat back grinning. The easy rapport with the employees in the other two offices had kept her from going mad when Max would be gone for a day or two, out on the field, as they had come to refer to his meeting with charities and clients in need.

She had yet to be invited to any in-person meet and greets but with every record she created, she'd imagine the faces of those being blessed. It would be nice to see the joy on the faces in person, but alas, that wasn't her place. Bargain shopping for needs every now and then was the closest she'd come to being involved outside of overseeing the financials.

Mariah stepped in a little further. "I'm just paying you back the box of staples we borrowed. Our supplies finally came in."

"They go in the bottom drawer of the filing cabinet." Mariah moved to put them away. "It's most likely locked. You can just leave them on Mr. Davidson's desk, he'll put them away when he unlocks it."

"No need," Mariah called out. "It's open." She headed for the door. "Thanks again."

Caught between shock and hospitality, Dream unable to speak, simply waved. She stood for what reason she couldn't say.

Mariah doubled back. "I almost forgot to ask. Our part time accountant is going on maternity leave. Do you think you could take us on for a few months?"

Dream snapped her trap shut, getting her glands working again. "Sure," she finally said. She'd been meaning to talk to Max about cutting down her hours. She felt like a fraud earning a paycheck for sitting at a desk shopping online. For the most parts, all of the record keeping had been a well-oiled machine that didn't require her full time attention.

"I'll let Albert know. Thanks again," Mariah said as she exited.

Dream walked to the door and waited for Mariah to disappear before closing it, and turning the lock into place.

Running over to the filing cabinet, she searched the files in Max's top private drawer. Two file folders dangled in the otherwise empty drawer. Two secret files, she'd never had access to.

Whenever she needed to input any data into the code named files, Max would email her the spending totals, never giving her an actual receipt. Not even the description of what had been spent was revealed to her. For the most part, she cared not, but with Pandora's Box wide open, her curiosity peaked.

Pulling the thinner of the two files from the drawer, Dream quickly opened it. A copy of a cashier's check for two thousand dollars with all pertinent information blacked out with marker. Rats. Placing it back in the drawer, she opened the healthier file.

A mortgage payment, the receipts for office supplies, including her laptop, copies of her paychecks, and every receipt for running the office. What was so secretive about this file? She slammed it closed and returned it back to its fortified resting place. Making her way back to the door, she opened it to find Max, readying to turn the knob.

"Max," she jumped. "I mean, Mr. Davidson, you scared me halfway to death."

Not too concerned that her heart nearly stopped beating, he narrowed his eyes to slits. "Why is the door closed?"

Time had proven that she was not good at thinking on her feet. "I was fixing my bra," she shouted as if she were on a game show.

His face blanched. "It's probably best you do that in the women's bathroom next time. I could have walked in on you." His mouth tightened into a straight line.

"You are absolutely right." She moved behind her desk and sat.

"How was your day in the field?"

Max hung the suit bag he'd carried on a hook by the filing cabinet and logged into his laptop. "Productive."

His usual answer.

"Question. Was the payment to the South Jersey Hospice a recurring or one-time donation?"

"One-time. Did I forget to email you the details?"

Dream checked her email. "No information about South Jersey Hospice."

"I'm sorry. It was a spontaneous decision and I've been out trying to find a tux last minute. I'll forward you the information in a bit."

Whenever Max would divulge such intimate knowledge about Mr. E.P.'s benefactors, alarm bells sounded off. More times than she could count, she could swear that Max was the elusive Mr. E.P., except Max couldn't afford to bless so many in such giving ways. Once again, she tossed the thought from her head. "Tuxedo? Sounds important."

"It's for a benefit dinner tonight. I'll be attending in Mr. E.P.'s place."

"Good choice. I used to volunteer there a few years ago."

Ripping his gaze from his laptop, he gaped at her. "I didn't know that."

"That's because you were off in California being a big shot photographer."

He sat back in his desk chair. "Why'd you stop?"

"My favorite patient died. Mrs. Ida. She used to be a Can-Can girl. Don't tell anyone, but I used to take my make-up bag over and do up her face. She loved it." Dream swallowed the lump in her throat. She didn't want to talk about Ida anymore. "Is that your tux?" She pointed the suit bag.

He nodded and regarded her with a sad smile. "Dream, would you like to be my date tonight?"

The invitation caught her unawares. "Excuse me?"

He walked over to her desk and sat on the corner. "I think Mrs. Ida would be proud if you made up your face in her honor and ate a dinner worth well over a grand."

Dream held the tears in check. Why they threatened, she wasn't sure. A date with Max, finally? Honoring Ida? PMS? It didn't matter. "I'd be honored Mr. Davidson."

"Good. Take the rest of the day off since, technically, you'll be working tonight." Max removed himself from her desk and moseyed on back to his own.

"I beg your pardon." His suggestion seemed so vulgar and inappropriate.

"I don't expect you to work all day and then come back to work tonight too. Besides, we can't afford to pay you overtime."

Dream snapped her gaping mouth shut. Max Davidson was a clueless, brute that didn't deserve her admiration. She turned off her computer and pulled her purse from the desk drawer. "I'll see you tonight."

"Meet me at my place and we can ride together. No sense in tipping two valets." He kept his eyes on the screen, as he spoke to her.

He wasn't even going to pick her up? It wasn't a date. She got that loud and clear. "Why don't you just put it on a billboard?" Dream trudged out the door, ready to spit nails.

"Dream, wait!"

Her heart raced as she stopped mid-step. Had he come to his senses? She spun to face him. "Yes?"

"It's a formal event so don't forget you need a gown. See you tonight." Max strode back into the office and closed the door behind him.

Brain working overtime she wondered how she landed in this mess. A black tie affair with only a few hours to prepare. No time to shop. No money to shop even if she had time. She had a mind to show up in sweats and running sneakers. It would serve him right. Pulling her cell from her phone, she called her mom. "Hey Mom. Do you still have my prom dress from junior year?" It was a long shot, but desperate times called for desperate measures.

They were worse than her mother, and that was saying something. For almost two hours, her friends, pulled, yanked, brushed and dabbed at her.

Nicole spritzed Dream's finished make-up. Tami stepped back after adding the last hairpin in place after following the YouTube tutorial to the letter. Her fairy godmothers to boot.

Slipping on the red, strapless mermaid gown with sweetheart neckline, she couldn't believe it still fit. Well mostly, fit. A little more snug than she would have liked, and the corset helped, but she doubted she could eat a hundred dollar's worth of that thousand-dollar dinner. She pushed down her womanly assets that had also grown a little more since high school. Nicole helped her slip on the rhinestone strappy shoes, she worn for Tami's wedding.

Tami removed diamond studs from her purse and hurried over. "I brought these in case you didn't have anything."

The hopeful look in her best friend's eyes cut right through her. She had a few pieces she could have chosen from, but how could she break her friend's heart? "They're perfect." A sheen in Tami's confirmed she'd made the right decision.

"If you looked this stunning for your Junior Prom and Max didn't pledge his love for you forever, than he doesn't deserve you." Nicole hugged herself, romance twinkling in her eyes.

"In that case he absolutely deserves her," Tami gushed.

"What do you mean?" Snapping from her daydream, she turned to Nicole.

"The day after prom, Max confessed his crush. I could hardly believe it." Tami unplugged her hair irons and began tossing hair tools and accessories into a black bag with lots of compartments.

Facing her friend, Dream faltered. "He did what?"

Tami exhaled deeply then shrugged. "It was so long ago, so I guess it doesn't matter now. "

"It matters!" Dream and Nicole said in unison.

Eyes wide, Tami sat at the vanity table facing inquiring expressions. "Then perhaps I shouldn't say anything."

"Get talking Preggo." It escaped a little more menacing than she anticipated but Tami didn't feel threatened, if her grin were an indication.

"Alright," she said with a chuckle. "Max told me that he had a crush on you and was upset that you were dating Ethan. He thought Ethan was bad news. I really don't see how ten years later it matters."

Turning to Nicole whose brain cells hadn't been compromised due to an invasion of a body snatcher, she dared hoped. "Do you think he still does?"

Scratching her brow, Nicole's brow furrowed. "I wish I knew." She stepped a few paces away. "I have to confess something too. Back during the week we were preparing for Tami's wedding, I asked Max if he were in love with you."

Dream waited for her to finish. Nicole stood silent. "And?" She asked impatiently.

"He didn't admit it outright, but it seemed pretty obvious to me."

Dream slipped her lipstick, license, and car keys into her clutch. She didn't have the time nor the stomach for way-back-whens and seems-like. She headed for the door and stopped in her tracks. "Perfume. I forgot perfume."

Nicole and Tami glanced at each other horrified.

"What?"

"Tonight is a special night. Why not wear something different?"

"What? Why?" Dream brushed past them and picked up the expensive bottle. It was almost gone and she couldn't afford a new bottle. Maybe she could go with something different just for tonight. Max didn't deserve her best, she said looking at her reflection. It was hard lying to yourself when the image peering back at you look pretty darn close to best.

Irritation replaced heart-warming self-reflection. It was too late to change but even if only for her own self-respect, she'd not wear her favorite perfume for the coward. Picking up the bottle her mother had gifted her, she dabbed behind her ears and on her wrists and drove herself to Max's house ready for work.

Chapter 21

Checking his watch again, Max paced slowly by the door. Dream was late. If she didn't arrive in the next five minutes, he'd leave without her. Served him right for inviting her in the first place. He'd lost himself seeing the melancholy in her countenance as she spoke about Mrs. Ida if he had heard her correctly through her choked up confession. The minute it slipped past his lips, he set out to do damage control and clear up any misconceptions. This wasn't a date but business as usual.

His mom had understood when he'd explained the reason for reneging his invitation. In fact, she'd been more than understanding, she'd been downright enchanted. Ignoring the cheer in her voice, he promised to make it up to her soon.

Dream's five minutes were up. Grabbing his keys and invitation, he stepped out into the crisp fall air. Dream's SUV idled out front. Reigning in his ire, he knocked on her window. "You're late."

The window lowered slowly. "I've been waiting for ten minutes. Now are you going to stand there and whine or are you getting in?"

She wanted to drive? The first thought savored much like machismo. Men didn't have to always be in the driver's seat did they? Besides, this wasn't a date. If she wanted to drive, so be it. He opened the door behind her and jumped in.

"Oh, no he didn't." She ineffectively whispered to herself

Oh yes I did. She was peeved and he was gratified. She wanted to play chauffeur, so he'd take full advantage, and enjoy every minute of her displeasure. Keeping his mirth to a limit, he tapped on her headrest. "We better get going. We're already late. Do you know how to get there?"

Working at keeping her cool, she exhaled deeply. "Sure do Boss."

Boss? Yeah, she was fighting fury. Max grinned and when she peered at him via rearview mirror, he masked how much he reveled in her exasperation.

The music was loud. Really loud, and when she attempted to sing even louder than the radio, he'd thought his eardrums would burst. Waiting at a red light, Max watched in horror as the cars in the lane beside theirs watched Dream and laughed. She cared not one iota. At the following traffic light, a man at the bus station turned toward the noise, he found himself surrounded by.

Taken aback, the gentleman jumped up and rushed to the car. Every nerve was on alert and before Max could warn Dream to lock the doors, the young man knocked on the window. Dream turned toward the source of the knocking and lowered her window. The woman didn't have a lick of sense sometimes.

"Hey Dream! Where you headed? You look fancy." She thanked the youngster that had done what he had failed to. Offer her a compliment.

"Thanks Derrick. I'm on my way to a dinner to raise money for Hospice. Where ya headed? Can I give you a ride?"

Max nearly jumped from the backseat and gagged her. No doubt about it she was mad. He cleared his throat. "Dream?"

Derrick's face brightened. "If it's no trouble?"

"It's no trouble," she said.

Opening the door, he jumped in removing the worn backpack from his shoulder and placing it on his lap, a familiar smell he couldn't place, wafting into the cabin of the SUV that took Max back to his youth. "Thanks for this."

"No problem." She lowered the radio and inquired after his mother and grandmother. Derrick went into full detail about his grandmother's health and his mom working herself into oblivion.

"I'm sorry, I haven't been around lately. Has someone come to take Elsie shopping?"

He nodded, shame filling his face. "I'm sorry Dream. If I had the money I'd pay you back."

She looked between him and the road confused. "Sorry for what? You didn't do a thing wrong and you certainly don't owe me any money. Ya hear me?" He nodded unable to look her straight on. "I mean it Derrick," she pushed.

The smile that emerged on his youthful face, visibly relaxed her shoulders. After settling that, she must have remembered he had an audience. "How rude of me. Derrick, this is my boss Max Davidson." Dream hooked a thumb and aimed it over her shoulder.

Surprised, Derrick looked back. "I didn't even see you back there. My bad, bro. I'm Derrick." He stuck out a hand, grease trapped in his nails. The hands of a mechanic. Max remembered those days tinkering with cars, spending hours under its hood.

"Nice to meet you. Are you working on a restore?" Max shook his hand, finally recognizing the smell. The mix of engine oil and gasoline.

Brows pinched, Derrick shook his head. "No. I work at a shop not too far from here. I do the oil changes. Trying to save for a car so I can take my mom to work and Grandma to her doctor's appointments. Dream helps a lot by taking Grandma grocery shopping, but we don't want to bother anyone. She's kind of bossy so Grandma just prefers not to argue with her."

Cackling, Dream kept her eyes on the road. "Wait until I get my hands on that old woman. She's going to hear a mouthful from me."

Fear skittered across his smooth face. "Please don't. She'll thrash me."

Her laughter intensified. "Ok, I won't. Only because the woman is fully capable of going twelve rounds."

A hearty laugh escaped the young man. "You could too. That's why you get along so well."

"Is that what you call our constant bickering?"

His smile faded and he faced her. "Seriously. She loves you Dream. Not many people will come out to our neighborhood to take an old lady grocery shopping a few times a month. And had I listened when you told me to watch the car while you helped take in the groceries rather than trying to get them up faster, than maybe your car wouldn't have been stolen."

Dream jerked to him and shook her head. The words snatched Max's attention paralyzing him.

"I think I know who did it, but the cops need proof. All the guys on the next block were bragging about it, but it's only rumors."

"You listen to me. I don't want you looking into this. It was found and fixed. No harm done. You are worth more than this car. Do you hear me? You let it go."

Hesitantly, Derrick nodded his agreement. "Alright."

"Your mom and grandmother need you. Focus on that."

Max looked to the rearview and briefly met Dream's eyes before she leaned to the left and away from his probing ones.

Turning his attention to Derrick, he recognized the pride of a young man. He'd been that young man. He didn't know where Derrick's father was and he supposed it didn't matter. The fact remained that for whatever reason, he was the man of the house as Max had been at a young age. A responsibility he took seriously, and identified in a fellow son trying to do right by his mother.

Minutes of silence later, Dream stopped in front of a row of homes, some boarded up, others very much lived in.

"Thanks. You saved me an hour. I can get some extra sleep." Derrick looked back and waved. "Nice meeting you."

Dream smiled. "Give your mom and Elsie my love."

"I will." He waved once more and trotted up the dilapidated stairs before disappearing into the house.

Words eluded him. This woman never stopped surprising him. In her presence, his heart soared then dived from one minute to the next. She deserved an apology, but how could he apologize for thinking the worse about her but never having said so aloud. Before he could figure it out, she raised the volume and crooned once more, pounding her closed hand against the steering wheel in tune to the beat much like her voice to his ears.

Their detour had cut into cocktail hour but they'd made it in plenty of time. Max let himself out of the car and naturally reached for the driver door but was stopped short by the valet. This wasn't a date and he would do well to remember that. He waited by the door and when he heard the clicking of heels behind him, he entered the ballroom satisfied she was nearby, but never looking back at the woman who had just struck a mighty blow to his already crumbling safety wall.

Polite conversation and the soft sounds of Bach, Mozart or some other dead composer were a far contrast from grand theft auto and Dream singing Chris Tomlin into decimation, with her goat-like voice.

"Max. I'm so glad you made it." Helena Rios slipped her hands into his pleased to see him.

"I'm happy to be here. You have a nice turnout."

Helena looked around and shrugged. She wasn't one to brag. "Where is your mother? I didn't see her at church last Sunday."

Heat crawled up his neck. "She was sick-"

Helena interrupted. "Oh no."

"It was a cold. She is better now, but I brought along someone else." Helena raised a brow, disappointment registering in her expression. He felt like a bad son. "I brought my accountant. She used to volunteer here a few years ago."

Helena removed her hands from his. "And who is this charmer that convinced you to abandon your mother," she teased.

There was no use in defending himself. "Dream Collins. She is Tamryns-"

"Best friend. Yes I remember her," she interrupted again. "A troublemaker, that one," she said a jovial quality to her voice. "She liked to do make-overs. Do you know one time I found her applying some cover up to a male patient?"

Shaking his head, he kept his amusement to himself. "I can't say that I did."

"Said the black circles under his eyes made him look like a zombie, then broke down crying. It was bad enough they were losing a family member, he didn't have to look like he was about to eat their brains too."

Laughter burst from his tightened lips. Dream Collins was a nuisance everywhere she went. He recovered quickly at Helena's glare. "Max Davidson. Death is no laughing matter."

She was right of course. And because he had to know, he dared ask, "What did the family say? About his appearance that is?"

"I didn't have the heart to tell them. They didn't seem to notice so I just left well enough alone. Of course, Dream was banned from bringing in her make up case, but she snuck things in. Her favorite patient forever wore ruby red lipstick whenever Dream volunteered." Helena softened at the recollection. "Those two were mischief makers of the worst kind." Helena's words betrayed the twitch in her lips.

She came back to present smiling up at Max. "I hope she keeps you out of trouble." Helena looked past him to the door and grinned. "Perhaps not. Excuse me. I need to greet the other guests and I believe your date is waiting for you."

"She's not my-" Max let his words trail off as Helena moved along. He turned in search of Dream and stopped short. His breath hitched. Standing by the French doors, Dream craned her neck in search of someone. Flashes of her prom and a red dress that had him picking his tongue up off the floor, skittered across his mind.

He exited the set of French doors closest to him that led to the foyer and walked toward her. She continued her search from the door, politely declining the champagne.

Max stood behind her and stuffed his hands into his pockets. A man, at least a decade her senior, approached her cunningly. "Excuse me ma'am. Are you looking for someone?"

"Yes. My date. Well, not my date," she clarified. "My boss."

"It seems that a gentleman that would leave a ravishing woman like you alone, date or employer, deserves to sit alone. My name is Thomas"

She giggled. "Dream Collins."

"Interesting name. Would you like me to escort you to your table Ms. Collins?"

"That will not be necessary," Max interrupted offering Dream his elbow. "I think I can manage."

Max nodded at Thomas then turned to Dream. "You look beautiful."

She smirked, but took ahold of his arm, pulling it to keep him from walking. "Thank you nevertheless, Thomas," she said before pulling Max alone.

Pulling out her chair, she side stepped him, pulled out his chair, and sat in it. He huffed before taking the seat.

"So Mr. Davidson. I can't imagine what responsibilities your accountant would have at a benefit dinner."

"To enjoy yourself."

"Splendid. I think I'll go find Thomas."

Max sat back and grinned. "I'm sure his wife would love that."

"His wife?" She asked appalled. "How do you know he's married?"

"Did you not see the wedding band?"

"I guess I wasn't looking for one." The zip from her voice was gone.

"But I'm-" A soft voice echoed from the speakers, Helena interrupting again. It was probably for the best. Whatever he was about to say was pure madness.

Helena spoke and spoke and spoke. Afterward, a few more speakers graced the podium testifying to the loving care and respect given to their loved one at the hospice toward the end of their lives.

Dream tried hard to keep it together but failed delicately. Max covered her hand with his for a few moments before she'd excused herself to the restroom. He wasn't surprised she needed a minute. He could bet that she'd been thinking of Mrs. Ida the whole time. She returned fresh as a daisy, the trace of red in her eyes the only proof of her earlier tears.

Dinner was served and she'd offered him a smile assuring him she was ok. He would have believed her had she eaten more than two bites of her dinner.

"Is something wrong with the food?" He leaned in and whispered.

She shook her head and grinned again, perking herself up. "No. I'm sorry I only ate about two-hundred and fifty dollar's worth, but it's all I can swallow."

Grieving Mrs. Ida must have tangled her stomach in knots. He didn't care what the plate costs, he cared about her welfare, but he'd leave well enough alone. At least she'd tried.

A few of the couples in attendance took to the dance floor as Dream looked on wistfully. "Would you like to dance?" Max stood, extending his hand to her. He could help take her mind off things for a while.

"I don't think that is such a good idea." Dream straightened, looking around as others watched them.

"Are you going to deny me in front of all of these witnesses? I don't think my ego can take it."

Dream offered a stiff smile and rose gracefully. Escorting her to the dance floor, he kept her at a respectable distance while instrumental versions of songs he was sure he didn't know played on.

"I meant it when I said you look beautiful."

Keeping her eyes over his shoulder, she thanked him coolly.

"This looks like your prom dress." He tried to engage her in polite conversation rather than dance in the awkward silence.

"It *is* my prom dress," she replied stiffly.

"I didn't mean to upset you."

"I'm not upset."

Oh! She was peeved alright, but he surely couldn't pinpoint why. He'd bet there was a whole list of offensives he'd have to answer for.

Pulling her taut to him, he whispered in her ear. "Are you going to tell me what's wrong or do I have to charm it out of you?" The unfamiliar scent she wore, pleasantly surprised him. Not that toilet water that made his stomach sour. With a slight twist of his head, he nuzzled her neck and inhaled it again. She shivered and his ego boosted at her response.

"You couldn't charm water from Old Faithful." The breathlessness of her whisper betrayed her retort.

Always sharp with her tongue. "So you are mad at me." They spun then continued swaying from side to side. "It is because I sat in the back instead of shot gun?" He teased. "Or perhaps because I didn't immediately recognize a dress from a decade ago." She tensed. He'd hit a nerve. "Why did you wear that dress Dream?"

The accusation hung in the air and he regretted it. Putting her on the spot also put him in the hot seat. Did she know how the dress had affected him years ago? How it did so now?

"Well Mr. Davidson," she said, the usual quality of her voice returning, "you leave a woman little time to find a gown when you invite her to a black-tie affair with only a few hours to prepare. It was either this dress or maid of honor gown from Tami's wedding. Imagine what you would have been thinking had I worn that one. You probably would have run out of here screaming."

The grin that spread across the span of his face couldn't be helped. Her sass was like the baskets of fish and bread, Jesus blessed. Never ceasing. And she wasn't done.

"If you would be so kind as to climb down the pedestal you placed yourself on, I'd greatly appreciate that. For the record, I had no ideas of catching your eye. You are my boss."

Max spun her and when she returned to him, she continued without missing a beat. "And if you like, you can sit in the trunk of my car, if that's what makes you happy."

Chapter 22

Only the streetlights illuminated the interior of the car as she drove down the vacant road, the trickle of rain, beginning to darken the pavement. He was quiet. She was quiet.

As requested, he removed himself from the heights of her adoration, as least in his estimation, and ended the dance with a bow thanking her for the honor. Before she could take a seat, she'd been requested for another dance, then another. Before she knew it, she'd made several connections on the business front. Of course, that dress got her in the door, but her God given mathematical skill would get her seated at the table. Overall, it hadn't been all bad.

From across the room, she'd spotted Max watching her before turning quickly as not to be noticed. He'd nuzzled her neck. She could still feel the warmth of his exhale on her skin, his arm wrapped around her waist as he held her tight. Remembering the sensation, her eyes drifted close and she swerved into oncoming traffic lane, before easing back into the proper one. Good grief, that was bad. He raised a brow but not said a word. The cad.

He's lucky he'd only gotten verbal retaliation on that dance floor, rather than physical retribution. She had half a mind to dip him backwards and kiss him until he couldn't breathe, everyone in attendance a witness.

If her words had stung, it served him right for being so narcissistic. As if, he were God's gift to women. Oh please!

Now if only she could have waited to speak her mind until after she'd requested to use his bathroom, she would be perfectly willing to keep up her scowling, but as it were, they arrived at his apartment and her bladder at its end.

"Thank you for the ride." Unclicking the passenger side seat belt, he let it wind back into itself and fished for his keys. "For what it's worth, I'm glad you came along." Was there some humble apology in those words and in that look?

Staring deep into them searching she was mesmerized, the green in his hazel eyes, she loved so much, was buried behind the honey color, but she found it didn't matter. She could stare into them all day and not tire from the task. Before she could say or do something stupid, he rescued them.

"I'll see you Monday morning." Opening the door, Max exited. Unfortunately for him, he couldn't get rid of that her that easily this time around. She turned off the ignition and reached for her duffle bag in the backseat.

"Max, wait."

He stopped and turned toward her. "Yeah?" His keys dangled from his hand.

"I need to use your restroom."

He narrowed his eyes to slits. He looked to his darkened apartment then back to her and she knew what he was thinking. "Yeah, Sure." he said hesitantly.

Relieved she could relieve herself, she locked her car doors and followed him inside. Even if he didn't know, he was safe with her. She'd had no intentions of ever making a move on him again. Being rejected once was enough to last a lifetime.

"What's that?" He asked pointing to her bag.

"My change of clothes."

"Your what?" He asked fumbling with his keys.

"I always keep an emergency bag in my car. Like a banana, once I peel this baby off, it's not going back on."

He nodded, her words doing little to calm him. It would have tickled her, had her bladder not insisted on being serviced. Once he unlocked the door, she made a mad dash to the bathroom only to return a minute later. "Max," she called out lowly.

The apartment was dark, the only light visible spilled from the bathroom she vacated, and what must have been his bedroom. She called out again. If he didn't come out soon to help unzip her dress, there was going to be an accident to the likes of which she hadn't experienced since first grade. A shudder ran down her spine remembering that horrific school year.

"Max! I need your help. Now!" Nothing. Inching toward his door, she knocked and called out again. Reaching for her zipper, she contorted to no avail. She couldn't reach that zipper had she been a circus act for Cirque de Soleil. How did she always land in these predicaments?

Closing her eyes, she knew she was asking for trouble, but what other choice did she have. She slapped a hand over her eyes as a second layer of protection and turned the knob. It was open. Inching it open, she called out lowly. "Max, are you in here?" She stumbled forward. No answer. Where was this man? The moon?

She uncovered her eyes and studied the room. No Max. Panic set it. Maybe if she made it back to the bathroom, the mess could be contained in the tub, except there was no tub in has half bathroom. The sudden appearance of Max emerging from his bathroom shirtless stunned her still.

"What are you doing in here?" He rushed to his dresser pulling a tee from his drawer and slipping it over his head.

Fully covered she found her voice again. "I can't get the zipper," she stuttered.

Moving closer, he nodded his understanding. "Turn around."

Complying without question, she turned and saw their reflection in his bureau mirror. Max studied her from behind, gazing at the slope of her neck. Was he unaware that she could see him? His attention seemed to be centered on her alone. He closed his eyes and stepped closer, quickly unzipping her dress the turning away from her. "You're all set."

Gaping at his back, Dream could scarcely move. He'd had the opportunity to sneak a peek and hadn't. Her respect for him had just grown, as had her love. Unfortunately, her bladder hadn't. Clutching her gown, she ran for the bathroom without a backward glance.

She'd been in the bathroom for twenty minutes and Max had probably thought she had the runs or the toilet had swallowed her whole. The latter wouldn't have been so bad compared to her other only option, stepping out of the bathroom to where anyone on the planet could see her.

Back in the summer, much to her mother's relief, Dream had packed her emergency bag and left in the car, after nagging for a week. Removing her corset, she could kiss her mom.

Up until she pulled out her backup plan from her bag. Much to her own displeasure, her execution of the plan was an epic failure. Dream stood in Max's bathroom in running shorts and tank top. With no other shoes, she bit the bullet, and slipped her feet back into her heels.

Moaning, she gathered her dress, rolled up the gown without a care, stuffing it into the bag against its will along with the corset. That dress had brought nothing but trouble.

Looking into the mirror, Dream huffed and turned away, unable to accept that the hot mess returning her gaze, was her. She looked like a ten-year old tomboy playing dress up with her mother's shoes.

Girding herself, she placed the strap of her duffle bag on her shoulder and exited the bathroom like royalty. Mind over matter.

Coffee brewing wafted through the air, settling in her nose, inciting her stomach to react. It smelled heavenly. Max worked in the kitchen, pulling the mug from the Keurig, stopped dead in his tracks seeing her in her state of dress.

So help her, if he said one word…

"You look nice. Is that all the rage in Paris these days?" With a grin, he set the coffee down on the table, opened the refrigerator removing a pink bottle of over the counter antacid from the door, and placed it beside the coffee. "Ladies choice. No questions asked."

As if she'd stay a minute longer to endure his ridicule. "Just my coat, thank you."

Sobering, he leaned against the kitchen counter and surveyed her from head to toe. The long hard look rattled her. What she would pay to know what he thinking?

"You look ridiculous."

She wanted a refund.

"Let me get you some sweats. I have a pair that will be a bit baggy but at least your legs won't freeze."

"Just my coat, please."

Ignoring her request, he disappeared into his bedroom. With a few minutes until his return, she took the time to survey the apartment freely. Black and white portraits filled a wall adjacent to the front door. None of the subjects she recognized.

Shelves lined the wall opposite the portraits. Framed photos of Tami and Jonah at their wedding, gazing into each other eyes reminded her vividly of the day. A larger frame held a candid photo his parents in their yesteryears, sitting beside each other laughing hysterically neither facing the camera.

On a separate shelf, a photo of Max and Emily Serrano, his current best friend, begged to be dusted and examined. Wearing aprons and hairnets, the two posed back-to-back, arms folded across their chests like kitchen help superheroes. The goofy grins plastered across their faces, invoked one of her own. She'd nearly forgotten the two had worked at Chunks, the local hang out, many moons ago.

The last frame, a group photo of all her friends together at a BBQ two summers ago, rounded out the collection. Unlike the other frames, dust hadn't piled up nearly as high atop this one.

Recollecting the night, Dream grinned. The photo captured everyone huddled close on and around the small couch. Max kept insisting they squeeze in tighter, inciting infectious laughter.

Max set up the camera's timer and ran to the couch before plopping himself across the laps of all the women sitting beside each other. The photo captured all of their personalities so well it instantly enraptured her. She picked up the wooden frame, running her finger over it as if it would transport her back in time.

Tami was caught laughing, as she smacked Max on the rear for the unexpected stunt. Nicole faced the camera smiling demurely as if she hadn't noticed a man sprawled across her lap. Drew stood beside Jonah, an arm around his cousin's shoulder as they bent lower to keep their heads from being cut out of the shot.

Jonah had both palms on the back of the couch as he laughed at his brother-in-law, his deep dimples always present.

And there she was, sitting at the end of the couch, looking down into Max's gleaming face, love evident in her eyes as she returned the rare smile he gifted her.

She'd never seen the photo before. Seeing it now, she felt exposed. Was her love for Max always so transparent? Not able to look at the picture a minute longer, she returned it back to its place.

She turned to head back to the table only to collide into Max. He held her steady, then offered her the sweatpants. Their gazes clashed and held for what seemed like an eternity before he swallowed and awarded the floor his fixed stare. Aiming a thumb over her shoulder, she gestured to the photo. "That was the inspiration for Sunday dinner. I've never seen it before."

He nodded. "That was the Sunday Drew was baptized. It's a rare one." He scratched his neck "There aren't many of all us together, aside from Tami's wedding."

She rushed passed him, the smell of masculine soap scrambling all good sense. "It's a great shot, picture," she said, the words fumbling them. He hadn't moved from where they'd exchange a longing she could feel down to her toes.

"It's one of my favorites," he said, kicking at a scuffmark on the hardwood floor.

"I'll just go put these on and then I'll be out of your hair." Holding up the sweats, she rushed into the bathroom and changed. She needed to leave immediately. The tension had been building, and she was liable to expose herself again. A fatal decision if there ever was one. Max had already made his decision. Then again so had she. Now was as good a time as any to inform him.

Dream exited the bathroom with the need to square things away with Max who sat at his kitchen table looking like he'd lost his dog.

"Hey. Can we talk?"

He hadn't bothered meeting her eyes, as he latched onto the mug of coffee.

"It's about work?" That managed to get his attention.

"Not exactly."

Not at all.

Chapter 23

Dread seized him and he couldn't say he hadn't seen it coming. Taking the seat across from him, Dream sat ready to say something sure to turn his world on its axis.

"Now that I've caught up on the finances and the budget has been in place for three months, I feel like I'm collecting a paycheck I'm not earning. There isn't a need for me to be in the office every day. Besides, it seems as if Mr. E.P. has decreased his donations."

Max closed his eyes slowly. Of all the things she could have said, she had to voice his fear. It had been a month since he should have come clean with Dream. The office should have been turned over to her.

Yet, he couldn't find the strength to break away. He'd been with her almost every day for two months. It had seeped into his soul and he craved her company more and more every day. He couldn't have her as anything more than a friend but he could have her everyday sitting across from him crunching numbers and bargain shopping. It had become a content existence.

The problem with superseding God's plan with your own was that the anointing God placed on it, ceased to exist. It had been nearly a month since Max had received a request for help. Desperate to keep up the façade, he'd searched out charities in need of donations without God's help. The South Jersey Hospice was such a charity.

It was a great cause to be sure, but his heart hadn't stirred as it always had. Now here he sat an hour after having donated thousands of dollars and for what? She wanted to leave him again.

"Dream, I need to confess something to you. A lot of somethings." He dragged his chair besides her and turned her to him. Their knees touched and she looked taken aback.

"You're acting weird. Are you alright?"

"No." He swallowed. "I'm going to tell you a lot of things but please hear me out until the end before you say anything."

"Am I going to jail? Is Mr. E.P. a crook and you've got me mixed up in organized crime, laundering money? Oh, Lord, you know my heart." Dream looked up heavenward.

"Can you please stop?" He touched her knee, trying to calm her. "This is why I ask you to wait to hear me out before you say anything. You overreact."

She inhaled. "Right. Sorry. Go on."

"You aren't going to jail and Mr. E.P isn't a crook. Dream, I'm Mr. Enigmatic Philanthropist."

Her eyes popped open and she covered her mouth. Pointing at him, she narrowed her eyes but managed not to speak a word.

"Four thousand dollars of the donation to your church from our Saturday basketball team was from me."

She blanched and broke his gaze.

"What? Tell me." He lifted her chin.

"I lost it. Your donation and the church's Sunday donations for two weeks disappeared the day I went to Delaware with you. I thought I left it in the safe, but it was gone. That's the reason I was removed as Treasurer."

Aghast he sat back. The eight thousand dollar check in Pastor Collins desk. "You paid it back didn't you? Your life savings and business start-up money. You threw away your dream."

Surprised, she asked. "How do you know that?"

"Why didn't you tell us?"

Plopping back in her seat, she shook her head. "It was my mess to clean up. Besides, how could anyone have helped?"

"I could have helped," he all but shouted.

Dream stood and paced. "How was I supposed to know you were passing off money like kids do germs?" Folding her arms into themselves, she peered at him. "Even if I had known, I don't want your charity. There are people who really need your help more than an unemployed accountant."

He pulled her back to the seat. It was time she knew everything. He needed to tell her everything. She wasn't going to like all he was going to divulge, but he saw no other choice.

From the reason he left to California, to Ava, to her temporary job to why he'd held back from moving the plan along to get her business started, he'd divested himself of every detail pertinent to whatever had brought them to this place of tug and pull between. Every single thing. The funny thing with pouring out your heart is that it's left feeling hollow and empty.

Tears streamed down Dream's face, but not one word passed her lips. Nothing. No screaming. No questions.

She didn't deposit into his emptied heart one way or the other. Instead, she left him sitting there alone with his confessions, feeling vulnerable and naked as all of his past lingered in the heavy air. The door closed softly as she walked through it and he'd let her leave.

Max fought the desire to chase her and make her understand why he'd done the things he'd done, but what was left to say that hadn't already been said. She'd heard every shred of what made him Max.

Staring up at the ceiling, he relived the hurt in her eyes. Even after all he'd already confessed to her the sympathy in her eyes hearing about Ava, had nearly broken him. In that moment, Dream shared his pain and everything he genuinely wanted in a wife manifested in her expression. Compassion and love. One accord with him. A bond.

Suddenly, a mother to his children, his quiet life, and lovemaking didn't matter if it wasn't with her. Dream was his dream. Even eating pizza everyday didn't seem so bad, so long as he was eating it with her.

Sleep evaded him night after night. His brain was bombarded with all things Dream and longed for a break. She had invaded his life and it no longer felt complete without her in it.

After several days in the doldrums of insomnia, his body lost the battle to sleep only to be tormented in his victory. Dream laughing. Dream in his arms as they floated in the Atlantic. Dream in a red dress. Sitting at her desk. Dream. Dream. Dream in his dreams. It had become difficult to differentiate between being awake and being asleep.

One Sunday turned into a month's worth and she hadn't shown up to a single dinner. He missed her. The gang missed her. The dynamic of the group shifted though no one dared voice it. Polite and careful, they each tiptoed around the disaster he'd exacted on them. Calling him out could have made it all more bearable as opposed to waiting for the shoe to drop. He expected it from everyone but Drew. Yet even he chose to remain quiet and only offered him looks of pity and sometimes an update.

According to Drew, Dream had taken to having Saturday morning breakfast with the women, including Emily who become a staple at Sunday dinner over the last few months. They'd meet at a café, Drew was forbidden from disclosing, and do Share Time.

Everything was falling apart, including the ministry God had birthed through his blessings. He hadn't blessed a poor soul since the benefit dinner. God urging him in the spirit had gone dormant.

Everything in life had become meaningless. He'd still had more money than he knew needed, and more than anything, he longed to give Dream a better life. It burned a whole in him to be so wealthy and she had yet to find a job. She'd even put her condo up for sale.

Rapping on the door to Pastor Collins office, Max knew Dream wouldn't approve but it was all he could to keep from going insane. If only she'd put her pride aside and accept his help.

He entered the office when prompted and took a seat. Pastor Collins didn't seem to surprise to see him there, as he lounged in his chair tapping a pencil against his finger. "I was wondering how long before you came to see me."

"You were expecting me?" Max asked bewildered.

Pastor Collins laughed. "Not exactly at this moment, but something told me you'd come."

Pastor Collins was under the impression Max sought counsel and wanted to talk. He didn't. There was nothing he preferred less, than pouring out more of himself. "I just came to drop this check off. I know she was held responsible for the lost donations, but I was to blame for interrupting her while she was working."

"By she, I assume we are referring to my granddaughter?"

Max nodded. "Yes. Dream repaid the church with the money she needed to start her future. I want to replace her donation with mine. Tell her you found the money and want to refund her. Give her back her money and take mine."

"You want me to lie to my granddaughter?" Pastor Collins hadn't budged from reclining in his chair.

That sounded bad when he put it that way.

"Why haven't you just given it to her directly?"

"Because she won't take it from me. From you, I'm sure she will." He'd put it another way. "I only want you to give your granddaughter the future she worked hard for. What does it matter how she receives the money, if the end result is the same?"

Pastor Collins raised a questionable eyebrow. "Well for starters, only God determines the end result and you are mistaken if you believe that all that matters is how you end up. The journey is just as important. That is how you learn and grow." Pastor Collins remained quiet for a minute and Max knew the cogs in his brain were turning. "I'm curious Max. A few months ago, we discussed the solution to your current dilemma. How did it go so wrong?"

What could he say other than the honest to goodness truth? "I Sauled it up."

"Sauled it up? What does that mean exactly?" Pastor Collins laughed.

"I took my anointing and elevated myself. God had a plan. I had a different one."

"I see. And is there a David waiting in the wings because of your folly?"

Shaking his head, he couldn't believe he'd walked right into that one. "I don't know? Is there?"

Finally sitting forward, Pastor Collins leaned in closer. "Thousands of years ago, yes. Today, I'm not so certain. Care to tell me when everything went haywire?"

"The day I met you granddaughter," Max complained.

Proud as a peacock Pastor Collins grinned. "She has that effect on people.

"No disrespect, but some people may consider Dream a menace to society."

The clergyman didn't bat an eyelash. "Do you?"

"I consider her a menace to my heart."

"Now, we're getting to the part of the onion that provokes tears."

Yeah. His granddaughter's. The same one's that drowned him in sorrow and regret.

"You know Max, I've wanted to ask you a very specific question for years now, and the timing never felt right until now."

"Alright." That sounded ominous.

"What's holding you back?"

Max considered the question for a long while. Did he mean from love? Life? Commitment? A million possible answers to a million possible questions flooded his head and heart, but only one truth answered them all. "I'm afraid of failure and not living up to the man my dad was."

A grin split Pastor Collins's face in half.

The confession came with a load of emotions he hadn't expected but humor wasn't among them. The man could be as right as rain one day and as cracked as mud in a drought the next. Then again, he was related to Dream. "Why are you smiling?"

"Because acknowledging the problem is half-way to fixing it. I didn't know your father well, but I know his children and his wife, and if they are a product of his influence as a dad and husband, he was a good man."

"He was," Max, agreed.

"Here is what I see, however." No longer smiling, Pastor Collins, straightened, removing his glasses. "You have placed your father on such a high pedestal, no matter how hard you try, you'll never be good enough to stand beside him. At least not in your own mind.

"On the other hand, you've managed to lower God to so low a platform, despite all He has done to put you in a place to serve in a mighty way, you made Him a small and indispensable God. That's quite a dilemma you've gotten yourself into."

Max contemplated the words that wrapped around his head and heart constricting it until it was ready to burst. Had he begun to idolize his father? Worst. Had he stopped trusting God with his life and lost all fear of Him? Had he not already gone through this with his life in California and determined to live his life right? Old habits did indeed die hard.

"I don't know what to do? I thought I'd already conquered this battle. This desire to forge my own way without anyone's help, fuels me to accomplish more."

"There is nothing wrong with forging ahead. We just find ourselves in trouble when we try to steer the car when God's driving."

"I guess that makes sense." Max stood, the need to be alone and process the revelation, consuming him whole.

"I should go." Despite Pastor Collins protests to stay, Max needed air. He felt an avalanche of conviction weighing down on him, crushing him. The rush of cold air on his flaming cheeks soothed him.

I know the plans I have for you.

The winter wind carried the words. Max searched his memory for the scripture as a whole. What was it? Yes, he remembered. Plans to prosper. For hope and a future. Not to harm him. God even declaring that was His will.

Vivid memories of floating in the Atlantic Ocean with Dream and God speaking those words to his heart warmed him. God had even spoken them to her. She'd said the words allowed hadn't she?

Like a fuzzy picture finally becoming clear, it seemed so obvious now. Dream was his hope and his future. Together they had prospered. It was only when he grabbed the steering wheel did he bring harm to them both.

The realization that God had been leading him to a better future than he had planned for himself all along, humbled him. How much time had he wasted running from his promised future? Years.

He and Dream could have been married now with enough children to start a singing group. Then again, if they sang anything like their mother, that couldn't be God's plan. The mere idea brought sunshine to his cloudy existence, steeling his resolve.

It was time to change a few things. First, he needed to clear out all of the old lingering garbage before he grabbed ahold of what God was leading him toward. Dream didn't know it yet, but he was about to sweep her off her feet.

Pacing the length of his apartment floor, Max wondered if God was speaking to him or if the crazy notion to speak with Ava, was his own. It had to be God. He'd never tell himself to do this. If he was determined to let God lead, now was the time to do so and not slink back into doing things his own comfortable way. Finally, picking up the cell, he searched for her number in his contacts and swiped to initiate the call. Two rings, then voicemail.

Leaving his number and a brief message, he asked for a return call, a little disappointed he'd have to wait a little longer to have the conversation he longed to get done and over with. It would happen when it needed to happen. Until then, he had something more important to address.

Max tossed his cell on the couch and headed for the shower. He hadn't seen Dream in two months and smelling like a gym wasn't going to put him back in her good graces when he finally took the plunge.

Max toweled his hair dry as he ran to the door barefoot. "I'm coming," he shouted in hopes of getting whoever was on the other side to cease their assault on his door. Any harder and it'd come off its hinges. Scowling, Max swung his door opened with indignation.

"Knock the door down why don't you?" Dumbfounded, he gaped around in search of anything amiss to indicate he was dreaming. An upside down tree. A talking horse. A deceased relative.

Much to his relief, the world was as it should be and the only dream was the one standing at his door. She looked peeved. But she was still as his door, nevertheless.

Ready to rip his head off, for a reason he was sure she'd come to yell at him about, she pinched her lips before exploding.

"How dare you?" She waved a check, his check, in the air before charging past him.

Max closed the door behind her. Oh, that. He should have known Pastor Collins would sell him out. He'd thank the man later for unknowingly sending this beautiful woman to his door.

"What are you grinning for?" None too pleased, she folded her arms across her middle. "You have crossed the line for the last time."

He stepped forward risking life and limb just to be close enough to her. "I missed you." Freely flowing from his lips, he hadn't meant to pounce so soon.

She stepped back a little surprised at his confession, not that he could blame her. Then again, why waste more time. They could talk about the check later. Right now, he needed her to know how much they belonged together.

Her brow crinkled, before turning away abruptly, a blush settling on her cheeks. "Can we start this conversation over? Like from the door. I'm going to go back out and try this again." Aiming a finger toward the front door, she made her way toward it.

The request was odd, but if it meant she'd listen, he'd grant her a million crazy requests. She was out the door before he could agree, its quiet click reminding him of the last time she'd been here.

Waiting for her knock, he inhaled deeply, calming the anxiety that had taken ahold of him. Instead of a pounding on the door, a folded piece of paper slipped under the door. The check. Max ran to the door in pursuit of Dream trying to make an escape.

No more running from either of them. She'd made it one flight of stairs before he caught up with her. Against her will, he picked her up and tossed her over his shoulder. Issuing threats, her screams echoed in the hallway of his apartment building, but he cared not. Setting her down inside his place, he closed his door, then locked it.

"Have you lost your mind?" She asked breathless and panting. "This is kidnapping!" She looked around for an alternate means of escape. Not likely since they were on the second floor.

He chuckled. "I guess you were right about Mr. E.P. after all."

"You think this is funny? Why you think this is a good idea is beyond me, but I can promise you isn't."

"I just want to talk."

"I don't."

He leaned against the door keeping his amusement at bay. "Here me out, then you can go."

She contemplated, then nodded. "Fine. I'll give you five minutes and not a second longer, but could you at least put on a shirt? You're distracting me."

Looking down and seeing his bare chest, he realized he'd rushed to the door, shirtless. Finding her eyes raking over him, a spark of appreciation in them, she froze before jerking her gaze away. Never had he ever been more attracted to any woman in his life, which proved he needed to don about ten shirts. Yet, if he'd left her alone for one second, she'd leave again. He couldn't have that. He grinned confidently as a solution presented itself.

"Any of my tees in the top drawer will do." The lazy wink was a bonus.

Chapter 24

Her tapered pea coat, skinny jeans, and heeled boots hardly qualified as a maid's uniform, no matter what Max was thinking. "You expect me, a single, respectable woman, to go into your bedroom? I don't think so. I don't know who-" She stopped. She knew exactly who. Ava was who. Well she wasn't Ava, and never would be, had never been, and didn't plan to start now.

The smug grin on his face was evidence he hadn't been in tune with her thoughts. Oblivion seemed blissful from where she stood. Not a care in the world. No qualms about stringing women along until they suited his purpose and then moved on to the next. On second thought, oblivion seemed awfully similar to selfishness, immaturity, cowardice and a list of a few more choice words.

She busied herself, pushing her cuticles back. Anything to keep her gaze from roaming up and taking in Max's chiseled arms and chest. Temptation always came wrapped in nice packaging. Once it peeled away however, you were left with a narcissistic know-it-all, with too much time and money on his hands.

The wisdom in ripping up the check and keeping her distance from Max, came too little too late. Here she stood trapped in Max's apartment, her heart pounding in her chest as he stood their half-dressed. A few months ago, this had been how she pictured her honeymoon, not a kidnapping. Make no mistakes about it. This was a felony being committed.

"The faster you get the shirt, the faster you can go." He crossed his defined arms and leaned against the door, crossing his bare feet at the ankles.

She wasn't proud enough to allow a little discomfort stop her from reaching the ultimate goal of fleeing this place. Heels clicking on hardwood floor, she marched into his bedroom determined. Overcast weather and a north-facing window offered little natural light. Just great. A dresser and a bureau. Dream walked to the five-drawer dresser, opening the top drawer with a yank.

Undergarments stared back at her and she quickly slammed it shut, the hardware rattling. She wasn't about this crazy life. Grocery shopping with elderly woman and part time accounting had filled her days now. If Gramps walked in right now, she'd been put on discipline for sure.

The fear of the Lord set her feet to moving as if rocket launchers had been attached to her ankles. Quickly opening the top drawer to the bureau she snatched a tee and escaped his room, the warmth of hell and brimstone nipping on her Jimmy *Ay-Chus*. Lord knew she couldn't afford actual designer heels without a real job.

Haphazardly tossing the tee toward him, he caught it midair, his athletic build responsive. She could slap herself for noticing. As he stretched the tee and slipped his arms into the sleeves, his eyes never left hers until that euphoric moment when the tee went over his head and his exposed chest and abs greeted her.

"Hel-lo," she whispered to herself.

Pulling the tee over and down, essentially covering his upper body, he ran a hand over his cropped hair and leaned against the door once more. "Did you say something?"

Heat crawled up her neck or was that the devil so close she could feel his breath on her flesh? It was time to go. "As a matter of fact I did? Goodbye." She motioned for him to unlock the door and step aside.

"You promised me five minutes."

"I promised you squat. I did offer five minutes, of which you have used up two and half on me running your errands."

The smug expression faltered slightly. "Fine. I still have two and a half minutes."

"Two minutes and fifteen, fourteen, thirteen." She tapped her foot.

"I only need five seconds, but I figured I'd take advantage of the opportunity to look at you as long as you'll let me."

"Take a picture. It lasts longer."

"Maybe I will. Mind handing me, my cell?" Max pointed to the couch. "Or you could take a selfie? Without the coat. Please."

Pushing off the door, he spread his feet and held his hands behind him like a soldier at ease. "I still have two minutes."

He had to be joking. This man had some nerve, but rather than being appalled, she found herself attracted to his confidence. She really needed to be anywhere but here. Releasing an exaggerated breath, she unbuttoned her coat and draped it over the arm of the couch as she picked up his phone.

Then again, two could play this game. Suddenly she felt a little clumsy. Removing the protective case, she nearly dropped it intentionally, making no secret of her threat. "Take it yourself." She held it out to him. "Or I can toss this too, if you prefer." Right to the other side of the room.

He tilted his head to the side and stared at her. Goodness gross profits that man had spent too many years on the wrong side of a camera! Perhaps she should be taking his picture.

Mentally slapping herself back to the dire situation at hand, she pretended to toss it, although he'd made no move to catch it.

Lifting his chin to motion to the phone he said, "I can buy a hundred of those if it falls and breaks, but I only have a minute left with you."

Ok, that made her heart jump. Drats! Emotions were worse than lusting for him. There was no denying she'd always be attracted to him, but she'd made leaps and bounds getting over Max Davidson, yanking the roots embedded in her core. Well more like hops and skips, but at least she wasn't where she was before. The prospect of going through that pain she endured again fueled her to save herself, but she'd remain cool in the face of confrontation. In less than a minute she'd be gone, never to step a foot through that door ever again.

She walked the phone to Max, handing it over to him from a safe distance. He looked to the cell, than back to her. Slowly, he brought an arm forward and held it just out of reach.

Flaring her nostrils, she stepped a little closer and slid it into his hand. Before she knew it, she was turned and pressed against a wall, Max imprisoning her, his face so close to hers she could scarcely breathe. His gaze bore into her so deep she could feel it in her bones as they held the phone between their palms.

Waiting a minute to compose herself, she closed her eyes to avoid the hazel eyes she'd fallen for so many years ago. "You have forty five seconds and then I'm leaving." Her steady voice masked the chaos erupting within her. Snapping her eyes opened she awaited his response.

The warmth of his breath tickled her ear. "Marry me."

Every wall she'd built up began to crumble. In a panic, she searched her memory for just one reason to run for her life, but every thought was a jumbled mess. "Is that a genuine request or have you lost your mind?" She whispered.

"Whichever keeps you with me forever." Dropping the arm he had pressed against that trapped her in, he brushed the hair over her shoulder. The ceiling could have caved in and she wouldn't have noticed.

Slowly and unexpectedly, he buried his nose in the slope of her neck and sniffed. His sudden laughter traveled over her skin.

"What's so funny?"

"You're back to the old perfume."

It shouldn't make her heart leap that he knew which perfume she wore, but then again he'd already lassoed and corralled it. What did it matter if he made it leap it too? Curiosity got the better of her nevertheless. "Why is that funny?"

"This one used to make me sick and gag. Literally. But it seems like I've been cured." He sobered the humor in his expression giving way to something else. His eyes darted between her eyes and lips. Desire, was the something else and it sparked in his eyes.

She'd seen it one time before. The scab on her shoulder was a constant reminder of a summer night not so long. Funny enough, it felt like a lifetime ago.

She narrowed her eyes in warning as his gaze focused on her mouth. He wouldn't dare. A frenzy of emotions consumed her when she had no doubt he was past daring and entering conquering.

Max closed the gap between them and captured her lips, exploring them with painstaking patience. When he abandoned his cell in her hand and snaked his hands around her waist to her back, her traitorous hands traveled up his chest and wrapped themselves about his neck.

The thrill of his kiss sent chills from her hand up her arm. She'd never experienced such a sensation.

"Just ignore it," Max whispered and continued kissing her passionately.

It took a moment to realize the source of the thrill reverberating up her arm was his cell phone vibrating, not a result of his skilled full lips. Max moved onto her neck as she craned to peer at who'd been calling.

A sickening motion roiled in her stomach threatening to erupt. She gathered her wits and removed herself from his embrace.

"Please don't leave," he begged. "You haven't given me an answer. Say you'll marry me." He urged her back to him, but she resisted. Holding up his phone , she forced him to face his caller. The expression of guilt was all she needed as confirmation. "It's not what you think. Dream, please." He tossed the phone to the couch, pursuing her.

"Stop. Just stop. It doesn't matter what I think. Just know that I don't want your money, and please leave my grandfather alone." She stormed passed him, her freedom so close, yet so far. She turned the knob and pulled it, only to have the door slammed shut, the sheer force of it startling her.

"Let me explain. Please." He faced her square on. "I love you."

"Sticks and stone may break my bones, but your words will never hurt me again." Not anymore. An ache worse than she'd ever felt flooded every fiber of her being. His cruelty knew no bounds and she'd had enough of giving her heart to Max Davidson.

Chapter 25

Exiting the salon, Dream had felt like a part of her had died. It was only hair, but it had been a part of who she was for so long, the bob haircut felt foreign. Running her hand through it would take some getting used to.

She inhaled biting back the emotion. She'd not cry about hair. Sixteen inches had been chopped off and donated to make wigs for children. If there were a reason to cry, children needing wigs would be it.

However, not today. It had been too long since she felt this alive and carefree. She hadn't told a soul of her plans for a new look, but Drew being honored for his Christian volunteer work with inner city children inspired her to do her part to make the world a little better. He'd chosen mentoring youth through basketball and inspiring a desire for discipleship, discipline, and teamwork and she'd cut her hair.

Dream walked to her SUV checking off the last to-do item on her mental checklist of things to be completed before tonight's gala. When given a proper amount of time, a woman could enjoy pampering herself in preparation for a night in fancy clothes and fabulous shoes that pinched but made legs look killer.

She clicked on her seatbelt as her phone vibrated on the passenger seat. "Good morning FauxPa."

His chuckle made her smile. "So we're back to that?"

"We never left it. Please don't tell me that in your old age, you're becoming forgetful. I think Rosita's rubbing off on you, God bless her heart," she added. Couldn't forget that, lest she'd feel his wrath.

"You'd think that at thirty years old, you'd have a little more compassion and respect for the elderly, being as you're nearly there yourself."

"Bite your tongue! I'm twenty-eight."

"Pish posh. It's all the same once you get to my age. A brat is a brat no matter her age and you are pushing old brat."

Dream laughed aloud. No wonder she had a mouth that wouldn't quit. What she hadn't learned from her mother, Gramps had filled in the gaps of her education. "What are you up to, other than being a bad influence? Did you pick up your tuxedo?"

"About that. I was wondering if you could meet me at Rosita's? She took a spill in the office and sprained an ankle."

"Wow. Is she ok otherwise?"

"That I know of yes, but she called me and wanted me to stop by. I figured you could come along. We should have plenty of time before the gala."

Biting the inside of her cheek to keep from laughing, she risked his ire. "Need a chaperone do ya?"

"Propriety is important in my line of work, yes."

"You are absolutely right. We wouldn't want an eighty-year old to steal a kiss, then force a shot-gun wedding with the Pastor of Christ Community Church." She teased.

"Do you ever quit?"

Truthfully, no. Especially when she managed to ruffle the few feathers he had left. She chuckled. "I'm on way. Oh and Gramps?"

"Yes?"

"FauxPa and Rosita sitting in a tree…"

His photo abruptly disappeared from the screen, him having ended the call. How rude. It only made her laugh all the more.

Rosita lived in a senior living facility near the medical district, a few small towns over. A convenience for the elderly, she supposed. The third floor smelled of mothballs and ointment and Rosita's neighbor had the volume to the television so high, she could hear the jingle to a car insurance commercial as if she were watching it herself. She knocked on Rosita's door, wondering if she could rise to answer it in her state. Pressing an ear to the door, she listened for Rosita's voice to welcome her in.

"It's bad manners to eavesdrop."

Dream jumped, her heart pounding like a drum. "Gramps! You scared me."

He grinned and knocked a little louder, his tall frame overshadowing hers slightly. "Finally took the leap?" He motioned to his chin referring the length of her new bob cut. "Never thought I'd see the day."

A lock clicked. Then two. A chain slid, before Fort Rosita lowered its drawbridge. The petite fireball welcomed them in before hobbling back to her chair. Marciana sat on the couch, arms crossed, face buried in the screen of her smartphone. Why hadn't she helped her grandmother by answering the door? Unbelievable.

"How are you Rosita?" Gramps inquired, as he lowered to sit beside Marciana on the plastic covered couch, air whooshing from the cushion as he did so. Dream opted for the loveseat beside Rosita, thankful it wasn't summertime yet, lest she'd stick to it.

"I good Pastor. Sank you."

"I'm happy to hear it, Rosita."

"*Dios te bendiga,* Rosita" Puckering up, Dream placed a loud kiss to Rosita's cheek, much to her amusement.

Slapping her hands to her knees, she gazed upon Dream. "Very pretty. I like it," Rosita studied the new hairdo from all angles as she asked Dream to model it for her.

"Thank you."

"*Quieren café?*" She asked, changing the subject quickly, never one to beat around a bush.

What did it matter so long as she could enjoy a nice cup of Spanish coffee. "*Si, por favor. Negro con un poco de azucar.*" Dream replied.

"Drain, *mija*! You Espanish is much better. *Muy bien.*"

"*Gracias, Rosita.*"

"Pastor?"

He sat forward on the couch like a mountain cat in sizing up his prey, ready to share news from what she could gather and seemingly of the juicy variety. Never had she ever heard Gramps gossip. It intrigued her more than disappointed. She'd work on that.

"None for me, thank you." He held up a hand to Rosita.

It must be extra spicy if he was refusing coffee.

"Marciana. *Café,*" Rosita ordered her jovial tone reserved for her company alone. "Black coffee and a little sugar for Drain."

Not attempting to hide her displeasure, Marciana set her cell phone down. "I understand Spanish, Grandmom."

"So English is you problem then? Because you no listen," she said raising her voice, gesturing with her chubby hand, the tips of all five fingers gathered.

"*Muchacha cabeza dura,*" she finally whispered to herself as Marciana disappeared into the kitchen.

Dream covered her mouth to cover her smile. Rosita would apprise the President of all his shortcomings on national television if she felt it necessary. Marciana didn't stand a chance.

The coast all clear, Gramps cleared his throat, eyes wide. "Rosita," he urged.

She nodded and tightened her lips before speaking.

Ah. Rosita had the scoop. That made much more sense. She was still intrigued, still not as disappointed as she should be, and still needed God to work on her.

"Drain, *mija*, I so sorry. You no lose the money. It no you fault it was missing."

Rosita didn't have to elaborate. She knew to what she referred. The donations had been gone for nearly nine months without a trace. To hear she hadn't been responsible felt like another chain breaking that bound her down to misery.

"Marciana hide the money. She was mad at me for no giving her money for-" Rosita motioned her thumb back and forth to her lips, as if she were sipping from a bottle.

"But I put it in the safe. I know I did." Dream offered, despite being shocked at the development.

"*Si. Si.* It was there. I forgot to write total *en mi reporte* and no remember the amount. I check the deposit slip, and asked Marciana to put it back in the safe. I watch her," She pressed, a feeble attempt at covering her lapse in judgement. "She put it in and then lock it."

"Except, she didn't," Dream clarified.

Gramps tapped Rosita on the knee assuring her that he'd explain the rest. "She pretended to put it back in the safe, but actually stuffed it behind it. Last night, in a drunken stupor, she confessed to Rosita what she'd done. I found it this morning and every cent is accounted for."

Dream could cry. That was the best news she'd heard all month. What was wrong with Marciana? How could one treat their grandparent so cruelly? "I'm sorry, Rosita." Would Marciana continue to embarrass her grandmother at every turn?

"No, *mija*. I sorry. You no deserve it."

She was too elated to be angry. Besides, tearing into Marciana would only make Rosita feel worse.

I know I am pain right here." She patted near her rump. "But now you speak Espanish, I can leave the church to you."

"Pardon me?"

"I retire. It's you turn to welcome our people to CCC." She patted Dream on the hand, her skin almost translucent, a web of veins visible just below the surface.

"But Rosita we have plenty of Spanish speaking people at church that can take over your job."

"*Es verdad*." She nodded. "But God make the plans."

The scripture made her heart constrict. It would be forever connected to Max and the Atlantic Ocean. She'd once thought that God's plans for her future, Max included. Why else would she have waited so long? Alas, she'd heard what she wanted.

"Yes, but what does that have to do with me?"

"The job is for you. I only hold for you until you were ready. Open you heart and listen. You will hear Him."

Nowadays she didn't trust she'd ever heard from God to begin with, let alone if she ever would again. Wasting twelve years of a wasted life would do that to a person. She wasn't about to jump into a new commitment because

Rosita said, God said. The conviction in Rosita's statement felt like truth but was it enough?

Dream grasped Rosita's hand. If wisdom could flow from one person to the next, she'd sit by her for days. "Rosita how do you know when God has a plan for you?"

The question caught her off guard and she looked to Gramps, who simply smiled and sat back, hands raised in defeat.

"God has a plan for everyone, *mija*."

"I thought God had a plan for me, but nothing turned out as I thought." So many hurts still touched her deep within.

Rosita chuckled, its quality raspy. "God had a plan, but you did too." She tsked.

"What do you mean?"

"*Muchachita*! God's way *es mas alto*, than whatever you thinking in here." She tapped Dream's forehead.

"I'm lost," Dream confessed.

"This is very true," Rosita said tired out and waving a dismissive hand.

Gramps chuckled. "What Rosita mean's, is that just because your version of the plan failed doesn't mean God didn't speak to you in the first place. Don't limit God to your limited abilities and thinking. He's a far greater God than any of us could ever be."

That truth settled over her like a warm blanket. She cozied up to it and gladly accepted it, because the alternative was too depressing.

The seed of hope burrowed itself deeper into her soul as she drove home to get ready.

"God I had doubts before and honestly, still do. Some confirmation would be nice right about now. I can't waste any more of my life."

The suddenness of her cell phone buzzing startled her. Was Jesus calling? Dream clicked on her Bluetooth.

"Dream?"

"Give the woman a prize!" A car zipped past cutting her off. "Jerk!" she yelled. "Terrible drivers."

"You have a delivery," Tami chuckled. "We're parked outside of your place with your gown."

"You are? Perfect, I'm pulling in now." Turning into her parking lot, she saw Nicole and Tami parked in front of her apartment. Seeing her SUV pull in, they vacated Nicole's car, Tami's protruding belly, leading the way and Tami with the light blue gown she'd found at seventy five percent off.

"Ahoy!" Dream shouted waving an arm in large arching motions, as Tami wobbled closer.

She reached Dream breathless and misty-eyed. "Was that a fat joke?"

Tami had put on some pounds, but that's what pregnant woman did. She didn't mean to offend her. Dream looked to Nicole for help. From behind Tami, she shrugged. Coward.

Damage control underway. "No! I said a boy! From back here, it looks like you are carrying a boy."

"You think?" Lovingly Tami rubbed her belly. "Jonah wants a boy. He'll be happy with a girl too, but he keeps referring to the baby as a he."

Dream grinned and nudged her along, placating her with nods and assuring grunts. Unexpectedly, Tami stopped and turned facing her friend, stunned. "You cut your hair?" There was definite disapproval in her thundering question, of which she didn't expect an actual answer. Shoulders dropping a fraction, she fingered the ends. "As much as I hate to admit it, it looks amazing. But you're going to let it grow back, aren't you?"

"Yes, but I also plan to make another donation for children in need of hair for wigs as soon as it's long enough."

Being side hugged, on either side, her friends expressed their approval, and because she was physically incapable of holding it in, Tami cried.

Inside, she wiped her swollen nose with a tissue as she reclined her feet on Dream's ottoman. Dream brought her a tin of cookies and two baby carrots as compensation for the joke made in bad taste.

"Eat the carrots first, Tami." Dream warned. "You know the routine. If you stuff yourself full of cookies, you'll leave no room for the carrots."

Tami shook her head as she opened the tin. "Jonah won't ask. He's too busy editing videos for our vlog."

Nicole slung the garment bag over the couch. "How many subscribers are you up to?"

"Thirty-five," Tami announced proud as a blue ribbon apple pie winner.

Sitting beside her, Dream snatched the tin and replaced the cookie Tami held, with a baby carrot. "Hey!" Tami protested before acquiescing.

"Are you guys all set for tonight? Is Drew nervous?" This was a big deal. She couldn't be more proud.

Nicole shook her head nonchalantly as if the question made no sense. She shared a look with Tami then cleared her throat. "He's not afraid of public speaking so, he hasn't mentioned being nervous."

Huh. Letting the matter slide, Dream changed the subject. "He wasn't singing that tune a few weeks ago. He blubbered like a baby when you walked down the aisle." Tami chuckled. "I've been meaning to ask how that beach date went last summer. I mean, obviously well, since you married four months later."

Glowing, Nicole plopped on the couch on the other side of Tami and giggled to herself. "I don't kiss and tell, but let me just say, he proposed again."

The riotous laughter the three shared lasted nearly a half hour as they walked down memory lane. She loved this. Them. Yet and still, a chunk of heart was void.

I know the plans I have for you.

Oh how she could get a glimpse into that future. Some evidence she was on the right track. But faith didn't work that way. She'd learned that back on the beach many months ago watching the sunrise.

"Well, we best start getting ready for tonight. I can't wait to see you dressed up. It feels like prom all over again."

"Except I'll be wearing a moo moo." Tami said breathless as she struggled to remove herself from the couch.

"You'll look beautiful."

"I'll feel like a cow," she held her back and winced.

Rubbing her back, Nicole creased her brow. "You alright?"

She nodded, her features pinched. "Sat on that Barbie couch for too long. I'll be alright."

A few minutes later, she was alone in her condo, the loneliness draped over it like a wet rag. Next month, she'd be all moved out. Another notch on her plan to move on.

Chapter 26

Crystal goblets and chandeliers sparkled, reflecting the candlelit centerpieces and the soft lighting above. A lavish affair on his account. How absurd. To be fair, Max wasn't the only gentleman being honored tonight. Not that he was ungrateful, because he had been touched that so many had nominated him for such a distinguished recognition. He just couldn't wrap his head around the fact that he'd only followed the Holy Spirit's urging, so technically the praise ought to go to Him. Surrounded by family and friends, he'd give God his glory. His speech insured it. The thought brought a measure comfort to his bleeding heart.

The evidence of life marching on without Dream in his life stung a little more today seeing the happy faces of everyone he cared most for. Everyone but her. Nine people seated at a ten-person table. Cecily, his mother of all people, had secured a date with her gentleman friend, Oscar. They insisted they were only friends, but the beginning of a bond had begun to form. He was a nice man. He wasn't his dad, but he digressed.

Nicole and Drew had been married in a quiet ceremony with just family and a few friends. Drew had eased up since then, Max couldn't pretend to not know why.

His very pregnant sister, Tami spoke animatedly into Jonah's recording phone relating, in detail, her first false labor contraction.

Much to his displeasure, Emily sat beside David, her date for the evening, engrossed in his trip to Spain a few years back and his misadventures with Spanish women. He was just grateful she was only interested in his stories and not the man himself. She was always thinking of her next character and plot. David turned out to be a treasure trough of cheesy romance novel dialogue.

Seated at the next table behind his, Max welcomed Derrick who had spent the last several minutes convincing Elsie that the candles had to stay. For some odd reason, she insisted that she'd always taken a centerpiece home at all her family functions as a parting favor. The proof lay in the wall unit covered in chachkies made up of mainly porcelain figurines sitting atop ribbon embellished styrofoam. Not the Philadelphia Museum of Art, but she was a proud collector, nevertheless.

It hadn't taken long for these people to infiltrate his heart and Max knew that the chance encounter of seeing Derrick again, was no accident. He'd bonded to them so quickly, his head spun. It was easy to understand why Dream held them in such high regards. Elsie patted Max on the cheek, her smile bright. He poured her a glass of water then knelt beside her as she spoke, basking in her affection for him. If only she could feel his pain.

No one really understood the depths of his hurt. He'd never been one to be vocal about suffering or joy for that matter. His feelings where his own and he had never learned to trust them in the care of others.

Except God. He'd been a constant friend. He filled a part of him that Max hadn't realized had become desolate. Dry and thirsty in need of God's living water and He'd given him to the full. It was a different love and affection he needed from and bonded him with Dream.

Since feeling her in his arms and on his lips, he'd felt starved of it. A famishment only she could satisfy. He missed her more today than yesterday, never growing accustomed to the emptiness, no matter how many days passed.

He hadn't seen her since Drew and Nicole's wedding. He'd spent half the night trying to catch a glimpse of her just to get his fill, to last him a while before he could see her again and the other half, avoiding her in hopes of starving out the need for her.

He sensed her, before he saw her. Max stood slowly, then surveyed the room with equal deliberation. She'd come after all. A vision in a white gown. Even if she would have worn rags, her confidence elevated her beauty above every other woman in the room. Pastor Collins whispered something in her ear and she blushed. Catching his breath, Max realized everyone was as mesmerized as he was. When she looked up and met his eyes, her smile faltered, the reaction as painful as a sharp knife to the center of his chest.

Pastor Collins greeted Elsie and Derrick, his parishioners, before making his way to Max's table, stopping to converse with them all. Once a pastor, always a pastor, and wherever you are, a pastor.

Taking advantage of the opportunity, Max donned his chivalrous coat and pulled out a chair for Dream. "You look amazing." And she did. She could have been in a bride in that dress. A lump lodged in his throat. His bride. She'd cut off all of her luxurious hair yet his fingers twitched to feel the silkiness that remained.

"Thank you," she said politely. "Excuse me. I want to say hello to the man of the hour and the gang."

Squeezing past, he nodded, her perfume grabbing him by the throat and bending him to her will. Clenching his jaw, he grew weary of this battle. Unsure which of the other recipients received the benefit of her smiles and pride, and not caring to spy their exchange, he re-gifted his smile to Elsie, before excusing himself to get some air.

Much to his dismay, the cool air didn't reach deep inside, where he burned with remorse for purposefully allowing too much time to slip by, wasted. For the coldness and distance that existed between them.

I need some help here, God.

Clapping resounded from within the ballroom.

"The program is about to begin."

Hands stuff in his pockets, Max casually peeked over his shoulder to Derrick, blowing warm air into his fisted hands.

"Thanks. I'll be right in."

Nodding Derrick left him alone. Max stared out over the expanse of the gardens, lifeless flowerbeds, and skeletal remains of bushes, their dry branches swaying in the breeze. Following the wind into the smallest tree in the north corner, newly sprouted leaves rustled in harmony with the whisper of a breeze. Among all of the barrenness, the hope of spring and new beginnings lay within a few leaves. Not because the leaves will the Spring season to come, but because God's plan was already established, even when the source appeared lifeless from a winter season.

The corner of Max's mouth tipped north at the hope of new things sprouting from what seemed dead. "Thank you God. I'll take it." Smoothing his lapels and collar, confidence resurged, not in himself, for that was a gamble he'd taken and lost, but in God who'd had a plan. Hadn't God been saying that all along? Well, this time would be different because this time, he'd trust the Lord.

Max entered the ballroom to dimmed lights and a video playing. A montage of pictures and footage of this year's honorary recipients of the South Jersey Christian Volunteer Association. Himself included.

Oblivious to the many photos ops, he'd hardly faced the camera in any of them. He was too focused on the joy on the faces of those he'd been able to bless. Silently, he thanked God for choosing him, then using him.

Half an hour later, he'd seen so many pictures of himself he doubted, he'd ever want to peer into a mirror again. The soft polite claps came from the tables in the back. Near him, a few shrill whistles and hardy clapping had ensued. You couldn't take these people anywhere, he thought as he laughed at the ruckus his guests created. That's who they were and he loved them all for it.

The music accompanying the photo slideshow faded away and the dimmed lights were brightened as a member of the SJCVA took to the podium and announced the first recipient. A chorus of claps bolted Kyle Staller from his seat. Max had only met him once. Nice guy. He simply didn't have the ability to end a conversation. With the same exuberance he'd noticed Kyle carried in abundance the first and only other time they'd met, he bounced on stage.

   The MC whispered in his ear and Kyle nodded all the while already talking. If she was smart, or the least bit kind to everyone in attendance, she'd keep a leash on the microphone. Max lowered his chin, biting back a smile when she hesitated moving away, as if she'd read Max's mind.

   Once Kyle reared off topic, Max turned his attention back to the photos silently playing on loop in the background. He wondered if Dream recognized a few of the items she'd purchased on line. The space heaters for the seniors. New bookshelves for the privately funded library that flooded.

   Discreetly he turned to face her. She watched the video too. When a photo of the child with the broken leg, who'd needed a wheelchair having been severely beaten courtesy of his stepfather looped again, she lowered her face as if unable to face it. He recalled that day clearly. It was one of the few times, he hadn't been greeted with child-like joy. Instead, Sean simply thanked him quietly staring off into space. Not that he could blame him.

   Kyle was finally wrangled away from the podium much to his consternation and to Dream's delight. She'd been duped into coming tonight in a dress she hadn't chosen but fit like a glove, even if it did look like a wedding gown. The surprise limo she and Gramps rode in, aided in making her feel bride-like. Every single one of her loved ones had set out to deceive her. What great storytellers they all were. Drew receiving an award, her foot.

To add insult to injury, she'd been seated at the table behind Max's. He had been in her line of vision during the entire montage and she found herself searching for his reaction whenever a photo of him appeared. She soon found herself enraptured in the photos as much as he had been. Matching faces with the items she'd shopped for, had gratified her spirit. To see her effort wasn't in vain had melted her heart. Before she knew it, she was thanking God for the opportunity she'd been given.

Helena Rios, petite and slender approached the podium and introduced Max with all the bells and whistles. She included a quip from his childhood that would have made any man blush but prompted Max to grin wide. Straightening his two-button tuxedo jacket, he fastened the top one and enveloped Helena in a motherly embrace, then held her hand as she descended the two stairs.

A woman a few tables away hooted and purred prompting a few whistles and remarks. Returning to the podium, he greeted everyone with a bright smile before a vocal, "Good evening and thank you. There are some very passionate volunteers here tonight."

Laughter sounded throughout, although Dream found the behavior of those women crude and his response improper since it only served to encourage them. Jezebels.

He sobered and began speaking of growing up in the church. His passion to volunteer had been planted in his life as early as children's Sunday service, where he acted as usher for a few years. He spoke of his father being his mentor, even after death, and finally his ministry, which he revealed was officially entitled, His Heart Ministries.

He thanked the numerous churches and organizations that worked hand in hand to help him help others.

Folding his speech back into squares, he inhaled deeply. "I have some people I would like to thank individually, if you all could bear with me for a few more minutes."

He was so charming and well-spoken she was sure they'd pay him to keep talking.

"First, I'd like to thank my mom. She has been a single parent to me when boys needed their father's most and she never made me feel like she was parenting alone. She kept my father's memory alive and for that, I will always be grateful. But, mostly for being the standard for which Tami and I should live our lives. Thank you."

Cecily sobbed, her date passing her his handkerchief.

"My sister Tamryn." He grinned. "Don't cry," he warned but it was far too late for that. "You are one of my best friends. I've never expressed how much I look up to you. You are gentle, and kind. When we were younger, your unabashed love for God no matter when or where helped me overcome my fear of not fitting in but encouraged me to stand out. Thank You."

He went on to thank Jonah and Drew for being the big brothers he'd never had, Emily and Nicole, his other sisters, and his Pastors and church.

Max spoke about H.H. Ministries, and all the organization accomplished in such a short time, citing statistics she'd personally drafted and sent to Max months ago.

He watched her intently and she returned his attention. "Having heard all of that, you all must know that I could not have organized all of that alone. I can hardly keep my tee shirt drawer neat & tidy." A few chuckles reached her but she ignored them.

Had she been eating, she would have choked. He was not doing this here and now. Hot hams! He was.

"Working closely with a large number of benefactors simultaneously can leave a two-man team tangled up with their backs against a wall a time or two."

Dream narrowed her warning him, as he studied her, awaiting a different reaction. She shook her head, a subtle plea to not continue.

"It can seem like floating the middle of the ocean. But when you build a rapport with someone and you're both in sync, both committing to hold on, and seeing it until completion, a two-man team could accomplish just about anything."

Her heart raced and she couldn't break away from his searing gaze. Which completion exactly? Marriage? Divorce?

Four months of retraining her heart, were gone in a few words and glances. The tux didn't help either.

She battled with her irrational heart. The man couldn't be trusted with the fragility of her heart. Why was part of her in such a rush to hand over her still battered heart to him?

"The success of His Heart Ministries could not have achieved all it has, without my friend and partner Dream Collins. From the bottom of my heart, I thank you." The applause although soft, rang in her ear like party horns.

He went on to give God glory, but she couldn't focus enough to figure out to what he was referring. Gramps patted her knee and comforted her with a wink. Blessedly, the last honoree was a man of few words. This night could not be done and over with fast enough. Dinner was served and she'd not eaten but two bites.

Dessert was served as was music, and dancing. The festivities relaxed as the lights dimmed. Dream stood, searching for Gramps. She'd had enough, but low and behold, he'd found a few fellow clergyman and there'd be no pulling him away now.

Nicole approached sheepishly. "I know this wasn't the dress you'd chosen, but it's perfect on you. You look absolutely gorgeous."

"As much as I love this dress, why bother. The other was nice too."

"Last year you did me a solid. You gave me some advice that worked like a charm." Nicole held up her hand, as she tapped on her wedding band. "I'm trying to help return it. Tami and I were hoping that if Max saw you in an almost wedding gown, he'd propose. And if you wore the dress and rode in the limo, you'd be giddy enough to accept him"

A hearty laugh pushed into the air. "Nicole, you are wonderful at many things but being fanciful isn't one of them."

"True. And this was actually Emily's idea but I got cat caught in wishful thinking. You and Max belong together."

Peanut butter and jelly belonged together. Dream's head was beginning to hurt. "Can we talk about this tomorrow? I just want to get out of here."

"Your knight in shining armor awaits." David sidled up slow and calculating. "I'll take you wherever you want to go."

Nicole crossed her arms, arrows shooting from her glare. "Aren't you here with Emily?"

"Just as friends. We didn't actually come together. Besides, she's with Max" Gesturing over his shoulder with his thumb, he kept his attention on Dream.

Nicole slipped away leaving her alone with him. Taking his time, he perused her, making her feel cheap.

"You look like you are getting ready to marry. How about it Dream? Want to jump the broom with me?" Uh. Even his words had begun to repulse her.

"I want to jump you with a broom. Does that count?"

"Dressed like an angel, but with a forked tongue. It's ok *Mami*. I don't scare easily."

Words that would have shamed her as a Christian were swallowed whole rather than voiced, when the warmth of a familiar arm snaked around her waist. "Hey babe." Max smiled at her flirtatiously.

Emily and Nicole joined them, smiling like hyenas.

The protest on her lips birthed from Max's liberties, crumbled to the floor, and would be vacuumed up later.

"Babe? Are you two together?"

Three yeses drowned out her single no.

"My bad bro. I didn't know. All this time you saw me acting like an idiot for weeks. Why didn't you say anything before?"

Grinning, Max straightened. "Because you were acting like an idiot."

"That's low, making me the laughingstock at basketball."

"I'm pretty sure you accomplished that all on your own."

A turn in the conversation left her a little lost. "Care to back the train up a little?" Dream faced both men reminding them she was still standing in their presence.

Red settled over David's face as he continued his conversation with Max. "I guess she told you we kissed. I swear I didn't know you two were together. I don't need to steal a woman, let alone my friend's."

The hand upon her waist tightened along with Max's jaw as if he had a right to care about who she kissed, but that didn't change the facts, David seemed to be twisting.

"Now you know and I think you just be leaving her alone from now on."

Nodding David was off in search of a new conquest, never looking back.

Max turned so swiftly, she'd nearly lost her balance. "You kissed that guy?" Stuffing his hands in his pockets, he'd looked ready to burst.

"It's none of your business what I do, and with whom I do it."

Emily cleared her throat. "Actually, he kissed her and she slapped him."

Darting his gaze to Emily, Max pointed a menacing finger to his best friend. "You knew about this?"

"Like she said, it's none of our business." Bumping into a waiter, Emily sped away, Nicole on her heels.

"That was subtle." Dream complained.

"He's gone isn't he?"

"Yes. Now if you could help me get rid of one more, I'd be set."

Max leaned back against the chair, grinning. "You want to get rid of me do you?"

"I thought I had."

"You slapped him." A smug smile graced his face. "You never slapped me."

"I'd say you're pretty close to winning that prize now."

Ignoring the jab, he crossed him arms. "Can we talk somewhere private?"

"Absolutely not," she chuckled, grabbing her purse from the table.

"Just five minutes."

Her chuckle multiplied. "Fool me once, shame on you. Fool me twice… Well, not likely."

"Two minutes?" He bargained.

"Not even five seconds." He smiled at the reference.

"If I recall correctly, that conversation lasted longer than five minutes, not that we did a lot of talking."

Was it suddenly hot in the room? No. She pictured snow-covered mountains. Ice cold water. Ice cream. "If I recall correctly, you were busy with a different conversation altogether."

Max straightened. "You don't want to be alone with me. That's understandable. How many chaperones will you require just for a few minutes of your time?"

Ha! "The whole room."

He grinned. "I'd thought you'd never ask." He tugged at her hand and wrapped his arounds hers, as he led her to the dancefloor, spinning her before he brought them together.

"One song. That's it," she whispered in his ear. "I'd say that's about five minutes."

"Two songs. You owe me. I chased David away." A temporary solution once he found out there was nothing between her and Max.

"This is payment for that temporary solution."

"Is that an invitation to make it a permanent one?" He spun her again and when she reunited again, he'd held her a little closer and a little tighter.

"You have three and a half minutes."

Max ran a finger along her hair pushing it aside and with no reservations looked her square on. "I'd rather have a lifetime."

Someone needed to get the wet floor sign because she'd melted into a puddle at his feet. This gorgeous man. Rich man. One that loved God. That wanted to be with her. Why was she supposed to say no again? Right! He misused her. She was back on track. That was close. That tux had some sort of power she couldn't see.

"You need to take that Tux off," she suggested.

Grinning, he glanced around before leaning in. "The honeymoon comes after the wedding, babe, but I appreciate your go get 'em drive. It speaks volumes about your work ethic."

Red faced, she slapped his arm. "I didn't mean it like that."

"By all means, please elaborate."

The song ended and another proceeded immediately. He held her tight to prevent her escape, little did he know, she hadn't planned on it.

"I just meant that the tux must give off some super power to make me agree to dance with you. Twice."

Thoughtfully nodding, he probed a little more. "So you are saying that you find me irresistible in this monkey suit and that this tux, not I, is what is charming you?"

Pretty much, but she'd remain quite. She'd already said enough.

"Silence. That usually means yes." He huffed. "I'll tell you what. My ego is a little bruised right now. No self-respecting superhero loses the girl to the sidekick. I demand retribution."

That was definitely trouble brewing. "Sorry, no rematches and our song is just about up, so I'm going to head on home."

He held her hand, absentmindedly running his thumb over her wrist, though she was painfully aware of each stroke as he led her to the empty area where a wet bar would have been set up. "We'll take a break and then just five more songs," he whispered. "You're half way in love with me. I can't stop now," he joked.

Attempting to pull her hand free, he held it a little closer. If he suspected for a minute that she was so far past love, he'd keep at it until she relented, and under no circumstance could she go back to that lonely existence of waiting for Max Davidson. Her smile faltered and she tugged harder.

Recognition set his green eyes ablaze. "You love me?"

She yanked away. She'd not give herself away this time. "I have to go."

"Don't do this. Why can't we just stop running from each other?"

"I'm not running. My feet are tired as is my heart and this topic."

He opened his mouth to speak, but a shriek ripped through the room. Tami.

Chapter 27

Sitting on a chair, breathing in and out forcefully, Jonah sank down beside his wife, confused. "What's wrong honey?"

"Is she in labor," Drew asked anyone and everyone.

Nicole crouched before her. Calm as if they were having coffee at the café. "Hey Tams. Where's the pain?"

"Everywhere," she finally said.

Concerned etched in how brow, Jonah lifted her chin. "How long have you been having contractions?"

"The painful ones? About a half hour."

Jonah rushed to his feet. "You have been in labor for a half hour and you are just saying something? I could have missed valuable footage Tams."

"Shut. Up," Tami growled, then apologized for being mean. Jonah turned on his camera and began filming to everyone's surprise except Tami's who waved as the pain subsided.

Cecily rushed over. "Let's get her to the hospital, shall we. Drew and Max can you carefully lift her?"

Outside in the cold, an illegally parked car prevented any cars from entering or leaving the lot. Dream spotted the limo and had Tami placed inside it. She'd arrive to the hospital in style if she had anything to do with it.

"Hospital. Please. She's in labor." Max pressed the driver who insisted he couldn't.

"Jumping into the parked limo, Drew sat beside Tami, while Nicole timed her contractions. Dream jumped in offering a hand to squeeze in exchange for the warmth of the car. Besides, it was her ride. Gramps decided against being present for the ordeal and accepted the lift home from Emily. "Bye Benedict Arnold," Dream shouted as he left. He waved, never looking back.

Tami yelled and squeezed Dream's offered hand, until her knuckles cracked. "Where's my husband," cried Tami.

"I'm here baby," kneeling beside her he kissed her hand, smoothing back the hair from her face. "Take this." Shoving the camera into Dream's midsection, he replaced her crushed hand with his. That was fine by her. She continued recording, but remained quiet.

Cecily, peeked her head in. "We can't find the driver who parked illegally. I'll call a cab."

Max walked back over to the limo driver and whispered in his ear. Nodding several times, Max clapped him on the shoulder, and returned to the limp. We're all set."

"I'll get there as soon as I can. Take care of my daughter."

"I will," Jonah promised.

Zooming the camera in on Tami, Nicole held her hand and waved. "Baby Wells is on the way."

Drew raised a quizzical brow aimed at his wife. She waved off his insinuation. "You'd be the first to know if I were," she promised as Tami's belly tensed, another contraction in full swing Tami screaming stealing her attention.

Pulling out his cell phone, Drew opened the bible app and searched for scripture on pain and health. "By His stripes you are healed," he recited over Tami's contraction. She slapped the phone to the floor and endured the pain.

Nicole raised a brow at her husband and Dream had gotten it all on video. She kept in the laughter to keep from ruining the audio.

"Nicole," a tired Tami huffed. "I need drugs. I don't want a natural labor. I'll take the processed labor. I don't need organic or whatever else these whack jobs offer, just numb me."

"I don't have drugs, honey," she smoothed Tami's perspired soaked hair breathing in unison with her.

Tami slapped her hand away. "Then leave me alone."

Drew chuckled. "Welcome to the club, baby." He held out his arms and embraced his wife.

Max checked his watch. "Just a few more minutes. Hold on Tams."

"What exactly am I holding onto Max!" she shouted. "Get me to the hospital," she growled.

"Another one bites, the dust," Drew sang lowly.

Nicole rubbed Max's arms sympathetically. "Your part of the club, now too," she teased.

"Jonah, will you be ok in the delivery room? I know you have a queasy stomach."

Jonah's jaw hardened. "Nothing is going to keep me from seeing my baby being born. It's one of the most important moments in my life. I'll be fine."

"Oh baby," Tami cooed, as she caressed his face. "That's so sweet."

The return of Dr. Jekyll and Mr. Hyde.

"It's nothing to be ashamed of," Drew continued. "Lots of people can't take the sight of blood. I'm already used to it, otherwise I'd probably be queasy too."

"Can you all please stop making nice conversation around a stinking campfire and get me drugs!"

A sudden gush trickled to the floor onto Jonah's lap. "What in the world is this?"

Nicole jumped up. "Her waters broke?"

Taking in the sight of his wet hand, Jonah's eyes rolled back before he passed out on the limo floor. Dream zoomed in her laughter barely contained before she zoomed back out.

Nicole began shouting out orders. "Max, pull Jonah back away from Tami. Drew help me lay her back."

Drew moved to where Jonah previously sat, felt the moisture, and turned to vomit in the corner.

Oh, this was amazingly perfect. You couldn't find this stuff on the big screen.

"Nicole's pulling in her last player from the bench," Dream called out unable to resist teasing Drew a little more. "Does he have what it takes?"

Max looked into the camera and smiled, then winked. Be still her beating heart. He adjusted Tami to lying and used napkins to clean up Tami's mess. No vomit. No fainting. Her kind of man.

The limo door flew open and the driver took one whiff and threatened all sorts of lawsuits. Nicole and Max helped Tami out of the car into a wheelchair. Dream followed with the camera in focus, as best as she could despite her gown and heels. Jonah was brought to, and was whisked away with his wife.

Left standing in the waiting room, Dream continued recording though the action had gone where she couldn't. "Hi Baby Wells. This is Auntie Dream. Today is your day of birth. You, your mom, and dad are upstairs somewhere and I am down here in the waiting area, waiting."

She faced the camera toward the window and outside. "Do you see that handsome guy over there? The one in the superhero Tux. That is your Uncle Max. He is settling something important. He's good at fixing problems. Remember that.

"And do you see that limo there? That is how you made it to the hospital. Auntie Dream hooked you up. Remember that too, ok? If you ever want to reward me, I love diamonds, baked chips, and pizza. And not necessarily in that order. And your Uncle Max, if I'm making a complete list." Panicked, at her slip of the tongue, Dream set out to do damage control. "Shoot. How do I stop this stupid-"

Dream looked for the start and stop button but there was no customary red record button. Flipping the camera up down and all around she had no idea how these things worked.

"Hey. You ok?" Max placed a hand on her shoulder.

She nodded, mouth dry. "Yep. Could you make sure Jonah gets this? I have to go."

Bolting, she didn't wait for his reply. Hailing a cab at three am would have been nearly impossible, but God always provides. No sooner did she wonder how on earth she'd hail a cab, had Cecily arrived in one.

In no time, she made it home contemplating what to do. With no other choice, she sent Jonah a text message explaining her predicament.. An hour later, and he had yet to reply. He was obviously watching his wife have their first child. Was Tami still pushing? How long did it take to push out a small baby? She wished her a safe delivery despite her own worries. She smiled. Knowing Jonah, he probably fainted again.

After a long hot shower, Dream slipped into her new favorite pajamas. Max's borrowed tee and sweatpants.

She checked her text messages again and found an update from Jonah with a photo. Tami had just given birth to a bouncing baby boy ten minutes prior. Nine pounds worth of chubby cheeks and hair.

Arriving a minute later, a text from Jonah, promised to erase the confession she was supposed to take to the grave. With her biggest fear relieved, and the news of Tami becoming a mom, she sent her congratulatory text to the happy parents, and let them know she'd stop by the following day to meet chubbers.

The long day caught up to her in short order. Now that the excitement had waned down, so had her energy. She climbed into bed, asleep before her head hit the down pillow.

The red digital numbers on her cell phone read ten forty-nine. She stretched and yawned simultaneously, a string of recollections trickled into her hazy brain. Sitting up, she immediately noticed the considerable weight difference in her hair. Namely, that most of it had been chopped off. She touched the length with both hands then ruffled the layers.

Swinging her feet to the floor, Dream's feet sank into the plush carpet. She'd miss it once she moved, but she'd always like hardwood floors. Maybe she could try that route.

Her phone buzzed but she ignored it. Nature was calling. Once in the bathroom she went through her morning routine minus makeup. She longed to crawl back into bed, but she had a very important person to meet.

Her best friend was a mom. Life for Tami and Jonah was about to change tenfold. A baby changed everything. Dream was sure the group dynamic would never go back to carefree days and impromptu lunches and vacations, but they had been fortunate in having shared many together. They squeezed the most of out their life as best friends as teens. Single and carefree. As young adults, childless and maturing. Now they'd adapt to being best friends with families. Before she knew it, they'd be the Golden Girls.

When she began picturing them with white hair and polyester pants, she knew she needed coffee. Pulling the throw cover from the couch, she wrapped herself in tight, only pulling out an arm to place her mug in the Keurig.

Once done, she cuddled on the couch, sipping her coffee. "Good morning Lord."

A peace always surrounded her mornings with God. Being unemployed had had its advantages. She spent every morning with God picturing herself wrapped in his loving arms. She reached for her bible, and found the last passage she'd read. The Psalms were definitely spiritual breakfast food. King David had some Dr. Phil type issues. Who needed soap operas when you could read about King David's drama? The man begged God more than a downtown panhandler begged a passerby. Then again, God had considered a man after his own heart, so there must have been some merit there.

Dream set down her coffee and looked up contemplatively at the ceiling, thinking of the heavenly realms beyond it. She thought about King David, and what she could learn from him.

She sunk to her knees, then thought better about it. If she were going to take a page out of King David's book, she might as well go for gusto. She lay faced down. "Ok God. This is me begging for direction in my life. A job. A place to live that I can afford and is not with my parents. Please. Please, not with my parents."

She wasn't as skilled as King David when it came to eloquent begging but she'd stay there another hour if it secured the chance she'd not be moving back to her childhood home.

"Bless Tami and Jonah and their new bundle of joy and my parents and Gramps."

She stopped herself. She was supposed to be begging. She cleared her throat. "Dear God. Dear God," she tried a little louder. "Don't forget about me! Remember me? Dream? We talk every morning. If you don't recognize me, it's only because I cut my hair and my face is buried in the carpet. I need a ticket out of Loserville Lord! If you could put one in the mail, oh God, I'd be eternally grateful. Oh and a pizza!"

It couldn't get any more pathetic than that. She wrapped it up with a thanks and an Amen but didn't make a move to get up from the floor that needed a good vacuuming. Laying there for a half hour She began to doze off when a knock on the door startled her awake. Peeling herself up from the floor, she wrapped herself in the blanket and looked through the peephole.

She couldn't see who knocked. "Who is it?"

"Pizza delivery!"

She didn't order a pizza and she had faith in God, but even that was too hard to believe, God sending her pizza delivery. "I didn't order a pizza! Wrong door."

He knocked again. "Is this a....Dream...Collins?"

"I didn't order a pizza!"

"Just doing my job lady. I'm leaving it at the door since it's already paid for."

Lady? No tip for his smart mouth.

After two minutes, and seeing a delivery car drive off, she opened the door to retrieve the pizza.

"Two whole minutes. I'm impressed." Looking like he'd stepped off a magazine cover, Max leaned against the wall casually.

"You set me up!" she picked up the pizza appalled.

"Someone could have been waiting to rob you or worse. You should have called the police."

"Good idea." Thumb and pinking pointing opposite directions Dream spoke on her finger phone. "Hello Police. Someone delivered a pizza. Please someone right away. Officer David Escobar is available. Yes, he'll do. Thank you." Hanging up, she raised a pursed her lips rather than outright calling him dimwitted.

His jaw flexed, but he didn't speak.

Holding the pizza with both hands, she turned to him. "Thanks for the pizza, but there's only enough for one."

"It's a large."

"Exactly." Entering the apartment, she reached for the door with her foot and pushed it closed.

He held it opened and waited at the door.

"I won't come in unless you want me to."

Of course, she wanted him to, which is why he needed to stay outside. "Go home, Max."

"Not until I give you a few things first."

Drats! That was a problem. She was nosey by nature so not knowing what he wanted to give her would keep her awake at night. She supposed she could tolerate him a few more minutes. Besides. It was gifts.

"Fine. But you have to stay at the door." Aiming a finger at him, she waited for him to agree.

He nodded slowly, his expression unchanging. "I can live with that."

"Alright. Make it fast. My pizza's getting cold."

Leaning against the doorjamb, he tsked. "Not so fast, beautiful. You answer a question, you get the gift."

Always strings attached. "What kinds of questions?" She opened the box and drooled seeing greasy pepperoni.

"Very easy ones. Yes or No. That simple."

She exhaled. "Fine." Funny thing is it wouldn't matter what sorts of questions. She would have agreed. Her curiosity was dangerous that way.

"Question one. Is it true that you love pizza?"

"Yes, but you already knew that. My gift please."

"Your pizza was the gift."

She fisted her hands on her hips. "Are you trying to jip me?"

He laughed. "No. The pizza was a prize. I was nice enough to give it you in good faith. Now, moving on to question two. Is it true that you love baked potato chips?"

Reluctantly she replied. "Yes."

He stepped out of the doorway and retrieved a grocery bag full of baked chip packages. "This should last you a day or two." He held out the bag to her.

Without a shadow of doubt, she knew he'd seen her video confession. Only two loves remained on her list and he'd ask her a gut-wrenching question. She stepped closer and accepted her prize. He reached for the blanket and pulled her within arm's reach.

"Question three." His voice raspy made her mouth dry. "Is it true that you love diamonds?"

"Max, I-"

He shook his head. "Yes or no only."

He repeated the question, his head tilted in that adorable way that she loved.

"Yes," she whispered.

Turning over his palm, a closed ring box stared at her. "Open it," he insisted. For a long minute, she waited. "Are you sure you love diamonds?" He joked. "The pizza and chips, you snatched up without hesitation."

"Those didn't come with strings attached."

"There doesn't have to be with this one either. Go on. Open it."

Dream opened the box and fought back the tears. A round solitaire surrounded by smaller diamonds on a diamond-encrusted band, sparkled up at her as if it were on stage performing especially for her.

"It's beautiful."

"You're beautiful," he whispered.

She didn't dare remove it from the box lest he assume she was providing an answer she wasn't prepared to give.

He pulled her closer still. "Last Question. Do you love me?"

It didn't take a genius to know the question was coming, yet it hit her like a ton of bricks. The short answer. Yes. But admitting it to him left her exposed and she didn't trust him with what was most vulnerable. Her heart.

She pulled free from the blanket he grasped with all his might. "I don't want to answer this question."

His laugh held no mirth. "You'll tell a newborn baby, but you want to tell me?"

Fear gripped her midsection but she remained silent.

"I know you love me. Look at you." His voice faltered. "You're wearing my clothes to bed for goodness sake's." He all but yelled. "That's intimate and purposeful. I know we're bonded and so do you. Why can't you admit you love me? Can't you believe I want to marry you?" He pointed to the ring she'd left in the box. "You won't need to replace me with my clothes. You'll have me there. Every day and every night."

If he wanted an admission, she'd give him one. "I don't trust you to keep my heart safe. Clothes don't try their hardest to push me away. They don't kiss me and then ask someone else to marry them. Your clothes are the safer choice and won't ever break my heart. They aren't expecting phone calls from their old bed playmates while kissing me."

Pain skittered across his features. He nodded but didn't look at her. "For what it's worth, I called Ava in search of closure. I've been angry for so long, I refused to see that I was wrong too. I knew better and sinned anyway. That falls to my lot. She has made some grievous mistakes but they don't negate mine.

"I did what I needed to do to move on with my life. I won't apologize for taking steps to heal my hurts and mend my spirit. Keep the ring. It was made for you whether its binds us or not."

The door closed quietly. If she weren't left reeling, she'd congratulate him on properly putting her in deserved place. She felt as valuable as gum on the bottom of a shoe.

She walked into the living room and did the only thing she could. Eat her pizza.

Hospitals were depressing and cold. Unless you were on the maternity floor. It was like Goshen in Egypt during the famine. Rather than tears of sadness, families shed tears of joy. Balloons weren't wishing a better result, but blessing the one that had come. And what a blessing Jeremiah Alexander Wells was.

Dream gushed over every little finger and toe as he slept. "Tami, he is absolutely perfect. I just want to put him in my pocket and whenever someone irritates me, take him out and stare at him until I feel better."

"He won't be in your pocket long," Jonah whispered,

"I heard that," Dream said smiling at Jaw, her special nickname for him. His initials.

"Oh please don't call my baby Jaw." Tami propped herself up in bed and smoothed the blankets.

"Are you kidding me? It's perfect! Awww, look at Jaw. See? It's perfect."

From her peripheral, Dream could see Jonah and Tami urging each other to ask her something that was surely none of their business. Tami finally found the courage to be nosey. "Speaking of perfect. That is a pretty perfect ring on your necklace. Where'd you get it?"

"Max."

They ogled each other in surprise before continuing their line of questioning.

"Max? My brother Max?"

Dream rocked the baby as she slipped his sock back on his pale foot. "Aha."

"Is it a special kind of umm, ring? A mood ring or maybe an engagement ring?"

"It's a ring around the rosy, why are you all so nosey, ring." She cooed. "Right Jaw? Tell them Jaw. Mommy and Daddy are nosey."

"He'll hate you for life if that nickname sticks. There is a boy in our church nicknamed Chunk. Can you imagine? Why would any mother do that to her child? Whenever his mom calls him, he practically melts right where he is standing. The poor woman has called him that name so long, she can't stop herself. It doesn't help that others have taken to calling him by the family nickname too. Poor kid."

"Nonsense! Jaw is strong. Intimidating. I bet no one will pick on him."

Jeremiah began to whimper and Dream passed him along as if he was a hot potato. Sleeping babies were cute. Crying ones, not so much.

Tami, cooed whipping out a breast without reservation, plopping little Jeremiah on it like she'd been doing it for years. Was it indecent to stay or insensitive to leave? Perhaps she could find an etiquette book in the gift shop. Yes. That worked.

Upon returning, Nicole and Drew had fallen in love with Jaw like anybody with working eyes would. Babies danced in Drew's eye, as Jeremiah held tight to his finger. "Oh, don't you dare, Drew," Nicole warned laughing. "We said we'd wait."

"Jeremiah needs a playmate," he teased.

"He has you," she elbowed and sat. Dream made her rounds and sat in the corner seeing how such a small little person could invoke such love and soften hearts. Babies really were a blessing from God.

A tap to the door stole everyone's attention as Max walked in a large teddy bear on his hip, his eyes for the baby alone. Handing Drew the bear, he washed his hands and waited eagerly for Nicole to pass him off. He gazed at his nephew and then Tami, sending a wink.

"I helped too," Jonah, added.

"Good job brother. He's a handsome little guy, but I think he gets it from his mom. Don't you bud?"

Max walked Jeremiah around the room for a while before nestling him into the bassinet, studying him. A thousand heartbreaks filled his countenance. He didn't have to tell Dream he was thinking of the child he'd never meet. Max dabbed Jeremiah's nose, who turned his face in search of something to suckle, before leaving the baby to stare out the window into the rainy afternoon.

Dream's heart broke for Max. She wanted to cry for him. With him. For him. If she could, she'd take his pain away. Tears streamed down her face before she realized she was already sharing in his suffering.

Leaving her seat, she approached Max wanting to comfort him, yet afraid he'd reject her. He'd be well within his rights. She'd done her fair share. When he began to quietly shed tears, she wrapped her arms around his waist without thought, and gave him, every part of her, without fear. "I love you, Max."

He tensed at her touch and then relaxed into the arms that sought to comfort him. Bringing her around to face him, he captured her in a crushing hug. Together they shared in the sorrow of the past and in the joy of no longer running from each other.

I know the plans I have for you. Two become one flesh.

Words of comfort and news of joy. She and Max were one flesh. The idea felt so right. When had it happened? The first time they'd admitted their feelings to one another? In the middle of the Atlantic Ocean? While ministering to the needy? When they shared passionate kisses? Now in their sorrow?

In everything.

In everything. None of it had been in vain. She relished in the thought. Max, the husband of her heart. And sooner than later, the husband of her everything, in everything.

In a little hospital room, in a little town, Dream thanked God for giving her the desires of her heart and for Him dwelling in hers. But in that moment for allowing herself to finally accept, that Max had always had her heart and always would.

Epilogue

4 Months Later

Dream knelt before the spill, frustrated. Her beautiful hardwood floors were covered in catsup. A handful of paper towels cleaned up the majority of the mess, but she'd still have to steam-clean it again. Another chore to add to the never-ending to-do list before the BBQ this afternoon.

Max and Dream were hosting their first event as a married couple. How often had she hosted Sunday dinner? Dozens? She could do this. Her mother-in-law and parents were coming, along with Gramps, and she wanted everything to be just right.

Tossing the saturated paper towels in the garbage, Dream washed her hands and tucked her basket of cleaning supplies under her arm. Her playlist sounded from her dock speakers. She turned the volume as loud as it could and sang to the top of her lungs as she dusted and cleaned glass surfaces. Admiring the photo of the first Sunday dinner among the friends, she wiped it down and kept working.

The next song, an up-tempo tune, took over her senses and she danced more than cleaned as she sang. Satisfied she wiped and spit shined anything standing, she turned down the volume. She turned to find too many eyes to count staring at her, laughter, and grins greeting her. Leaning against the doorjamb was her husband, gifting her a silent clap.

Using the back of her hand, she brushed flyaway hair from her face. Breathless she asked, "What are you all doing here?"

"We came to help before the guests arrive." Tami set a baby bag down and cooed at J. His official nickname. She removed him from the carrier and kissed his cheek. "Say hi to Auntie Dream."

Dream melted seeing his chubby cheeks and quick smiles. She divested him of his mother's arms and tickled him with kisses. Oh if only she could cuddle with him all day, but she had guests coming.

"You guys are lifesavers!"

"We have mother-in-laws too." Tami raised an eyebrow. "My first time hosting was a disaster."

"Hey. My mother is the sweetest woman on the earth." Jonah said as he lifted his son from Dream's hold.

"You are such a momma's boy," Tami joked before walking into the kitchen, Jonah at her heels.

"My mother-in-law is a gem." Nicole shrugged.

"It helps that she lives in a different state." Drew laughed.

"That is probably true." According to Drew's offended expression, Nicole had agreed to heartily, but didn't seem to care. "What do you need me to do?"

"Could you steam the kitchen floor? I spilled catsup. The steamer is in the closet by the laundry room. Drew I have a job for you." Dream grinned.

"So help me Dream, you'd better not have me cleaning out little candle holders or arranging flowers or something equally frilly."

"No. I need you to set up the inflatable movie screen with the projector and speakers."

He clapped his massive hands. "Skills I have. Yes, I can do that."

Dream smiled. If he only knew which movie she'd chosen.

Picking up the basket, she headed to the bathroom. "Are you just going to walk by your husband and not say a word?"

She stuck her nose up in the air and entered the bathroom pulling the window cleaner from the basket.

"Mrs. Davidson, in this house, we speak to our spouses or there will be consequences." He closed the door behind him, and then locked it.

"What are you doing?" She hissed,

"Talking to my wife in private."

"Open it before they think…the wrong thing." Dream reached for the doorknob. He caught her hand and placed a kiss to her palm.

"I don't care if they think we are printing fake money and rolling around in it. It's none of their business," he wrapped his arms around her.

"You need a timeout," she said placing the cleaner back in the basket before weaving her arms around his neck.

"That is the smartest thing you've said since we walked into this bathroom. Let's go."

"Where?"

"Did I forget to mention that timeout's can only be served in private, preferably in a wider space, and since we are one, we have to serve them together?"

Dream chuckled. "That is very specific."

"That's today's rule. It changes daily."

Taken aback, she gave him a questioning look. "Do you plan on being on timeout that often?"

"And twice a day when I haven't learned my lesson."

Dream's bubbling laughter echoed in the bathroom.

A knock sounded on the door and she covered her mouth. "We know you're both in there!" Tami yelled.

"Go away, Hami-Tami," Max yelled.

Dream held in her laughter. "Max you'll pay for that. Dream, I'm going to start the sides and Jonah has started the grill. Don't rush on our account newlyweds."

Dream launched herself to the door only to be pulled back by Max. Jonah was on the verge of ruining her first time hosting and would have to serve her parents the nastiest BBQ on earth, and just so happened to also taste like it.

Dream walked out to the yard and spotted her parents socializing and being merry. No one looking peckish or faint was always a good sign.

She headed for the grill to be stopped by Cecily. "The garden looks beautiful Dream."

"Thank you. I would take credit, but I can't keep a plant alive. How are you feeling? Any stomach pains?"

Cecily looked confused. "I feel good. Thanks."

The woman was probably used to her son-in-law's subpar fare. "Could you excuse me for just a second?" Dream smiled and bee-lined to the grill.

Jonah smiled and greeted her. "Hey. Hungry?"

"Depends."

"Ok, well, if you make up your mind, the food is over on that table." Jonah winked.

Shifting over to the table, Dream lifted the lid to see perfectly grilled meats, burgers, hot dogs, and vegetables on skewers.

Not sure what to make of it, she served herself before whatever Jonah cooked made it over. Night fell and they were ready to watch her movie. Gathered around the screen, laughter filled the air in her new home.

"I know it's not Sunday dinner, but I'd like to do a special Share Time." Everyone in arty agreement cheered. "Who'd like to go first?"

A consensus volunteered Jonah for the honor.. He happily disengaged from his wife's side and stood by Dream putting an arm around her shoulders.

"Something I need to share." He huffed and grinned. "For the past five years, I have been competing and winning BBQ competitions all over the country. I purposefully burned your food as retribution for all your barbs."

Dumbfounded, she gaped at every person before her. Some having the decency to look sheepish. Others barely containing their laughter.

Focusing on each face, she tightened her lips. "And you all kept that from me for five years?" Tami covered her mouth hiding her laughter. Max raised an eyebrow and nodded."

"Well Bravo!" Dream yelled. It was about time someone bested her. She was still the queen, A chorus of cheers made her chuckle. "I didn't think you had it in you Jonah. I've had it coming for a long time. I call a truce."

Jonah nodded agreeing to her suggestion for peace.

"Anyone else?"

"No one can top that!" Drew yelled!

"Is that a challenge? I love a challenge." Dream cleared her throat urging Max to step forward. "Max?"

He nodded and stood beside her calm and collected as usual. "I have something I want to share. As you all know, since moving our headquarters to CCC to make it easier for Dream to do both of her jobs, God has planted a seed in my heart to establish headquarters in churches around the area, using CCC as the model. Well, not only have we found a church in Pennsylvania working with us to get it started, my client, the one that owns the beach house we rented last summer, has signed on to be a benefactor."

"I stand corrected," Drew, said smiling. "That is awesome!

Max moved to sit, but Dream held his hand. "There's only one thing I love more than a challenge, Drew. A double challenge."

Confused, Max turned back to her. "Did I forget a detail?"

"No," she grinned. "I have something I want to share too."

"Ok. But it better not have anything to do with this afternoon," he winked at their loved ones.

"Honestly, Max," Cecily said a little shocked, as she bounced J. on her hip.

"He's only teasing," Dream assured her as she playfully slapped his arm. "Behave or no timeout for you."

"I think you have that backward." Jonah twirled one of Tami's curls around his forefinger.

Dream shared a private laugh with Max before turning back to the crowd.

"In case you haven't noticed, God seems to be blessing Max and me with more than we could have imagined.

When He led us to buy this house, we were a little hesitant. Why would we need such a big house for just the two of us? I guess that's because in about seven and half months, Max and I are going to have company. The kind that doesn't leave until college and even then will most likely return."

The shock registered on Max's face couldn't compete with the elation in his eyes as they began to water. He kissed her soundly as everyone cheered.

"J.! You hear that handsome. You will have someone to play with," Nicole shouted as she jumped up looking for him.

Drew laughed aloud pulling his wife down to his lap. "He can never have too many cousins."

"I couldn't agree more," Dream said laughing. "Because you all know I have never been one to do things half way and for whatever reason God has chosen to bless in doubles. I went from one job to two. H. H. Ministries is now operating out of two churches, and apparently J. will be playing with twin cousins."

The cheers and gasps crescendo. Dream only half ignored her mother when she offered to stay over to help out, choosing to focus on her husband, giddy with delight as he placed his hands to her belly. He enveloped her in a hug and let his earlier tears fall.

"Two babies? I'm speechless." He ran a hand down his face and laughed.

After everyone offered their personal well wishes, Gramps said a prayer over them, as her dad began rearranging a conference he had booked during the time of the birth.

"So Dream. What movie are we watching?" Tami asked.

"I hope it's a comedy." Drew passed around a few cans of pop, tossing bags of popcorns among the crowd.

"You can say that," Dream said.

"Was it in the theaters?" Jonah asked.

"Nope. Straight to video and doing well online too." Dream pushed played and watched the look of surprise on their faces seeing a fully edited video of J.'s day of birth. Including a movie title and opening credits.

"You didn't?" Jonah stunned, couldn't break away from the big screen.

Oh, but she did and seeing Jonah pass out and Drew vomiting on the big screen had to be funnier than seeing it on her laptop.

"We did," Dream said, sending Max a conspiratorial wink as he took his seat.

"Why is my name listed?" Drew asked, sitting at the edge of his seat.

"I wouldn't leave you out Big Shot. Get it? Big Shot? Basketball?"

"Got it," Drew snapped

"How did you get the video? Baffled, Jonah kept his eyes to the screen.

"Max had a copy for some odd reason," she joked.

"You do know this means the truce is null and void?" Red faced and ready to burst, Jonah clasped his hands atop his head.

Dream sat down beside Max, popcorn spilling from her bag. "I wouldn't have it any other way." Ok, so she was reneging on her promise to let Jonah be. God was still working on her.

Max chuckled and tossed some popcorn in her awaiting mouth. She couldn't quit now that she had a partner in crime.

"Oh! I almost forgot. Jonah, one of your videos has finally gone viral."

"Dream!" They all shouted.

Max squeezed her hand, their lawn chairs touching. "I love you crazy lady. Thank you for sharing your life with me."

"Sticks and stones may break my bones, but your words never cease to heal me." Dream had never been more proud to be called a lady.

The End

Thank you for taking this journey with
Dream & Max

If you've enjoyed this story,
please consider leaving a review!

Other Titles by Cynthia Marcano

Spring Love Series

Eyes On Him (Book 1 - The Teen Years)
Hand In His - (Book 2)

Acknowledgements

Putting together a novel is some hard work and I couldn't have done it without some super people on my life.

First, to my husband Phil for putting up with writer Cynthia who missed out on some quality couch time to write one more chapter. I love you.

Cailyn & Christian, you did a wonderful job keeping Camryn busy when Mommy needed to get some writing done. That's team work! I'm so proud of you guys. Love you both.

To my sister Delma, for volunteering to proofread my, often times, nonsensical gibberish and doing it in record speed!

To Kelly for putting up with my cover methods and my text messages asking strange and random questions throughout my book-writing journey. Thank you for inspiring some of Dream's story.

ABOUT THE AUTHOR

Cynthia Marcano is a native Jersey girl enamored of Jesus, reading, and cake. Born and raised in Southern New Jersey to Puerto Rican parents. Her writing incorporates South Jersey culture blended with life as a Christian and Hispanic woman.

When she isn't designing graphics or reading a Christian Fiction book, you can probably find her volunteering and praising God, or at home avoiding the dishes.

More years ago than she cares to admit, she met a man, fell in love, and got married. His name is Phil. Together they moved to the suburbs and spawned a few kids.

Her three beautiful and loved children have made it their life's mission to drive their mother crazy but luckily enough for her, Cynthia has a husband who poses as her part-time knight in shining armor when he isn't at his day job. He manages to tame the wild things. Sanity aside, Cynthia wouldn't have it any other way.

Made in the USA
Middletown, DE
20 January 2017